THE FEARLESS

STAR LEGEND BOOK TWO

J.J. GREEN

1

Airless and zero-g, the umbilicus snaked out from the *Cornflower's* starboard airlock. A steel scaffold protruded from the open end, a cage holding the molecular scalpel that would slice into the hull of the *Fearless*.

Major Wright pulled himself closer to the ship, hand over hand along grips lining the interior wall of the umbilicus. The crew responsible for attaching the scaffold to the BA's former flagship were taking their sweet time about it, and he wanted to know why.

The *Fearless* hung silent and enigmatic in space, adrift in the Asteroid Belt. In the five weeks it had taken them to reach her, she hadn't answered a hail, run her engines, or betrayed any other sign of life. None of her airlocks were responding to security override codes, so they had no choice except to force entry.

"Corporal Marks," Wright said, "is there a problem? You should be through that hatch by now."

"No, no problem, sir!" she replied.

Her tone was way too cheery and confident. Something was bothering her.

The corporal was one of eight Marines assigned to the task of gaining entry to the ship. All looked nearly identical in their EVA suits, their pulse rifles slung across their backs, but he spotted her as she turned to face him.

Marks would be accompanying him into the ship along with others. He was to conduct a preliminary search to discover the state of things in the interior. Aside from lots of dead Space Fleet personnel, he had no idea what he might find. The last thing he needed was a jumpy Marine.

He grabbed a strut and came to a halt.

No one else was looking his way. That wasn't so strange. They had to concentrate on what they were doing. But their movements seemed slow and reluctant. Whatever was bothering Marks, the rest of the team felt the same.

"Marks," he said, "leave that a minute and come here."

She pressed the magnetized square on her power tool to a pipe and propelled herself in his direction. Catching onto one of the bars used to manipulate the scalpel, she stopped in front of Wright.

Through the tint of her visor, he was surprised to see fear in her eyes.

This was the Marine who had courageously helped him blast into the mountain in West BI to find Arthur. She had also ventured out with him under fire to rescue Ellis, who had been immobilized.

He switched his comm system to one-to-one.

"What is it, Marks? What's going on? Whatever it is, you can tell me. You won't get into trouble."

She broke eye contact. "It's just...Shit, I feel dumb saying it."

"Come on, spit it out. We don't have forever. The EAC would love to get their hands on the *Fearless*, even in her current state. They could be on their way right now."

Wright heard her swallow and then say, still looking away

from him, "It's just, some of the others are worried about what might be inside."

He guessed she was also one of the 'others'.

"S-some people have been calling it a ghost ship."

"A ghost...?"

Dammit.

He'd heard it all: Gremlins causing system failures; mysterious alien predators living on moons with no atmosphere; and zombie hostiles rising from the dead.

Now it was ghost ships.

You could train Marines to keep on fighting against hopeless odds, to put their lives on the line every day, but you couldn't train them out of being superstitious.

"Okay," he said, "everyone on the *Fearless* probably died when the black cloud took her, or if they didn't die then, they blued soon after. We're going to find dead people, for sure. It isn't going to be pleasant. If it's any consolation, as long as you keep your visor down, you won't smell them. But ghosts? Come on."

His skepticism didn't appear to have any effect on the corporal, who continued to look at him with dread behind her eyes.

"I've never seen a ghost," he said. "Have you?"

"No-o."

"Anyone in your family ever seen one?" he asked. "They're miners, right?"

"Last I heard. I blocked them after they signed up with the Antarctic Project. I don't remember any of them saying they saw a ghost—"

"There you go."

"But they did used to talk about brownies that would take revenge if you accidentally broke into one of their caves."

Wright suppressed a sigh. "All right, look at it this way: If there are ghosts on the *Fearless*, they're BA ghosts. They're going to be friendly, not try to hurt us. They'll probably stay out of the way, in fact, to make it easier for us to give their bodies a decent burial. Makes sense, doesn't it?"

"I guess so," replied Marks, not sounding at all reassured.

"Good. Get back to work. If I don't report to the brigadier soon that we're beginning the search, she'll come out herself from the *Valiant* to see what's happening. We don't want that, do we?"

Though the larger vessel, the *Cornflower's* 'parent' ship was only a few hundred kilometers distant, Colbourn would be mightily pissed off if she felt it necessary to make the journey.

"*No*, sir," exclaimed Marks. She thrust off with a hand and returned to the edge of the scaffold.

The brigadier was scarier than any ghost.

Wright addressed the team. "As you know, the *Fearless* is still maintaining an atmosphere, so we can expect some nastiness once we're inside. You might see someone you once knew." It was doubtful any of the corpses would be recognizable, but it wasn't impossible. "It's going to be hard. I want you to remember the real people who manned the ship are long gone, and what you see is only the shells they left behind. When we've figured out the situation, they'll be given all the respect they deserve, but for now, I want you to focus on doing your job."

"Sir," said Cole, "permission to speak."

"Go ahead."

"Should we expect to encounter hostiles, sir?"

"If anyone aboard her wanted a fight, she would have fired on us when we came within range hours ago. That answer your question?"

"Yes, sir," Cole replied doubtfully.

Was the private imagining a space creature lurking on the former flagship?

"You have your rifles just in case," said Wright. "But think before you shoot. The ship still has pressure. I don't want one of you blasting a hole in the hull."

When the scaffold was secured and the molecular scalpel was in place, the two engineers on the team guided the scalpel's nozzle to the ship's hull and started her up. Pre-programmed, the machine moved smoothly, slicing a vertical line through the thick skin, severing the layers like a razor passing through silk. Gases erupted from the slit, instantly condensing to ice. The scalpel turned a corner and swept along the horizontal, silent in the vacuum.

The molecular scalpel's progress continued until the square was complete. The emerging clouds of frozen condensate faded. The engineers withdrew the machine, and then applied magnetized paddles to detach the excised section. The movement caused the motion-sensitive interior lights to blink on. They slid the thick slice of hull away and captured it in a net before securing it to the side of the cage.

The airlock looked normal. Beyond the small oblong window on the far side, the passageway lights were on, which Wright found odd. He'd been expecting the ship to be in darkness, though he didn't really know why. Unanticipated nervousness hit him. Until that moment, he'd been focused on the task ahead, but now the oddness of the scenario reared up in his mind.

The *Fearless* had disappeared in the midst of battle, 'swallowed' by an amorphous mass of unknown astronomical matter. And now here she was, inexplicably hundreds of millions of kilometers from her original position.

How had she come to be here? What force had transported her and then abandoned her? What had killed everyone aboard?

"Major Wright," said one of the engineers from inside the airlock, "the control panel appears to be working normally. Do you want to bring the team in so we can seal the breach before we open the inner hatch?"

"Affirmative."

2

The Marine approaching Taylan seemed familiar. He was tall and burly, and he had a look on his face that told her she better not beat him.

Huh, tough.

Ah!

She remembered him. He was the guy the instructor had teamed her up with the first time she supported a training session—the guy she'd thrown on the mat and punched to keep him down.

The burly Marine lunged. Taylan stooped, preparing to drive her shoulder in low and unbalance him, maybe even upend him as she had before. But he'd learned from his earlier encounter. He went lower, and swiped at her with a fist. If it hadn't been for her fast reflexes, his longer reach would have caught her. She pulled her head back just in time. His knuckles swept past her nose.

She shot out a hand and grabbed his extended wrist, quickly twisting it and stepping to the side, trying to get his arm up and behind his back. He was too strong. He resisted the twisting and kicked out at her knee.

A shout of protest went up from the audience of new recruits. She jumped left a fraction, just enough that he didn't make contact, while maintaining her grip on his wrist. *What a jerk.* The big guy could break her knee and put her out of action for weeks.

She hauled him forward, taking advantage of his temporary imbalance, and quickly got behind him, shoving him the remaining distance to the floor. In another beat she had a knee on his back and his elbow pushed up.

The downed Marine cursed and tried to rise, but she forced his arm higher. Even his thick muscles couldn't protect his shoulder from the pressure. With a yell of pain and frustration, he slammed the mat with his other hand, conceding the match.

Taylan released her hold and climbed to her feet, panting. Her opponent also rose, and she saw him hesitate. Was he planning to pull a fast one and attack her while her guard was down? She glared at him, hard-eyed.

I dare you.

After another moment's hesitation, he slunk off, walked right past the gawking recruits on the mat, and barged out of the gym.

The instructor went after him, yelling.

She shook her head. Her partner's behavior was unacceptable, but it was also a symptom of a wider problem that affected the BA's military forces. Arthur's influence had gone some way to improve matters, but the cracks were still evident.

The instructor returned, without her demonstration partner.

What was his problem? Everyone lost sometimes. It was nothing to be ashamed of. Her dad had beaten her more times than she knew. He'd taught her to accept defeat graciously and try to understand what had gone wrong so she could avoid making the same mistake. Maybe that was the difference. The guy was used to winning all his matches due to his size. He didn't know *how* to lose.

"Session's over," said the instructor. "Dismissed."

She jogged to the showers. If she was lucky, she might be able to find Arthur and spend some time with him. Ever since he'd learned English, she'd been getting him to tell her about his life and the world he'd lived in. Though Wright still refused to accept the man was *the* Arthur, King of Britain, the former name for the Britannic Isles, she didn't need any more convincing. No one could make up the number and range of things he'd told her over the weeks, and no one could maintain the facade so effectively for so long.

What she didn't understand was how he was still alive. Arthur's existence was *impossible*. But he couldn't explain it either, so she'd given up on trying to figure it out.

After putting on her clothes, she left the changing room and headed for his cabin.

When she arrived, he wasn't home.

She had no way of reaching him. He had no comm implant. The docs hadn't wanted to put him through the operation as they were still trying to figure out how the hell he was alive. He also didn't carry a comm button. The devices freaked him out. He could watch vids, but disembodied voices coming out of nowhere made him turn pale and tremble. It was just one of the many aspects of his new life he would take time to get used to. He'd only just begun to accept the *Valiant* floated in the sky.

Where could he be?

She walked down the passageway, trying to think of likely places.

First, she went to the mess. Arthur loved eating and would eat anything and everything he was offered. But there was no sign of him there. Her next destination was the entertainment lounges. He wasn't in any of them, but then she remembered he'd complained about the noise and lights. Along from the entertainment lounges was the main fitness center. Her hopes rose as she walked inside and surveyed the exercise machines. Arthur came here quite often to work out, though he didn't seem to have to do as much as regular people to put on muscle.

He wasn't in the fitness center.

Bummed, she left.

Where else?

Taylan wandered the *Valiant* for another half an hour before she finally found Arthur in the sick bay, of all places. It had been the last place she'd looked, and then only because she was bored. She hadn't thought he could actually be there. He was probably the healthiest person on the ship.

"Hey, what are you doing here?!" she asked as she spotted him sitting outside the medics' office. Even if it hadn't been for his size, the torcs he wore around his neck and bicep made him stand out.

"Hi," he replied, "it's good to see you too."

His English had improved a lot over the weeks since he'd undergone the speed learning program, and he'd developed quite the talent for sarcasm.

"Sorry, I was just surprised to see you in the sick bay. Did you hurt yourself? Are you ill?"

"Neither. I'm not here for me."

"Oh." She looked around the room, thinking she must have missed the patient, but the place was empty.

Then the door to the medics' office opened.

A doctor emerged, carrying Boots.

"I'm here for him," said Arthur.

The doc placed the cat in his arms. "I've checked him over, and there's nothing to worry about. I guess he must have thrown up a hairball. It's pretty common for cats."

"That's a relief. Thank you."

"No problem. Examining cats makes a change from treating

war wounds. Hello, Corporal Ellis," added the doc. "How's your back?"

"I get a twinge now and then, but it's pretty good."

"You hurt your back?" asked Arthur.

"Yeah, but it's fine now."

"The option to exchange the artificial replacements we used for natural ones grown from your stem cells is still open," said the doc. "Now might be a good time, before shit really goes down. You should ask permission."

"Thanks. I'll think about it."

The doctor shrugged. "Up to you." She returned to her office.

"What did she mean, *before shit really goes down*?" asked Arthur. "What shit are we expecting?"

"Uh, you don't know?" Taylan hadn't been aware he was so out of the loop. She hadn't said much to him about BA stuff, preferring to listen to stories of ancient West BI. "Come and get a coffee with me. We need to talk."

"Sure." He stood up. Despite the fact that nowadays he wore ship-printed civvies and his red-gold hair and beard were clipped short, he still managed to retain the appearance of an Iron Age warlord. He towered over most everyone else on the ship and his chest and shoulders were proportionate to his height.

Boots climbed from his arms onto his shoulder before leaping the considerable distance to the floor and running out of the sick bay.

"I guess he doesn't like coffee," said Taylan.

～

"I like this drink," Arthur said as they sat down in the mess with their mugs of coffee, "but I prefer ale."

"Most of the ship agrees with you," Taylan replied, "but drinking alcohol is against regulations."

"It is?! Why?"

"Because it makes you drunk. And when Marines get drunk, bad things happen. Sometimes we're allowed a few beers for a special occasion, but mostly we can't drink unless we're on surface leave."

A twinge of sadness hit her. The prospect of surface leave in the near future was currently a dim and distant hope.

Arthur gave a snort of surprise. "Every day I learn something new. In my world, everyone drinks ale from the moment they're weaned. Though the beer children drink is very weak."

"Kids in your time drank beer?" asked Taylan, astonished.

"Why not? It's safer than drinking water."

"Huh, well, you don't need to worry about the water on the *Valiant*. It's very clean." She didn't go on to explain that it had also passed through other shipmates many times. Some things, it was better he didn't know.

Her curiosity sparked by his reference to 'his world' she asked a question she'd meant to ask him for weeks. "Arthur, do you still think you're dreaming?"

He took a sip of coffee and put down his mug before answering, "If I am, it's a very long dream. But perhaps dreams can seem to last a lifetime. Honestly, Taylan, I'm no longer sure. Everything I experience feels real." He smiled. "The way I see it, I might as well behave as if this is reality."

"That sounds a good way of handling it, and I'm glad for another reason. You see, we need you. The people of this time, I mean. Do you know the prophecy about your return?"

Once again, he took his time to answer. "I know something of it." He didn't elaborate.

What was he holding back?

Taylan decided not to press him. "Your story, as it was passed down to me, was that in your final battle you were mortally wounded, and you were carried from the field to an unknown place. There, you were to sleep until the people of the Britannic Isles needed you again. I'm from West BI, where we found you. My land was invaded by the EAC. I escaped to Ireland, along with my..." She paused and swallowed as memories popped into her mind. She went on, "The timing works, you see? After thousands of years of independence, the Britannic Isles fell to a foreign invader. And, within a couple of years, you were found and brought back to life."

Arthur was frowning and staring into his coffee.

"What are you thinking?" she asked.

He looked up and smiled again, the skin around his kind eyes wrinkling. "I think my timing could have been a little better."

"What's two or three years between friends?" Taylan quipped. "Seriously, though, I can't think of any better explanation for what happened. Can you? You're here to help solve the crisis and restore the Britannic Isles to its people. After the military coup attempt and destruction of the BA's Parliament in exile on Jamaica, the Space Fleet was going to secede. The Britannic Alliance was falling apart. Everything was breaking into pieces—until you gave your speech in the gym. You restored Colbourn and Wright's faith in their cause, in themselves. And you gave the *Valiant's* Marines something to believe in. We didn't manage to force the EAC off Jamaica, but when the rest of the Fleet saw what we were doing, it changed minds. Now, people have begun to pull together again."

"I only spoke the truth as I see it."

"But it was a truth we'd lost sight of. Words can be powerful when you've lost hope and a sense of purpose."

Arthur sighed. "I'm happy I helped, but it wasn't by design. I just did what you asked me to do. As to freeing the Britannic Isles, as you call them, I'm ill equipped. I don't understand how you fight, how your weapons work, or how to operate any of your strange machines. I don't know who your enemies are or what strategies they use. I'm at a loss. Give me a sword, armor, and a battlefield, and I'm your man. But your world is too different and too complicated for me."

"I understand. Everything you say has already crossed my mind. But the prophecy was correct. That much, we know. Only the most stubborn would deny it." Taylan thought of Wright. "On the other hand, what you say is true too. Your fighting skills aren't so useful now."

"Maybe I could talk to the other knights of the Britannic Isles."

"That would probably help, but there's no Camelot anymore, Arthur. Millions of men and women were on active duty in the BA military not so long ago, in all parts of the globe. I don't know how many are contactable now. They'll be fighting their corners in the remaining BA territories and protectorates, or they will have gone to ground, waiting to see what happens."

"A million knights? I can hardly imagine such a number."

"It doesn't matter how many there are if we can't reach them," said Taylan. "I don't know what the answer is. We're missing something."

3

———

The passageway was silent and empty. According to the figures on Wright's HUD, the *Fearless's* life support systems were functioning normally.

He lifted his visor.

Something his suit's sensors would not register was the odor of death, but the air smelled normal. He expected he would be picking up the awful smell soon enough, but at least no nasty surprises seemed to be awaiting them in the immediate vicinity.

He wasn't expecting an EAC or AP trap out here in the Belt. Both had fled the battle scene after the *Fearless's* disappearance, so it was unlikely they had anything to do with what had happened to the ship. He decided to split the team into small groups to expedite the search.

After dividing them up, he said, "Proceed with caution. At the first sign of something suspicious, halt and comm me before going any farther. And make sure your cams stay on. Service access tunnels only. I don't want to waste time trying to figure out how to get you out of a faulty elevator. Sergeant Elphicke, your team takes deck four." He went on to portion out the other areas. Finally, he said, "Marks and Cole, come with me."

"We're searching deck six, sir?" asked Cole. It was the only deck Wright hadn't assigned, and the site of the *Fearless's* bridge, where they might be able to access the ship's log.

"Affirmative. I want to start at the bridge and work forward." He led them toward an aft maintenance hatch.

A blueprint of the *Fearless* was an overlay on his HUD, and dots signified the search teams. They were crawling steadily along the ship's lines. His comm remained quiet.

As they passed by an elevator, it dinged. Marks jumped.

"Hey,' Wright admonished. "Cool it, Marine."

"Sorry, sir," she replied, though her eyes remained wide as she stared at the elevator doors.

They opened, but it was empty.

She visibly relaxed.

The doors closed, and the elevator descended. Wright felt Marks tensing at his side. No doubt she was wondering if ghosts were operating it.

A few minutes later, they climbed out of the service hatch into an empty passage on deck six.

"Where *is* everyone?" Cole asked. "They just disappeared?"

Wright didn't reply, thinking the disappearance of the *Fearless's* occupants would be a better alternative than what he expected to find. A ship's infrastructure and systems might survive being flung millions of kilometers, but the people aboard would not. It was only a matter of time before his team or another would stumble upon the smears that were all that remained of anything organic.

He stepped toward the nearest door, which led to the bridge. At the time of the battle, the former admiral, Yorkson, and many of the ship's officers would have been here.

Partly expecting the door to not open, he approached it slowly.

As he reached it, it slid back.

The wide, semi-circular room spread out before them.

Empty.

Cole was peering over Wright's shoulder.

"Nothing here, sir," he said, sounding relieved.

The bridge wasn't the kind of place people left things lying around, especially not during a battle, so it was unsurprising there were no signs of human occupation. The ranks of consoles and seats appeared as they would on any large BA starship. From long experience, Wright knew where each officer would sit: Helm, navigator, weapons officers, comms, and so on. At first glance, no damage appeared to have been inflicted, and there was no obvious explanation for the absence of people.

Perhaps whatever had moved the *Fearless* across the Solar System had caused everything living aboard her to vanish?

Wright walked to the captain's seat, from where the admiral would have directed the BA fleet. The interface screen was dead. He tried to open it, but it didn't respond.

"Check the consoles," he told Marks and Cole. "Tell me if anything's working."

He went to the navigator's station.

Here, the screen reacted to his touch. He gave it the security override code.

Instantly, a holo flashed up in the center of the room.

Marks started. "*Shit!*"

"Steady, Corporal," said Wright.

She muttered something about pissing her pants, but he ignored it.

The holo was of the battle where the *Fearless* had been lost. They'd been on their way to attack the *Bres*, Ua Talman's colony ship, when the AP and EAC had closed in on them.

From the positions of the ships, he guessed the scene was about a minute from the moment the black cloud had reached out. From the perspective of the flagship, the cloud was behind, above, and to the left.

He watched. Cole and Marks had also stopped what they were doing to witness the replay of the disaster.

The finger reached out.

It seemed so purposeful, like it wasn't only a living thing, but also intelligent. It had targeted the *Fearless* and removed it for a reason.

The finger touched the ship and flowed over and around it, enveloping it.

The holo died.

"Okay," said Wright. "Finish checking the other consoles. Then we try the mess."

THE BRIDGE YIELDED no clues about the fate of the *Fearless's* personnel, but the mess room doors opened on a scene from a horror vid.

They'd found some of the missing men and women, and they were alive...ish.

Several hundred people were crammed into the space. All were heavily emaciated. Their uniforms hung from their bones, and their faces were hollowed and fleshless. Some were lying in corners, out of the way of foot traffic, many sat listlessly at tables, and a few wandered about aimlessly. The room stank of body odor, unwashed clothes, and other smells Wright didn't want to dwell on.

What was most remarkable was no one appeared to have registered the Marines' arrival. No faces turned toward the door, no one said anything. In fact, aside from the sounds of movement, the mess was eerily silent.

Something very, very strange had happened. But at least some of the ship's personnel had survived.

Wright comm'd the news to Colbourn immediately. As he was speaking to the brigadier, Elphicke tried to contact him. He asked Colbourn to please wait.

"Sir," said the sergeant, sounding shocked, "we've found some of the crew."

"Where are you?"

"Mess hall. Deck Four."

"Don't tell me, they're alive but only just?"

"Yes, Major. How did you know?"

"Stand by, Sergeant."

"We've located some more of the personnel," Wright told Colbourn, "in a similar state. I'm guessing there are still more to find. They all seem to have migrated to the messes. There are so many of them, it'll probably be easier to send the medics here."

"Yes, that makes sense," the brigadier replied. "Is the ship secure? I want to come and see things for myself."

"We're still assessing the situation, ma'am."

"Let me know when you're ready." Colbourn closed the comm.

Now that he'd carried out his orders, pity for the poor souls gnawed at him. He approached one of the *Fearless's* crew, a private. The man was slumped at a table, his head barely upright, gazing unfocused into the middle distance.

"Hey, what's your name?" Wright asked.

But the man didn't seem to even hear him. He also didn't seem to have noticed that the person he was sitting next to was too still and turning black. Not everyone had survived.

Wright reached over the table and grabbed the private's shoulder. It felt like pure bone under his hand. "Name, rank, and number," he said, hoping the formality of the request might trigger a response.

His demand provoked no reaction, except perhaps the tiniest glimmer of consciousness deep in the man's eyes.

Of all the situations Wright had imagined he might

encounter on the *Fearless*, this one had never entered his mind. The crew were alive and present, but in body only. Whatever had happened to them had affected their minds. They must have been taking on fluids or they would all be long dead by now. But they hadn't been eating, or only very little. Brain damage seemed the likely answer. The docs would figure it out.

4

———

Dwyr Kala Orr lived in darkness. The heavy curtains of her bedchamber were permanently closed, and she rarely left the room. When she worked, she lit only one candle to see her books. She had ordered that every mirror in the castle be removed. If she went out, everyone had to remain in their workplace, and if she passed near them, they had to avert their gazes. Even Perran was banished from her company.

It was not enough.

In her rage during the BA's invasion of her Jamaican mansion, she hadn't realised the extent of her injuries. The soldier who fired upon her in the secret tunnel had set her robes alight. The flames had engulfed her torso, arms, and head as she fled, and even the herbal ointments of her medics had failed to prevent severe damage to her skin and face.

The moment she'd first seen her injuries replayed again and again in her mind. She couldn't shake the image in the mirror of her stretched, red face and neck, distorted and twisted, from her thoughts. It horrified her.

She had been *beautiful*.

Now, she was a burnt-up husk, and every day her injuries became more painful as her scars grew tighter.

More disturbing even than her damaged appearance was the fact that someone had managed to hurt her, *she*, who was inviolable. The fact went against everything she'd always understood about herself. It meant Perran was in danger too. Had she misunderstood all these years? It made no sense.

There was one way to find out, but she was reluctant to attempt it. The cost and risk might not outweigh the benefits. She could lose everything she'd worked so hard for. On the other hand, what was the alternative? Could she face living out the rest of her life hidden away or, even more unimaginable, facing the world in her altered state?

Her books provided no other answer than the one she feared. But was she ready to go that way yet? Were things bad enough?

There was no way back to her partnership with Ua Talman. She had burned her bridge to him when she had turned upon him, and now she'd earned his deep animosity. He had aided the Britannic Alliance in their attack upon Jamaica, his ships defending the BA destroyer as it waited in orbit above Earth. And her assault upon his colony vessels had failed. She'd lost ships from her fleet, though thankfully not the *Belladonna*. Her flagship remained intact and was patrolling the neutral zone beyond high Earth orbit. She'd given her commander and the other heads of her military forces free rein while she dealt with the distraction of her personal crisis.

She could expect repercussions of her failed partnership with Ua Talman to continue. The only advantage she had was the intel Perran had brought back from his visit to the *Bres*.

And she still hadn't ended the threat from the mythical man the BA had extracted from his sealed cave in the West BI mountain. She'd been warned about him long ago, and it had taken her decades of research and investigations to find him, only to have him snatched from her just as she reached out to grasp him.

She was also desperate to discover who had succeeded in hurting her. She had to find out how it had been possible, and, then, she wanted vengeance. When she found out the identity of her attacker, she would do everything in her power to locate and then kill them, in the most long-winded, painful way possible. Her own sufferings would be nothing in comparison with those she would inflict.

Unfortunately, her contact within the BA had gone silent. Why, she didn't know. It was possible the woman had died in the invasion of Jamaica. Or she was hiding for some other reason, perhaps to protect herself. The upshot was Kala's reach into the Alliance was shortened. She needed a new source of intel.

She walked to her chamber window and opened a curtain a little, enough to peek out. Outside, life went on. Workers passed to and fro in the courtyard. The sun lit a square of grass. She could hear the ocean surging against the castle stones. She wanted to be out there, in command, leading the EAC, not ensconced in her room.

She would never find her attacker and enact her revenge as long as she spent her days ruing her ravaged visage.

She had no choice. It was time to act and take the feared path. She would leave her room early tomorrow. She could only hope the risk would be worth the reward.

THE APOTHECARY HAD to be an old man by now. Kala wasn't even completely certain he was still alive. Since she'd granted him a lifelong place in her household, the man kept to himself, carrying out his experiments late into the night and rarely speaking to anyone. In other places where she'd lived, she'd often seen a light shining from the window of his room in the early hours of the morning, but in her current abode she wasn't even sure where his room was.

It was time to find him.

The cook would know which room was the apothecary's. The woman knew everything that went on in the castle. Kala put on a dark, woolen cloak and pulled the wide hood over her head, drawing it low so her face could not be seen. Outside, the sun was rising. The cook would be in the kitchen already, preparing breakfast, but most of the rest of the castle would be asleep.

Kala walked down the stairs and into the quiet hallway. She crossed to the doorway at the back of the hall and descended another, narrower, staircase. As she'd predicted, the cook was already at work, bent over a large wooden table, rolling dough. A young girl was there too, on her knees, starting a fire in the stove.

At Kala's entrance, the cook's gaze quickly took in her presence and then flicked to the girl. She sharply told her to go to fetch the day's milk. When only the cook and Kala remained in the kitchen, she said, "Good morning, mistress. Is there something I can do for you?" all the while keeping her eyes firmly focused on her task.

"I'm looking for the apothecary, Jonathan. Do you know where he is?"

"Jon the Alchemist?"

"Is that what he's calling himself these days? Yes, that's who I mean."

"I know his room, but he'll be asleep. When Mary comes back I can send her to wake him up and bring him to you, ma'am."

"No, I'll wake him myself."

"In that case..." The cook gave her directions.

The apothecary had—predictably—chosen a room in an

out-of-the-way section of the castle, where few people would have cause to go. Kala crept along the passageways until she reached the winding stairway that led to the man's remote living space. The air seemed chillier here. She drew her cloak tighter and ascended the steps.

A single door stood at the top.

Rapping her knuckles on the solid wood made little sound, and there was no knocker.

"Jon," she called out. "Jon, wake up! It's Kala."

She listened.

Silence.

Had he even heard her through the thick barrier?

"Jon! Wake up! It's me."

Still, nothing.

Could she hear snoring?

She turned the iron ring to open the door.

Jon's room was small and round. A bed occupied one quarter of the stone wall. On the opposite wall stood ranks of shelves lined with transparent jars containing liquids and strange, dried materials. The rest of the space was taken up with tables full of scientific equipment. The air was filled with a heavy, sickly, chemical scent, probably from the experiment that was running on one of the tables. A tiny flame was heating yellow liquid in a spherical glass. A box sat under the bed, clothes spilling from it, and on the bed itself a lump rounded out wrinkled, messy covers.

"Jon!"

Even at close quarters, her shout provoked no response.

She stepped to the bedside and leaned over the sleeper. His bedclothes were pulled up to his chin, and a nightcap had been pulled down over his ears. A thin, scraggly, white beard covered his cheek, and his nose was a map of broken capillaries.

He looked much older than she remembered him. How

long had it been since she'd used his services? It had to be ten years or more.

She grabbed his shoulder and shook. "Jon, wake up, you old goat."

Sleepy groans issued from the elderly man. He shrugged her hand off his shoulder and pulled the covers over his head.

"Jon the Alchemist," Kala said sternly. "Your Dwyr commands you to rise immediately."

"Ughhnnner," Jon muttered. "Whaaaadyou...Dwyr?" A shock seemed to run through him, and he jerked awake, throwing off the covers and leaping up. Kala had to leap backward to get out of his way.

Wearing a grubby nightshirt that hung to his knees, he stood legs akimbo and arms spread out as if to ward off an attack from an unknown direction. Stick-thin calves poked out of his nightshirt, leading to bony feet and hairy toes. He swiveled his head from side to side.

"Wh-where is she? Where's the Dwyr?"

"Put on your glasses, you silly fool."

Jon appeared to waken up some more. "Ah, glasses. Yes."

Turning to the small table next to his bed, he patted it until his hand alighted on a pair of spectacles. He put them on, tucking the thin wire frames behind his ears. When he turned back and spotted Kala, he started, and then sat on the edge of his bed. "You-you gave me quite a fright."

"Well, don't have a heart attack," Kala said. "I need you."

"Hmpf!" Jon pulled out the box of clothes from under his bed, rummaged around, and found a holey cardigan. He put it on, and then thrust his feet into fluffy slippers. He peered at her more closely. "Why are you hiding under that cloak?"

Taking a breath, she pulled the hood down onto her shoulders.

The old man only raised his eyebrows slightly. "If that's the look people are going for these days, I can't say I like it."

"Don't joke," Kala replied bitterly, drawing the hood over her head once more.

"I'm sorry, I can't help you. I don't provide medical treatment these days. I've been concentrating on—"

"I know you can't help me. I didn't come here for that."

"I'm sure the BA and AP have the technology to treat scarring. If you asked nicely, they would probably give you the surgery."

"I said, don't joke!"

Jon had never approved of the Earth Awareness Crusade. It had long been a bone of contention between them and was one of the reasons Kala avoided him.

"What are you going to do?" he asked. "Have me executed? Have me *burned alive*?"

The news of what she'd done with the two BA military leaders must have gotten back to him. She didn't care. He didn't understand and never would.

She allowed him his taunt. He was the only person in her domain who could get away with it, with the possible exception of Perran. She would never hurt him, and he knew it.

"I want you to prepare me another draught of the formula."

The querulous old man, who had been picking at the holes in his cardigan, grew still. After a pause, without looking up, he said, "No."

"It wasn't a request. I'm ordering you to make it."

"No. I won't do it."

Kala sighed. "Move over."

He slid along the bed, and she sat down beside him.

"I need you to do this for me, or at least give me the recipe."

"Again, no. To both. No one else could make it anyway. They would only mess it up."

Kala sighed again, trembling. Her gaze traveled the room, taking in once more the glass instruments, bubbling liquid, and peculiar ingredients. Jon's other room had looked much the same when she'd broken into it as a young girl, fascinated by the weird and wonderful things. Her resulting experience had been the beginning of her journey.

The EAC hadn't been her idea. Others had begun the organization as a reaction to the activities of the AP, when no one else had seemed to care for the sanctity of the Earth any longer. But after her experience in Jon's room, her young eyes had been opened to the direction the Earth Awareness Crusade needed to take. It didn't have to be only a society of nature lovers. It could be so much more. It only needed someone to show it the way, and she'd known with absolute certainty she was that person.

The EAC was her life. It was *her*. And it was slipping from her grasp. She had to have another boost, another delve into the source, if she was to overcome this latest setback.

"Jon, *please*."

"I won't do it. It could kill you. I should never have done it again after the first time. I don't know what I was thinking. I was too enchanted with the tales you told afterward, I suppose. But you're older now. Less resilient. Look at you. You're injured. You must be in pain. How can you withstand—"

"I cannot go on without it. I simply can't. I'm begging you, as one friend to another. You have to. You're the one who started me on this journey. You can't abandon me now."

"If I could go back in time and reverse what I did, I would. Do you know how many times I've regretted leaving that concoction out on my desk, for any adolescent burglar to find?" He shot her a gap-toothed grin.

Kala relaxed. He was coming around. The apothecary had always had a soft spot for her, ever since she'd been an urchin on the streets of Berline, sharing his lunch with her and giving her his cast offs. It was no wonder that one night when the temperature fell to -15C, it had been his shop she'd picked to sneak into for warmth. She knew if he found her, he wouldn't have her arrested.

Neither of them could have guessed what would result when she'd sampled the experimental mixture he'd left out to cool overnight.

She put her arm around his old shoulders, skeletal under her touch. He'd always cared more about his work than eating. "I think this will be the last time."

"You've said that before."

"I know, but...I need answers only she can give. If I don't have them, I won't know how to go on and finish what I've started. The EAC will fall apart. All its members will lose their livelihoods, their way of life. You won't have this cozy little place or free access to everything you need for your experiments. I'll take full responsibility for whatever happens."

"I don't care who will be held responsible. I care about *you*. Your practices have become more and more questionable over time. I'm not comfortable with the way things are going. I don't want to encourage you."

"Perhaps I have lost my way. Perhaps I need her help to guide me back to the truth path."

Jon groaned. "You have a will of iron and the persuasive powers of a serpent. No matter what I say, you have a counterargument. Ah well, why put off the inevitable?"

"Then you'll do it?"

"Do I have a choice? Come back in a couple of hours. I already have all the ingredients."

Kala wrapped her other arm around the old man and hugged him.

5

Living in a cramped bamboo cage and eating only scraps had left Hans Jonte a shadow of his former self. His arms and legs were brown, mosquito-bitten sticks. His stomach was a concave hollow above his jutting hips. Sores on his buttocks and back, arms and sides, made most resting positions agony. The only way he could sleep was by lying on his stomach, his knees folded up at one end of the cage and his head pressed against the other. Once he developed sores on his chest—probably only a matter of a few days—he would have no places on his body remaining where he could touch the bamboo without being in severe pain.

Death would probably come soon after.

How long had he been here? Weeks? Months? He'd lost track of the passing days.

He remembered the night of the military coup and the EAC attack that quickly followed. Mariya had said she knew a place they could hide, and she'd driven them into the mountainous jungle. They'd left the car and walked down the trail that led to the cave entrance. Mariya had followed him.

When her car's headlights were no longer shining, it was

hard to see where to go, and Hans feared he would miss his step in the dark. The people in the mouth of the cave seemed to be watching and waiting for him, though he could only make out their silhouettes.

Mariya had gone strangely silent. He would have expected a *Be careful, Mr Jonte* from her, or a *Watch where you step*, or something equally solicitous. It was what he'd come to expect from her. In that, she was very like her deceased identical twin.

But she only followed him quietly, without speaking.

He stepped from the end of the path onto the roughly flat stone that marked the beginning of the cave where it emerged into the lush, verdant vegetation of the tropical mountainside. The faces and bodies of the people waiting became more distinct. These were people like Mariya—Jamaican locals, dressed in swathes of brilliant color. They were young like her too, young, strong, and vital.

"This is him?" asked one of the men.

She must have nodded as a reply. Immediately, the man who had spoken and another young man strode forward and each grabbed one of Hans's biceps. They pulled him so roughly he stumbled, and then they dragged him.

"What-what are you doing?" Hans protested. He fought, but his captors' grips were too tight. "Mariya, what's going on? Mariya!"

He was dragged into the back of the cave. There, hidden in shadow, was a cage made of bamboo, the canes lashed together with vines. He was thrust inside so hard he hit the opposite side, nearly overturning the light structure. But it rocked back to the horizontal. The door slammed shut and someone tied another dried vine around the door and its frame, doubling and tripling the knot before sitting down with his back to Hans.

Grabbing the bars, Hans yelled, "Mariya, what are you doing? Who are these people? Why are you doing this to me?"

His—former, he guessed, now—PA was talking quietly with

the others. They were all ignoring him. He shouted several more times before giving up. His mind was whirling with shock, and he felt weak and clammy, despite the heat of the night.

What would they do to him? Were they going to kill him? Or were they planning on giving him to the EAC?

The only person who might possibly answer his questions was his guard.

"You," he said, "who are these people? Why have I been brought here?"

The man, who seemed younger than the rest, didn't react.

Hans reached through the bars and touched his back.

"Hey!" the man yelled, leaping to his feet and spinning to face Hans. He pulled a knife from a sheath at his waist and thrust it at Hans, who jerked backward involuntarily.

"Touch me again and I'll slit your throat," the youth threatened.

He sat down again, facing away as before but at a greater distance from the bars.

Hans dropped to his knees, instantly regretting it as his kneecaps hit the bamboo canes. He tried sitting, but the canes ground into his buttocks. He was forced to squat on his haunches instead, resting his back against the bars.

The people at the front of the cave were deep in discussion. They'd moved farther out, and someone was starting a fire. He could hear them speak but could only make out the odd word, not enough to understand exactly what they were saying. He heard *Dwyr Orr* several times and *the BA*. That was only to be expected. Mariya's reasons for bringing him here and imprisoning him were clearly something to do with the EAC's invasion of Jamaica.

It had all been a lie. Her taking over from Josie, her 'hero worship' of him, her work for SIS. The entire time she'd had some other agenda. But what was it?

He gritted his teeth and knocked the back of his head against his prison. How could he have been so stupid? He'd been seduced by her appearance, disarmed by her flattery. He, the head of SIS, a man whose entire career had centered around espionage and the gathering of sensitive intel, outwitted by a young woman.

Just as his shame and anger were peaking, Mariya separated from the group beyond the cave's edge and walked over to him.

"Speak of the devil," Hans muttered.

But he bit his tongue, deciding against railing at her or upbraiding her for her deceit and disloyalty. Any understanding he held and didn't share with her could help him in the future, so he held onto his advantage, small though it was.

"Mariya," he said, trying to sound amazed and pathetic. "What's happening? Why have your friends locked me up? Don't they know I'm no danger to them? That I want to help them?"

She smiled her lazy smile, her eyes hooded. "You're confident for an imprisoned man. How could you help us, Hans? You have no power anymore. All your associates in the BA are dead, or soon will be. You're nothing now."

He hung his head, partly to hide the rage that was building despite his best efforts, and partly to give the impression of sadness and despair. "You're right. I'm nothing. The Britannic Alliance is finished. It'll never recover from this invasion. The Caribbean was our last major stronghold. Now all the others will fall too, either to the AP or the EAC and the days of the great BA will come to an end."

Mastering his expression, he looked up. "But I don't understand why you've brought me here if I'm so worthless and unimportant. What difference does it make to you if I live or die? Wouldn't it have been simpler to leave me for the EAC to find? Why did you go to the trouble of coming out to my villa and tricking me into leaving with you?"

She shook her head. "You're a monkey in a cage, and I don't give monkeys answers. You'll find out in time why you're here, and when you do, you'll probably wish you didn't know." She turned to leave.

"Mariya," he called. "One thing, I beg you. About Josie."

She'd begun to walk away, but she halted at the name. She didn't turn to face him.

"Was she really your sister?" he asked. "Or was that all a lie too?"

He barely heard her reply above the call of the cicadas and whining of mosquitoes. "Yes, she was my sister." Then she left him.

The fire outside grew brighter, and meat was speared onto sticks to roast over it. More people came out from the inner cave and joined those around the fire. They were smoking the local herb. The sweet, heady smell of it drifted over. They'd also brought drinks and other kinds of food. Hans was desperately hungry. He hadn't eaten any supper. His excitement over the military coup had stolen his appetite. But his current predicament made him ravenous for some reason, and the gin and tonic had worked its way out of his system, leaving him thirsty too.

No one paid any attention to him. Even the person who brought food and drink to his guard didn't spare the prisoner a glance.

"I need water," he complained. "And I'm hungry. Aren't I going to get anything to eat?"

But he might as well have been speaking into the ether.

It must have been two or three o'clock in the morning when the gathering around the fire began to break up. Another guard arrived to relieve the first, who went inside the cave with the majority of the men and women. Others lay down around the fire, wrapping themselves in blankets.

By now, Hans's body ached from contact with the bamboo

canes. They were three or four centimeters thick and the gaps between them were only just large enough to accommodate his fist. No matter how he sat or lay, or even leaned his back on them, he couldn't get comfortable. Within minutes, the pressure points would begin to hurt. After hours of this, he was nearly mad with discomfort. He'd tried asking for a blanket or grass or anything he could place between himself and the bamboo, but he'd been ignored.

The man who replaced his original guard was older than average in the group. He settled down facing the cave front and took something out from his shirt pocket. A little fiddling around with something else, and the lighting of a match, and the older man was puffing regular tobacco in a clay pipe.

Hans inhaled the rich scent. He loved a nice cigar himself, and had often rewarded himself with one at the end of a long day's plotting and maneuvering. He let out a long sigh and rested his forehead on the cage door.

"Water," he said. "Could I please have some water?"

When the guard continued to ignore him, he added, "Whatever you have planned for me, I won't be much use to you if I die of thirst."

"You be a'right till mornin'," the guard replied, in a heavy island accent.

"Please, I beg you. As one human being to another. Just a little water."

The man took his pipe from his mouth and spat on the sandy cave floor. "Shut your mout or I'll get some folks t'elp me move you out tere, away from t' fire, where t' skeeters'll getchu."

Hans didn't need telling twice. He was a mosquito magnet. As it was, the insects were already bothering him. He didn't fancy facing a night of their predation without the benefit of smoke to deter them. Resting a shoulder against a gap in the cage wall, he tried to get comfortable.

Exhaustion and hunger sent him into a light doze. He was

vaguely aware of people softly passing in the darkness, murmured conversations and snores out at the fire, and the smacking of his guard's lips as he puffed on his pipe.

A crick in Hans's neck drove him to full consciousness. He let out a groan and shifted position. His muscles and tendons sent out pain-ridden protests. He opened his eyes and dug his fingertips into their corners, removing crusted sleep. The sky was lightening, and the camp was quiet. Even the snorers by the fire had turned on their sides and were sleeping quietly.

Hans's guard had let his pipe fall from his hand. It had gone out, leaving a small scorch mark on the ground. The man's head was hanging on his chest and his ribs moved rhythmically.

Hans didn't waste any time. He moved quietly to the cage door and the knot his captor had tied in the vine that secured it. At the time, he'd thought it a slack method for preventing his escape. A knot could be untied easily. The greater challenge would be passing the sleepers without waking them and getting far enough away that they wouldn't catch him after they saw he was gone.

Being alone in the jungle with no food or any survival training would be a challenge, but it was preferable to captivity and an unknown fate.

He began to tug at the knot, trying to find a section of vine that he could loosen and thereby eventually work the whole knot open. Only none of them seemed any looser than the others. He tried to peer at the knot more closely, though it was difficult to see from inside the cage.

His digits roamed the puzzle. Perhaps he could feel its structure and so figure out how to undo it. But he couldn't interpret what he was feeling or imagine it in his mind's eye. He breathed a quiet curse. A knot! A freaking knot was all that stood between him and his chance of escape.

Minutes passed. His hands became slippery with sweat. His

fingertips were becoming as sore as the rest of his body with effort.

Then he heard a chuckle.

The guard was awake. Without Hans noticing, he'd been watching his attempts for—how long?

"You won' get tat open," he said. "Tat knot weren' made for untying." He stood up and stretched, and then walked to the edge of the cave where he pulled down the front of his pants and pissed into the vegetation.

Hans knelt down, hunched over, gloom and anguish gripping him.

6

Wright hadn't been exactly elated when Colbourn had tasked him with finding out what had happened to the *Fearless*. He was a Marine, not a detective, and though he had the services of scan data expert Corporal Singh at his disposal, he still felt he would be more useful doing something *military*.

But orders were orders, and it beat having to deal with the problems on the flagship.

All except twenty-five of the *Fearless's* personnel had survived their ordeal, though many lives hung in the balance. More survivors had been found at the ship's other messes, and they'd been in the same state as the first to be discovered. After assessing several of the crew, the *Valiant's* CMO reported the victims seemed to have retained sufficient brain function to gravitate to water and food sources, but they hadn't been capable of much more. At present, some could answer simple questions and obey basic instructions, while others appeared almost comatose and were close to death from dehydration and malnutrition.

Crew from the *Valiant* and *Cornflower* had been seconded to help care for the sick and meet their basic needs. Meanwhile, medics were treating the men and women, but whether they would ever return to normal mental function was a question that remained unanswered.

The *Fearless* herself, on the other hand, had only had her circuits scrambled a little. Otherwise, she was unaffected by what had happened to her. The flagship could return to her fleet. The BA only had to find another seven and a half thousand personnel to crew her.

The return journey to Earth had begun, though as far as Wright knew, there had been no updates from the admiral on what would happen when they arrived.

"What have you got so far?" he asked Singh, who was analyzing the data on the flagship's disappearance.

"Still nothing more than we already knew about the cloud," the corporal replied. "And all we have on that is the reduced light levels. I have found some more information on the ship, though I'm not sure how useful it is."

"Something's gotta be better than nothing."

"You know how we lost all trace of her until the *Gallant* noticed her by chance?"

The *Gallant* had been held back from the attack on Ua Talman's colony ship, the *Bres*. She'd been sent to a rarely frequented sector and had happened to pick up the *Fearless's* anomalous heat signature in the vastness of space.

"Uh huh."

"I found an old space telescope that's still operating, though no one's listening to it anymore. When I pulled its data, I found it happened to have registered the arrival of the *Fearless*. She appeared in the Belt at exactly the same time she disappeared from the battle."

"*Exactly* the same time?!"

"Uhh..." Singh checked his screen. "It depends on how exact you want to be. Point zero zero two seconds later."

"Exact enough." Wright rubbed the top of his head. "How far is Ua Talman's shipbuilding site from the Belt?" he asked, but as Singh began to check, he added, "Don't worry about it." Even if the distance were only a few meters, it was impossible for a starship to disappear from one place and reappear in another simultaneously. With the BA's flagship out of the picture, Talman could have gone for the kill, but he hadn't. His tech might be cutting edge, but he hadn't had anything to do with this.

Whatever had happened to the vessel, it had stopped her engines but allowed most of her other functions to continue normally. Unless that was entirely by chance, it indicated some kind of intelligence, as if the intent had been to remove the ship from the battlefield but not jeopardize the lives of the people inside her. Only the people *had* been harmed, some of them fatally, and it wouldn't have been long before they all would have died if the ship hadn't been discovered by chance.

Wright was reminded of a toddler playing with a pet and unintentionally hurting it. He softly cursed. What the hell was he supposed to put in his report?

As far as he was concerned, the biggest, most pertinent question had been answered. Whatever the cloud was, it didn't belong to the AP or EAC. If either organization had been in control of it, they would have used it repeatedly on the BA ships.

"Sir," Singh said suddenly, "can I ask what's going to happen now? Are we going back to Jamaica?"

Wright grimaced. "You're asking the wrong person. I don't think even Brigadier Colbourn has heard anything yet." He wasn't sure the higher ups even *had* a plan. Admiral Kim was new in her position, and the military coup had thrown her a curve ball. He guessed that might have been behind her hasty decision to secede. Now, if the BA wanted to drag itself back to some kind of position of power on Earth, it had a long, hard road ahead.

"If we were to try to take back a territory," Singh ventured, "it might make more sense to focus on the Britannic Isles. It *is* the homeland, after all."

"Hm, yeah." Wright knew of another corporal who would agree with the idea of re-taking the BI. "But the EAC has been there for a couple of years now and has a firm foothold. Whereas in the Caribbean they're still establishing themselves."

He didn't elaborate. Wherever the EAC invaded, its usual MO was to murder the local inhabitants, either directly or via imprisonment or slave labor. The appalling treatment of the local workers shortened their lifespans dramatically. Immediate converts to the 'Crusade' were sometimes spared, depending on the whims of the military leaders. Within six months to a year of an invasion, only a fraction of the native population remained.

"I heard EAC forces are gathering on the west coast," Singh said.

Wright sighed. "Preparing to push into Ireland."

"Yes."

"I'd heard that too."

As the cult had spread across Europe, the invaded had been driven into neighboring countries. Then, as the refuges fell, they often had time to flee by sea or air. In the Britannic Isles, the only place to go had been Ireland, which, Wright had heard, was suffering a massive refugee crisis.

"If they do attack Ireland," Singh went on, "it's hard to know where people will go from there. The nearest landmass is the States but that's an awfully long way away."

"No, Iceland and Greenland are closer, but they would never cope with masses of refugees. You're right. They'll try to get to the States somehow."

"If Ireland does fall, that's where I'll look for my parents, the port cities in the Eastern States."

"You have family in Ireland?"

"I hope so. I lost contact with them when the BI were invaded."

"I'm sorry."

"How about you, sir?"

"My parents passed while I was a teenager. I was an only child."

"That must have been hard."

"Not as hard as not knowing what's happened to them." Wright clapped Singh on the shoulder. "Take fifteen minutes. Go get a coffee. I'll try to think up something to tell the brigadier."

Singh thanked him and left, but he hadn't been gone a minute before he rushed back into the room.

"Sir, have you heard?!"

"Heard what?"

"The black cloud's just been sighted again. It's heading right at us!"

7

———————

Aboard the *Bres*, in his private suite, Lorcan Ua Talman was writing with pen and paper. His grandmother had taught him the art when, as a young child, he'd waited at her house after school for his father to pick him up. Since then, he'd kept up the practice because it helped him get his thoughts and feelings in order.

Dear Grace

I'm happy to report things are progressing well since Dwyr Orr's treachery. What a deceitful witch she turned out to be. But then, I should have known from the beginning she would betray my trust. In a funny way, I believe I did know, yet something compelled me to go along with her schemes anyway. And it was not only expediency. I can tell you that much. The woman has something about her, a force of will that invades your soul. If you aren't careful, you find yourself agreeing to whatever she proposes.

•　•　•

FINE PAPER for writing was becoming more and more difficult to source, and its increasing rarity made it more expensive too. But Lorcan indulged himself with few luxuries, so he made an exception in this case. He'd bought reams of the stuff from a paper mill still operating somewhere in North America. As soon as his researcher had discovered it, he'd purchased the entire stock in every color and transported it to his private storage units on the *Bres*. Paper production would be a low priority in his new home, if it was ever required, but he didn't want to be without it. He had a vision that, if he didn't use it up over his lifetime, he could bequeath it to the colony's children.

YOU WOULD HAVE SEEN her for what she was immediately. You would have warned me about her. I can almost hear you. "Lorcan, that woman is trouble," you would have said. "I wouldn't trust her as far as I can throw her." And you would have been right.

HE'D ALSO PURCHASED MORE fountain pens and ink than he could ever possibly use. None of the colonists had the flexibility for such frivolity, not even his heads of department. One kilogram of personal items was all they were allowed. He wondered what people like Kekoa, Jurrah, and Steadman would bring. It was a measure of what was most important to an individual— what they would choose to bring and what they would leave behind. He was glad he didn't have to make the choice himself. He would take everything that meant anything to him. After all, he had irretrievably lost the most important things in his life long ago. The bits and bobs he had were all that remained, and his only way of reconnecting with them.

. . .

Aʜ, well. She did help me free our operations of BA interference and aided in the defense of the Bres when the Alliance attacked. All in all, the Project is in a better position now than when we first teamed up with the EAC, the losses we incurred when they turned on us notwithstanding. Production is up across most of the mines, all three ships are ahead of schedule, and we're discovering more and more fascinating genetic code to harvest and bring along.

Hɪs ᴅᴀʏᴅʀᴇᴀᴍs of humanity's expansion beyond the Solar System had been growing stronger lately. Some days, he thought about little else. During regular working hours he sat in the control center as always, but he paid little attention to what was going on. After years of his close scrutiny, his presence was enough to keep the staff on their toes.

He particularly liked to think about the later years of colonization, after the hard work of settlement had been accomplished. He imagined moving through the streets of a young city, most of its citizens born on the planet, and seeing what kind of society and culture they created for themselves. This was the true unknown of the Antarctic Project—would the people whose parents and grandparents he'd carried to the stars create the same kinds of lives? Or would the influence of the alien planet shape their behavior, motivations, and desires in different, unpredictable ways?

As ᴛʜɪɴɢs ᴀʀᴇ ɢᴏɪɴɢ sᴏ well, I've decided I can afford to take a little time off to visit the surface and see some of the code harvesting in action. I was thinking I might also take the opportunity to do some recruitment. There are a few individuals who would be an enormous benefit to a new world colony. I want to see if I can persuade them to come and explore the galaxy with me.

Surely that's an offer too good to refuse?

. . .

Giving a heartfelt sigh, he read over his letter. It contained just about all he wanted to say. It was time to finish it off and send it on its way.

I certainly think so, and I know you do too. Do you remember the long nights when we used to contemplate our future in the stars?

I miss you, my love.

Lorcan

He read the letter again, then, satisfied with the contents, he pulled a small cylinder from the many stored on a shelf underneath his coffee table. One end was closed and the other covered by a lid. He popped the lid, rolled up the letter, and slid it inside.

Turning out the lights, he stood and faced his window, one of the few on the ship. In the darkness, the starscape had become bright.

In the bulkhead next to the window was a round portal a little wider than his palm. He opened it, slid the cylinder inside, and closed it again. The button next to the portal lit up, indicating it was sealed. He pressed the button. There was a hiss.

A beat later, the cylinder containing his letter popped out on the other side of the window. The small amount of propulsion lent by its ejection ensured it sailed smoothly away from the ship.

Leaning on the glass, Lorcan watched until he couldn't see the cylinder any longer.

8

"You had better stay here while you take it," said Jon, somewhat reluctantly.

Kala knew the reason for his reservations: If she died while under his care, there would be hell to pay. The castle's inhabitants would blame him for the loss of their Dwyr, and who knew what they might do to him in their passion for revenge?

"I have a few remedies that might be effective," he added. "I'll try them if you seem to be slipping away."

"Please don't give me anything to bring me out of it," said Kala, "not unless you feel my life is seriously in danger."

"You're putting yourself in danger simply by doing this, young lady," he admonished.

She smiled at him calling her 'young lady'.

He gave a snort of annoyance and frustration. "It'll take me a while to make it."

He went to his jars of ingredients, unscrewed the lid from one, dipped in a spoon, and dumped the spoonful in a mortar. He didn't look at her, displaying his anger by the set of his shoulders while he worked. After watching him for some time, she grew bored and turned her attention to the view through the leaded window. Jon's room was high up, as high as the chamber where she made her blood sacrifices, but he over-looked a field, not the sea.

She saw some of the castle's children were already up. They were playing a ball game before breakfast, and Perran was among them.

She hadn't seen much of her son since the attack. She didn't like him to see her new appearance, especially not after he'd shrunk back at the sight of her. He was too young to be able to disguise his feelings in her presence.

As she watched the children play, Perran ran at another boy and pushed him to the ground. He snatched the ball from the other boy's grasp and held it over his head triumphantly. The other children shouted and tried to fight with him. Clutching the ball to his chest, he struggled free and sped away, heading towards the castle. Kala leaned forward, pressing her head against the leaded glass to see what happened next. When Perran reached the moat, he threw the ball into it. Then he disappeared from her view. She guessed he'd come inside.

Kala knit her brow and returned her attention to Jon, who was now grinding the ingredients together with a pestle. Her stomach rumbled.

"If you're hungry," said Jon without looking at her, "eat some bread. There's a bit in that basket covered with a cloth. You don't want to be taking this on an empty stomach."

She found the bread and munched on it, though her mouth was dry. The determination she'd gathered earlier to go down the dangerous route was fading. Was she doing the right thing? Would her body withstand the strain? Jon was not prone to exaggeration. If he was concerned, it was because he thought she really was putting her life at risk.

On the other hand, what else could she do? Things could not continue as they were. Her people needed their Dwyr.

Without her, the impetus to drive the EAC on to greater victories would fade. They needed a figurehead, strong and confident. The Earth also needed her to return to its proper state, to unleash the potential of a new future. Only she had the vision to carry out the enormous task.

"It's ready," said Jon, his tone heavy.

He was holding an earthenware cup full of a blackish, unappetizing liquid. Whatever had possessed her to try it all those years ago when she was only a young girl? But then, she'd always been the curious, risk-taking type.

"Are you going to drink it all?" Jon asked. "Perhaps you could try—"

"Yes, I'll drink it all. I can't risk this not working."

He shook his head heavily. "Have it your way."

She took a breath, put the cup to her lips and tipped back her head. It was impossible to avoid the foul-tasting fluid passing over her tongue, but she managed to minimize the effect by downing the entire cupful in one go.

Fighting the urge to vomit it back up again, she lay down on Jon's crumpled blankets. Too late, she noticed the smell of unwashed sheets.

Then the formula began to take effect.

She was passing down a dark passageway, gliding, apparently without the need for wings. She remembered this part well. The tunnel angled downward. She followed it, sinking deeper. Things became murky and uncertain. She lost her sense of time passing. How long had she been traveling? It could have been a few minutes or several months. She had no past or a future, only existing now.

She hit an obstruction. A substance as dark as the passage, soft and spongy, blocked her way. She plunged into it and found it didn't entirely halt her progress, only slowed her down. She was moving slower and slower, inching onward, then, a moment later, she was through.

At her release, she impacted solid rock and slid to the floor, unhurt.

A subtle glow surrounded her, and as she rose to her feet and her eyes adjusted to the light, she saw she was in a dark, hollow chamber. The glow seemed to come from phosphorescence, perhaps bacteria or fungi on the walls, roof, and floor. Although she could see and feel, smell the musty, stale odor of ancient air, and she could hear the slight movements of her body echo back from the cave walls, she didn't feel as though she was really there.

"You've returned," said a voice.

Kala spun around, trying to find out where the voice had come from, but she couldn't see anyone. Only darkness edged by faint light.

"Why did you stay away so long?" asked the speaker. "I've been lonely."

"I can't come here often," Kala explained, pieces of her life coming back to her. "It's too risky. It nearly kills me."

"I would never allow you to die."

"You said that—you say it's impossible for me to be harmed, but I almost died. I was horribly burned, and now..." She looked down at her arms. The burn scars had gone. Her skin looked whole and healthy again. A sob of relief welled up, but she forced it down. It wasn't real. It was an effect of the trance. She was in the Other Place, a deeper reality. "Someone hurt me. How did that happen if what you told me is true? You lied to me."

"I did not lie!" said the voice angrily.

The darkness in one corner of the chamber began to shift. It drew in tendrils, became thicker and darker, shrinking down and congealing. The absence of light became solid. Kala blinked, and suddenly she was looking at a woman. Black-haired and also dressed in black, only her face was clearly visible, a triangle of ivory floating in ink.

The woman stepped toward her. Kala drew back, fear overwhelming her fascination with the strange female. She remembered her clearly now. She'd never learned her name.

All her memories of her previous encounters were flooding back. She knew when she awakened, she would only remember bits and pieces of her time with the woman. A sentence here, an impression there. As before, she would be left desperately trying to string everything together.

Clearest in her memory was the first time she'd drunk the concoction Jon had left on his table. Then, as a young girl, she'd been transported somewhere different, though the place had been equally dark and dismal. The woman had been the same. The woman was always the same. More than thirty years had passed since then, yet she hadn't aged a day.

"Who burned you?" she asked gravely.

"I don't know. A BA soldier. I couldn't see their face through their visor."

The woman regarded her steadily.

Kala's heart pounded under the stare of those non-human eyes.

"Did you find the man I told you to seek?"

"No—well, yes, but the BA got to him first. He's with them now."

The woman turned and walked away. "This is bad news," she said softly.

Everything Kala learned was coming back with the clarity of a new bell. The woman was her ancestor from hundreds of generations ago. Of all her descendants, her blood ran truest in Kala's veins, she'd said. The formula enabled her to break the barriers of the conscious mind and travel to the place of the woman's incarceration.

No. That part was wrong. She had *many* prisons. Whoever had imprisoned her somehow moved her between many secret places, the timing and frequency controlled by an algorithm the woman hadn't figured out. She never knew when she might suddenly find herself in a new jail.

Each time Kala had traveled to see her, she'd been in a different chamber. How the woman survived without food or water for thousands of years, she'd never explained.

"But I was burned," Kala complained, standing her ground. Few things scared her except her strange acquaintance, but she was angry over the betrayal. She was determined to stand up to her and demand answers. What else had she been told that wasn't true? So much of her philosophy and actions were due to what she'd learned in these encounters.

The woman swept around and stalked closer, so close Kala could see her eyes clearly. She gasped. They were entirely black, except for the depths, where iridescent colors shimmered.

Summoning her courage, Kala reiterated, "What about my burns? You said—"

"You are near me!" exclaimed the woman, her black eyes growing wide. "I feel you. You must come to me quickly and release me before I'm moved again."

"What?" Kala was confused. Was her companion only trying to avoid answering her question? "How can I rescue you? I don't know where you are, and I never remember..."

Wordlessly, the woman snatched Kala's arm and drew on it with a long fingernail.

Searing pain leapt from the scratching. Kala tried to snatch her arm away, but the woman's grip was tight. Where her fingernail moved, numbers appeared on Kala's skin. The scent of burnt flesh rose. Kala screamed.

"Come to me. Soon."

The woman was gone.

9

———

There was nothing that could be done, but they were trying anyway. Everyone aboard the *Valiant* knew what had happened to the *Fearless*. Everyone knew about the vessel's personnel, turned virtually vegetative by the black cloud. Even if they hadn't seen the recording, all the *Valiant's* crew members knew it could move faster than any starship; that outrunning it was impossible.

But they were still running.

Taylan had managed to get Arthur and herself to crash seats within a half a minute of the announcement. The brigadier was going to burn the engines to get away, and everyone had to take a seat to help withstand the acceleration. The ship had begun moving as soon as the announcement finished, and by the time Taylan and Arthur reached their seats near Airlock D, they were already fighting to move.

Plenty of crash seats had sprung from the bulkheads, but only a few were occupied. The ship carried many more than were needed to avoid playing musical chairs in a crisis. Plus, a thousand or more personnel had transferred to the *Fearless* to help the victims there. At least they would be safe for now. The flagship was already tens of thousands of kilometers away.

"What's happening?" asked Arthur as he snapped the clips on his harness.

Of course, the ancient king had no idea what was going on. It hadn't been that long since he'd accepted that he was in space.

"Uh, around the time you woke up, we were in a battle," Taylan replied, "Something weird happened to one of our ships, and now it looks like it's going to happen to us."

"Something weird?"

"A cloud enveloped a ship and it disappeared. Then we found it again, a long way from its original position."

"Ah. The *Fearless*."

So he wasn't as clueless about what had been happening as she'd thought.

"That's the one."

"Where all the sailors were sent mad?"

"Um, not exactly, but basically, yes. Now the cloud's approaching us."

"What is this cloud?" asked Arthur.

"No one knows."

"You don't know? But I thought your people knew everything about what exists beyond the Earth's sky?"

"No, not at all. I'm no astronomer, but we don't seem to know much about space." She gasped. As they'd talked, the ship had been piling on Gs. She felt as though her flesh were being forced into her bones, despite the G dampening field. Arthur's face was beginning to distort under the pressure. She pitied anyone who hadn't made it to a crash seat in time. "No human has ever left the Solar System, for instance," she said with an effort. Then she took a deep breath, trying to prevent herself from passing out.

"The Solar System? What's that?"

"It's...never mind. I'll explain later." Not that she was likely to be in a condition to explain anything later, assuming they survived the effects of the cloud. Where would it send the ship? The *Fearless* had been transported all the way out to the Asteroid Belt. Would the *Valiant* end up as far out as Jupiter's orbit? Or even farther? Would they be the first humans to leave the Solar System?

Blackness encroached the edges of her vision.

This was gonna be it.

"Hey, Arthur," she wheezed. "It's been nice—"

She was thrown forward, and her stomach contents threatened to erupt from her throat. Their acceleration had abruptly ceased. She and others in nearby crash seats looked around, trying to figure out what was going on. The ship continued to quickly reduce speed.

"Does the cloud have us now?" asked Arthur.

"I-I have no freaking idea *what's* going on."

But she felt normal, for now. She understood and remembered everything she had before, she thought. Maybe the *Fearless's* personnel hadn't been affected by the jump right away. Maybe they'd lost their mental faculties later.

A Marine sitting across from her asked, "Does anyone know what we're supposed to do?"

No one replied.

Taylan hadn't received any orders either, and nothing was coming from the overhead speakers.

"I guess we just sit tight and wait to hear something," someone else remarked.

Taylan unfastened her harness. "Wait here," she said to Arthur. She began to make her way up the passageway, fighting against the decreasing acceleration.

"Where are you going?"

"To the bridge."

When she'd learned Arthur's true identity, she'd decided

things: Firstly, he needed an advocate and the best person for the job was her, and, secondly, that he had some kind of role to play in the future of the Alliance. She didn't want to deal with the upper ranks in the BA's hierarchy, but she was compelled to by her association with the ancient king.

She had to find out what had happened with the cloud and what Colbourn planned next, though the brigadier was a hard nut to crack. If Wright was old school, the brigadier was pre-education system.

It wasn't far to the *Valiant's* bridge, but before she reached it, the door slid open. Colbourn marched out, accompanied by Wright and a corporal she vaguely knew via Abacha. His name was Singh.

"Ellis," barked Wright the moment he set eyes on her. "What are you doing out of your crash seat?"

"I—"

"Forget it," he said. "Suit up, get a rifle, and meet us at Airlock D."

Airlock D? That was where she'd just come from.

The *Valiant* had now slowed so much she was able to move normally. She raced to the nearest armory. The major must have given the same order to several Marines because they were there before her. She hastily got battle ready, and then ran back to the airlock.

She encountered Arthur, walking toward her. Airlock D was about thirty meters away. Colbourn and Wright were standing together a few meters from her, and Singh was hanging about, looking nervous.

"Where are you going?" she asked Arthur.

"T.J. told me to move away. I don't know why."

"T.J.?"

He pointed at Wright.

So Arthur and the major were on first-name terms?

"Did *T.J.* say anything else?"

He shook his head.

Taylan walked over to Singh. Something was bothering him. The color had gone from his face and his eyes stared.

"What's happening?" she asked, speaking quietly so Colbourn and Wright didn't overhear.

"There…" he swallowed hard "…there's someone out there."

"Outside the ship?"

He nodded, apparently struggling to speak.

"After all that acceleration?! How the hell did they manage that?"

She guessed the person must have been outside working on a repair when the black cloud appeared, and they hadn't managed to get inside before the ship accelerated. But that didn't explain why Singh looked so scared.

He gulped again, closed his eyes, and shook his head. "N-no. The cloud disappeared. So Colbourn said to cut the engines. I suppose she thought we'd escaped it. Then…then I got some weird data from the sensors. It indicated something was moving on the hull. So I checked the maintenance cameras, and I-I saw him. He was clinging on, like, like a limpet! Crawling on the outside of the ship."

"Wow. That's a miracle."

"Y-you don't understand. He isn't wearing a suit."

"He…? He isn't in an EVA suit? Then, how is he…?"

Singh simply looked at her, the whites of his eyes showing all around his irises.

As they'd been speaking, the six or seven other Marines Wright had ordered to suit up had also arrived. The major and brigadier moved away from the airlock. He told the Marines to aim at it, but not to fire unless ordered.

"You too, Ellis," he added.

Her mind whirring, she lowered her visor and took a place at the front of the team with two others. She knelt down and took aim.

Singh's fear had infected her. What on Earth was clinging to the ship, able to survive without atmosphere or heat? But of course it wasn't from Earth. Singh had described it as a man, but no human could live longer than a minute or so within the vacuum of space.

And Colbourn was about to allow it aboard the ship.

She was allowing an alien to board the *Valiant*.

Who knew what it might do? Even if it intended no harm, it might release a deadly gas or do something else that would endanger their lives.

But, Taylan seemed to remember, BA regulations stated that first contact with extra-terrestrial intelligent life had to be non-hostile, unless the life form proved dangerous. The brigadier was predictably sticking to the script. But had the script been written with this kind of scenario in mind?

A subtle *clunk*.

The outer hatch had opened.

From her position, Taylan couldn't see through the small window in the inner hatch. In the stillness of the passageway, the quiet *clunk* that signaled the closing of the outer hatch seemed loud. She gripped her rifle and focused on her HUD, which told her where the pulse round would hit if she fired.

The inner hatch lock clicked open, and the door began to slide sideways.

"Steady," came the major's voice over her comm.

A man stepped from the airlock—a man not wearing an EVA suit, but instead dressed in a red robe that fell to the ground, defining his long, slim body. A short gray beard covered the lower half of his face, but most of the rest of his hair was hidden under a thin black hat that hugged his scalp.

Taylan sucked in a breath. Her visor allowed her a close up of the man's face despite the ten meters' distance. His eyes were entirely black. It was like looking into an abyss. Then he blinked and they became normal, his irises green.

A shout came from behind. Arthur suddenly barreled past her, bumping her into the bulkhead.

Ignoring Wright's shout to stay back, he ran to the alien creature. His thick arms enveloped him and he lifted him up so high his feet entirely left the floor.

Confusion followed. Arthur and the newcomer chattered in Arthur's tongue. The Marines relaxed from their positions and checked over their shoulders, looking for guidance from the officers. Colbourn, Wright and Singh stared, turned dumb by the scene.

Taylan realized she recognized the word Arthur had shouted.

Merlin.

10

Mariya hadn't spoken to Hans since that first time after his capture. He'd called out to her, the only familiar face among strangers, but she'd ignored him. Now, he'd given up on ever reaching her. She was not Josie. She'd never been like her sister. It had all been a lie, though he'd never figured out what Mariya's true motivations were. He didn't care anymore, not about that or anything else, such as who all her companions were or why they were there. He only wished for blessed release from his torture.

The natural fibers of the vines that bound the bamboo canes and secured the door were impossible to break through. They were covered in tiny hairs that knit to impenetrable felt when they came together. All that resulted from his attempts to untie the vines were bloody fingertips and aching hands. He was allowed out twice a day for a toilet break—oh how he looked forward to those precious few minutes when he could stand upright and walk. To open the cage, the guard would slice through the knot with a knife. When Hans returned, having dragged out the duration of his brief freedom as long as he possibly could, a fresh vine would be used to tie the door to the frame. He'd given up any hope of escaping.

In the early days, he'd watched his captors, figuring that if he understood them, he might argue his way out of captivity. Around thirty-five to forty men and women were living in the caves, though they belonged to a larger group. He'd noticed new people arriving and others leaving. All were locals. In the evenings, they would gather around a fire and eat, drink, and smoke long into the night. In the mornings they would rise early and go to the stream to wash and collect water. They spent the hot, humid afternoons asleep, as far as Hans could tell, in the cool of the cave.

The visitors would bring supplies, including weapons. For defense? Or were they part of a group resisting the EAC occupation? One day, he saw things from his house being carried down the path from the overhang. He guessed Mariya had taken her friends there to ransack the place. Of all she'd done to him, all her betrayals, this one hurt him least. He would have gladly given the people whatever they needed or wanted. He appreciated a fine aesthetic and he understood how the wealthy related to luxury, but he was not materialistic himself. His goals in life were nobler.

The day had come when Hans woke up and saw the beginnings of sores forming on his chest and hips. He knew the signs well by now, and his morale, which was already nearly at rock bottom, sank a notch lower. He knew that night's sleep would be even more uncomfortable, and when he awoke the patches would have grown redder. Perhaps the skin would already have begun to break open.

Meanwhile, his other sores were not healing. Starved of nutrition and worn down by fatigue, heat, and persistent insect bites, his body had lost its ability to repair itself. He almost wished for a proper infection, something that would finish him off, once and for all. He was not the type of person who gave up easily. If he had been, he couldn't have risen to his former position despite all the obstacles stacked against him. But he was near the end of his tether.

He gingerly prodded the red marks on his chest as he sat awkwardly to avoid putting pressure on his buttock sores. The sun had risen beyond the ridge at the edge of the hollow and was shining directly into his cage.

Suddenly, something cut out the light.

He looked up. A figure was standing before him, dark against the sun's rays.

Mariya.

In his preoccupation with his sores, he hadn't heard her walking up to him.

"How are you feeling, Hans?" she asked. Ever since she'd tricked him into coming to the cave, her tone when she spoke to him had utterly changed. She sounded confident and strong. She sounded like an entirely different person from the one he'd known.

Hans couldn't reply immediately. His old hurt at her deception and treachery welled up. What had he done to her that she should treat him so badly? He thought he'd always been a kind, generous employer. How could she justify her cruelty?

His vision blurred, and as he blinked, to his shame, tears slipped from his eyes.

"Open the cage," she said to the guard.

The man took a knife from a sheath hanging at his side and slit the knot.

When the door was open, Mariya said to Hans, "Come with me."

She waited as he crawled painfully out. Slowly, he stood to his full height, his nerves pricking painfully in reaction to the unusual position.

Mariya walked away, heading for the burnt patch where the fire was lit nightly.

She walked without looking back to check he was following her. His guard had taken the opportunity to be relieved of his tedious task and gone into the cave. No one else was around. It was Hans's chance to escape.

But he was so weak, he could barely support his own weight, let alone run away. And where would he go? He had no food and couldn't see any lying around that he could snatch before he left. Even if he'd been entirely healthy, he didn't know how to survive in the wild. He might last a few days, assuming he could evade recapture, but that was all.

On the other hand, when he died, he would be lying stretched out on soft leaf mold. He could die a free man. Dire though it was, the prospect was inviting.

He watched Mariya's back as she sauntered toward the fire, her hips swaying.

Then he understood.

She was giving him a choice: Leave now and die on your own terms, or take a chance with me, despite everything I've done to you.

The sun was creeping higher, soaking into his weary bones. He stood still, relishing the sensation of standing tall, stretching out his aching muscles.

Mariya had reached the fire pit and was sitting down. Still, she didn't look at him. She removed the cloth covering a small basket and began taking out small pots, which she placed on the ground.

Hans began to walk slowly toward her.

11

———————

The Republic of Suriname was a little close to the Caribbean for Lorcan's comfort. The last he'd heard, Dwyr Orr was currently subjecting the islands' inhabitants to her usual reign of terror. Nevertheless, he'd fixed upon the South American country for his expedition to gather unusual and rare genomes and, if he was lucky, people.

Places like Suriname drew him like a magnet. The difficult, mountainous terrain meant some areas had barely felt the touch of a human footprint. Scientists believed many indigenous species remained uncatalogued. It was like visiting an alien planet.

After brief tours of his bauxite and gold mines, he flew via his private shuttle to a tiny airport at the feet of the Wilhelmina Gebergte. He'd arranged for trail motorcycles, supplies, camping gear, and other equipment to be waiting for him and his companions, a couple of strong, fit manual workers from the *Bres*, named Bourke and Jeffries.

They rode along dirt tracks for two days, working their way slowly up toward Juliana Top. The motorcycles' wide and soft but extremely tough tires clung well to the sloping, loose surfaces, despite the weight of the trailers they pulled. Lorcan hoped to bring back specimens from the jungle, but these would take the place of food in the storage containers for the shorter trip down.

At the end of the second day, it was clear that they would go no farther on the bikes. The trail had shrunk to no more than a meter wide, and thick tree roots and overhanging branches intersected it.

The second half of the journey proved to be grueling. They carried the essentials on their backs. Humidity in the high 80 percents and the temperature constantly hovering around 35 C, the only relief came at night. Lorcan was not a young man, and he was paying, so he would wait while his companions set up camp and then rest in a tent cooled by a portable aircon device. Luckily, streams were common on the mountain, and the water was easily made safe with UV treatment.

During the daytime, he didn't speak much. He needed to save his breath for climbing, but he was also lost in memories of other, happier, times. In the early years of their relationship, Grace and he had undertaken similar journeys, supposedly prospecting for their burgeoning mining company. But their real pleasure had come from traveling in strange places. They'd been alike in that, though his wife had been kinder and gentler than him. He'd always considered her literally his better half. They'd sometimes joked they were like explorers from the old times, discovering new lands and people.

In the mid-afternoon of their third day of hiking, Bourke, who was in the front, halted and said, "It's another three hundred meters from here, according to the last available report anyway. But that's years old."

"Right," said Lorcan, appreciating the chance to rest. He was breathing heavily. He drew the back of his sleeve over his face to wipe away the sweat stinging his eyes, and then took a long drink from his water bottle. Much as he tried to ignore the fact, he was feeling his age. "Another three hundred meters, eh?" He squinted at the sunlight through the trees. He guessed it was about two hours to sunset. Encumbered and tired as they were, and hiking the difficult trail, it would be nightfall before they reached their destination.

"You two make camp somewhere hereabouts," he said. "I'm going on by myself. If I need anything, I'll comm you."

"Are you sure it's safe, sir?" asked Jeffries, who was bringing up the rear.

"I'll be fine," replied Lorcan.

He didn't want to wait until morning to approach his subject. He was excited to meet her and discover what she might have to offer the Antarctic Project. He also had a feeling he would have a better chance of success if he approached her alone.

Bourke began to slice through the vegetation that walled them in on each side of the track with a machete, looking for a piece of flattish ground to pitch the tents. Lorcan waited another few minutes to catch his breath, and then set off again.

The temperature had cooled as they'd climbed higher, though the air remained thick with moisture. Still, Lorcan was on the edge of collapse by the time he came upon the small house in the jungle. He knew, intellectually, how far he climbed, due to an implant he'd had fitted years ago that told him his position and progress as well as other useful information. But he felt as though he'd toiled for a kilometer or more. He was near the end of his strength.

He staggered into the forest clearing like someone lost in the desert for days without food or water. Falling to his knees, he was acutely aware he was making a spectacle of himself. He hated being at a disadvantage in this first encounter with the person he wanted to meet, yet he couldn't help it.

Assuming she was home.

"Hello!" he called out.

The door of the simple home opened, and a woman stood in the entrance, scanning the clearing. When her gaze lit upon him, he heard her give a soft exclamation before she ran down the steps. But then she suddenly halted, returned up the steps, and disappeared into the house.

What was she doing?

Lorcan was too exhausted to get up and follow her.

A few seconds later, she reappeared, flanked by two huge dogs and carrying a long-barreled, old-fashioned firearm. She stepped toward him slowly, sweeping the forest with her rifle. The dogs were well trained and stuck to her sides like glue.

"Are you alone?" she asked.

Lorcan nodded.

"Answer me. Are you alone?"

He realised he was kneeling in a patch of shade and probably nearly invisible next to the brilliant sunlight in the rest of the clearing. "I'm completely alone. I have two companions, but they're away down the track."

She must have said something to her dogs or given them a signal because both animals suddenly leapt toward him. The next second, they were at his side, sniffing him all over and softly growling. He froze. He'd grown up with dogs and liked them, but it had only made him keenly aware of what they could do to protect their owners.

The woman joined him in the shadow, her rifle aimed at his chest.

"Who are you? Wait." She peered at him more closely. Her demeanor changed and she relaxed. "Huh! I've been wondering when you would turn up. Darwin, Banks, heel."

The dogs zipped to her side.

She put the barrel of her rifle over her shoulder. "Can you stand?"

The short rest had given him a little energy. "Yes, I think so." He forced himself to his feet.

"The climb takes it out of most people," she said. "Come on, I'll help you inside." She came to his side and put his arm over her other shoulder. Slowly, they walked to her house.

It wasn't until Lorcan was indoors, sitting down, and drinking cool water, that he got a proper look at Iolani Hale. He'd read her name so many times at the top of scientific papers, but he'd never seen a photograph of the well-known recluse. She was short, and though she wasn't overweight, her face and bare arms were plump. She was wearing a printed floral dress and was barefoot. Her clothes made sense in the climate, despite the air-conditioning in her home, but the look wasn't what he'd expected from the world-renowned scientist.

"Here," she said, offering him a towel.

He took it and wiped the sweat from his face, neck, and arms.

"You'll feel better soon, Ua Talman," said Iolani. She crossed the room to a kitchenette in the corner, where she picked up a knife and resumed chopping vegetables.

The room was small and multi-purpose. Lorcan was sitting on a sofa in the living area. The tiny kitchen was diagonally opposite, and a dining area faced him. The fourth corner was occupied by a desk and chair. He guessed one of the two inner doors led to her laboratory.

"I see my reputation precedes me," he said. "How did you guess who I was?"

"There aren't many humans alive today with red hair," she replied, "and given who *you* are and who *I* am, it's kind of inevitable you would come to find me one day, isn't it?"

"I suppose so. I am a great admirer of your work."

Iolani only acknowledged his remark with a nod, as if it was exactly the kind of thing she expected him to say.

She put down the knife and turned to him, saying with some anger, "Look, I'll save us both a lot of time. My answer is no! Never. Not in a million years. So don't bother asking."

Lorcan chuckled uncomfortably, taken off guard by her vehemence. "After I've gone to all the trouble of discovering your location and climbing all the way up here to see you in person, almost killing myself, you won't even allow me to ask you the question?"

She shrugged and resumed her task. "I know you're a busy man, and, to be frank, I didn't ask you to come here."

"Touché," he replied. "But I'm not only here for that. I'm interested in what you've been doing."

"What I've been doing?"

"It's been a while since you published anything."

"My research? Global conditions aren't conducive to scientific work at the moment and haven't been for a long time. Unless it's to measure environmental destruction. She added, with bitterness, "As I'm sure you know too well, given that you're personally responsible for a lot of it."

She clearly wasn't going to pull any punches. Lorcan had known his proposal could be a hard sell, but he hadn't quite expected the brick wall she had instantly put up. Perhaps he'd been spending too much time around people who worked for him and were relying on him to leave the planet. He wasn't a man to give up easily, but as he'd grown older, he'd developed an instinct for knowing when he was beaten from the get-go.

"It seems we don't have much common ground on which to open a discussion," he said.

She said nothing but hacked viciously into a bunch of leaves on her chopping board.

Not wanting to entirely waste his expedition, Lorcan decided to try a different subject. "I didn't only come here to invite you to join the Project. I'm also interested in the species you've discovered in the forest."

"You're not taking any animals from here, Ua Talman."

"I didn't intend to." It was a blatant lie. He would have liked some live specimens very much. He'd even brought along some sedative to keep them under during transportation. "A sample of their genetic code would be sufficient. I'm sure an influx of funds would be a boon to your research."

Hale raised the knife in her hand and paused, as if considering something. From the look on her face, her thoughts were nothing to do with whether to sell him genome samples.

"No."

He put down his glass. "Very well." He was disappointed, but it couldn't be helped. Some adverse publicity had obviously poisoned her against him. It was hard to defeat negative press. "If you don't mind, I'll rest another few minutes and then I'll relieve you of my presence. The journey downhill will be easier than coming up."

Suddenly, her demeanor changed again. She returned her attention to her chopping board and became businesslike. "Did I say I was kicking you out? Why not rest a while longer? You can stay for dinner. Darwin and Banks will accompany you down the track later and make sure you get to your tent safely."

Surprised by this unexpected kindness, Lorcan said, "I'd be delighted."

Perhaps there was hope he could persuade her to sign up to the Project after all.

12

———

Cool, soothing bliss spread from the ointment Mariya was applying to Hans's sores. He closed his eyes, relaxing into the sensation. A minty scent wafted over him. The pain he'd suffered for weeks had even invaded his exhausted dreams. To finally lie at full length, stomach downward, on the rattan mat by the fire site brought him joy. He didn't understand what was happening or what his former assistant had planned for him, but he didn't care. If he were to die in the next minute, at least he wouldn't die in the miserable discomfort he'd endured so long.

Mariya's soft fingertips moved to the worst of the sores on his back, and he tensed. This one had ulcerated. When he could bear to touch it, his finger slipped inside to the first joint. His back muscles became rigid, anticipating a stab of agony, but the application of the salve only hurt a little.

"You're done," Mariya stated abruptly. "Sit up."

Hans heard the scrape of a lid being screwed onto a ceramic pot. "I don't think I can."

While she'd been treating his sores, he'd been looking out

into the trees, which were alive with insects and birds. Now, he turned his head toward Mariya.

She was sitting cross-legged, dressed in khaki pants and a yellow tank top. She regarded him with half-lidded eyes. "Then do what you can."

Hans managed to pull himself up to a sitting position by resting on the side of one buttock and propping himself on his arm.

"Can you drink?" she asked.

He nodded, but when he took the cup she poured for him, he hesitated.

"I am not going to poison you, Hans. If I wanted you dead, I would have killed you in your villa the night of the EAC invasion."

Keeping his eyes on her, he sipped the liquid. It was plain water, lukewarm from sitting in the sun.

She slid a plate containing something ashy over the mat toward him. He put down the cup to pick it up with his free hand. It was a kind of unleavened bread that must have been baked in the remains of a fire. He brushed off the worst of the gray dust and bit into it. His mouth watered, but his weakened jaw muscles struggled to deal with the tough, stale substance.

"Supplies are getting low," Mariya explained. "We mostly only have flour left. A group is going out to raid Kingston tomorrow."

Hans chewed and forced down the contents of his mouth.

"Are you going too?" he asked. "Sounds dangerous."

She shook her head. "Food isn't my responsibility. And it isn't that dangerous yet. The city's in chaos."

Feeling emboldened by her unexpected change in attitude, he said, "I thought I was good to you, Mari—"

"Don't you dare!" she snapped. "I am not and never was your underling. I didn't need you to be good to me."

"I'm sorry. I didn't mean to insult you. I simply meant I

thought we had a good professional relationship. I've spent the last few weeks wondering what I did that was so bad I deserved to be tricked, locked in a cage, half-starved, and brought close to death. Look at me. I doubt I would even recognize myself."

"Hans Jonte, are you *really* sitting here and criticizing *me* for being deceptive? You, the former head of SIS?"

He hung his head. He couldn't deny there was some justice to her words. "I never locked anyone in a cage," he said quietly.

"Maybe not, but how many people died in the coup you engineered? How many people were you prepared to sacrifice for your cause? *I* didn't kill you."

Again, he felt the cut of her retort. "What can I say? I was trying to do away with the monarchy and the Establishment. I wanted to create a better world, a more just society. I wanted to make the Britannic Alliance a republic, where everyone had a fair chance in life and didn't have to spend their days with the boots of the autocracy on their necks."

"And *that* is why you were not executed," said Mariya. "I came to your villa the night of the coup and EAC attack to make sure you didn't escape. I was supposed to deliver you to the EAC soldiers, but everything had changed by then. I decided to give you a chance to tell me what lay in your heart. Do you remember? I asked you why you set up the coup. You wouldn't tell me at first. It was only when we were in the car, fleeing the fighting, you told me the truth. You talked about the privileged upbringings of the BA elite, how everything had been handed to them on a silver platter. You said, *I'd hoped to put an end to all that, hoped Hennessy, Montague, and Beaumont-Smith would be the last of their type with any kind of power.* I realized you weren't quite as bad as the rest of them, and that was why I spared your life."

"You were going to take me to the EAC?" asked Hans, astonished. "Why would you do that?"

Then the penny finally dropped.

"You were working for them?!" he exclaimed. "You...That was how Dwyr Orr knew exactly when to send in her forces! She knew the BA would soon be at its most confused and vulnerable. You told her about the coup. She was prepared, waiting for it to begin."

"Not me," said Mariya. "I didn't tell her. Josie did. As far as Kala Orr was concerned anyway."

"Josie? But she..." Hans's head hurt, and it wasn't only due to his weakened, starved state. If he hadn't been so feeble and sickly, he would probably have quickly figured out what Mariya was implying, but not today. "Please, explain."

She broke off a piece of unleavened bread, took a bite, and chewed and swallowed before she began. "You have to understand I loved Josie very much, and she loved me. We were very close, but though we looked identical, our opinions on many things were different. Most of the time we managed to put our differences aside and get along." She sighed heavily. "I miss her, but maybe it's for the best she isn't here to see what's happening to our country.

"One thing we agreed on was that Jamaica should leave the Britannic Alliance. I thought we should be entirely independent, not under any other nation's control. Josie thought we should join the Earth Awareness Crusade. She was into nature and rejected modern conveniences. Loved camping and wildlife. She was also very spiritual but in the sense that she thought everything had a soul. You know the type?" Mariya smiled and looked away from Hans into the forest. Her eyes glistened and she rubbed one of them with the heel of her hand. "She would have loved this place.

"I didn't trust the EAC and was dismayed when she told me she'd joined them," Mariya went on. "I'd heard what they'd done in Europe and the Britannic Isles. Josie told me they wouldn't do that here. She had assurances that things in Jamaica would be different, she said. I asked her what she meant, and after some pushing she finally told me. We couldn't keep a secret from each other for long. She revealed she'd been recruited by Dwyr Orr herself. She was to use her position as your assistant to spy on the BA Government. All the time she was working for you, Hans, she was feeding the Dwyr information."

"Not Josie!" Hans was rocked. He'd never suspected her for a minute. Not for a second. But then, he'd never suspected her sister of any subterfuge either.

What a pair of agents they would have made.

Mariya didn't react to his surprise. She continued her story. "When Josie was killed in the attack on the General Council, I was shocked and outraged. She couldn't have known about the attack or she would have faked a reason for her absence. But Dwyr Orr should have guessed she might be there. She didn't warn her to stay away. She let my sister die, as if her life was worth nothing."

He wondered why the Dwyr hadn't told Josie anything. She would have needed a very convincing excuse to not attend. *He* would have been suspicious about her afterward, assuming he survived. Perhaps Kala Orr had been willing to risk her agent's death rather than revealing she'd infiltrated SIS. That would make sense, given the woman's callous attitude.

"You took over from your sister," he said. "Not only in working for me, but in becoming an EAC agent. Dwyr Orr didn't know Josie had died. She wasn't important enough for her death to make the vidnews, so you took her place and began reporting to the Dwyr as Josie. But you said you were going to take me to the EAC soldiers? If you were so angry about Josie's death, why did you begin working for them?"

"I often ask myself that question." Mariya looked into the distance for a moment, narrowing her eyes against the sunlight. "I don't have a good answer yet. Have you ever met the Dwyr in person?"

"No, never." The woman was famously cloistered, reserving audiences only for her followers.

"She's oddly persuasive. She gets inside your head somehow. I only met her a couple of times, but each time I came away feeling dazed and muddled. I'd only gone to see her out of curiosity, but I found myself doing her bidding. I don't want to ever meet her again. But maybe what I did isn't so strange. I wanted the BA out of the Caribbean forever. I thought the EAC could be a means to achieve that."

"But the BA was protecting the islands. Why would you want it to leave?"

"Hans!" she said angrily. "Don't you know anything about our history?"

He *had* read up on Jamaica and the other major Caribbean islands before the BA Government transferred to them. Their past was heavily besmirched by exploitation of the local people, both in ancient times and during the resurgence of the Britannic Isles' power two centuries previously. "I do know something of it, but that was a long time ago. Things are better now, surely?"

"Old wounds cut deep. We have always been an underclass, no matter what changes the ruling governments make. What you endured in your cage is only a taste of what my ancestors suffered, and what my people continue to suffer in other ways."

So that was it. Mariya had wanted to take out her revenge on him for the grievances of the Jamaican people.

"Then you've been targeting the wrong person," he said bitterly. "*My* ancestors were immigrants. They had nothing to do with what happened here."

"No, you don't get off so lightly," she retorted. "You were the head of SIS, a member of the Establishment, you were—"

"Working to destroy the Establishment!"

"To create a republic that would still control the Caribbean!"

"No! Well, maybe." He couldn't think straight. He was too ill and malnourished. But he was glad he was out of his cage and Mariya no longer seemed intent on torturing him. "What happens now? Are you letting me go?"

Her features switched from anger to solemnity. "You would never survive. As we all should have guessed, Dwyr Orr has reneged on her promise to spare the local population after the invasion. Tens of thousands have died already, and the slaughter goes on. We are safe here in the mountains for now. The Resistance has teams of people shooting down the drones the EAC is launching to find our hideouts."

She frowned at him sternly. "I have the others' agreement that now your punishment is over, you can stay with us. I should warn you, though, several of them agreed only because they see you as someone useful to us. If the EAC find us and begin to close in, they want to use you as a bargaining chip in negotiations. The Dwyr made a spectacle of Hennessy and Montague's executions. She may want to do the same with you."

13

———

"I don't like him," Taylan said, panting. She was training with Abacha in one of the *Valiant's* fitness centers. She turned off her treadmill and slowed her running pace while it came to a stop.

"Let me guess," Abacha replied. "You're talking about Merlin."

"Yeah." She'd been lost in her own thoughts and had accidentally spoken the last one out loud.

"Why? Because of what he did to the *Fearless*?"

"Is that what people are saying? Was that him? Or was it another black cloud alien, one of thousands of black cloud aliens floating around the galaxy that shape shift into human beings?" She paused to take a breath, bent over and gripped her knees. That had been entirely too much to say after a fast 5K run.

If Merlin had condensed from the same opaque cloud that had snatched the *Fearless*, no one had told them so. Colbourn had spent hours with the creature and Arthur in her office, but she'd made no announcements. Everyone was expected to carry on as normal, while a potentially deadly extraterrestrial life form roamed the ship.

"Who knows?" Abacha replied. "I'm thinking he can't be the same creature, or if he is, he isn't saying. Or Colbourn would have put him in the brig."

"Yee-ah," Taylan agreed reservedly. "But what would be the point? He could just transform into a cloud again and send us halfway to Betelgeuse." She straightened up, grabbed her towel, and wiped her neck.

She'd tried working her mediocre charm on Wright to find out what was going on, but without success. Whenever she'd managed to track him down and probe him for information, relying on the somewhat informal relationship she'd built up with him, he'd put on his 'major' face and walked away.

"Good point." Abacha also turned off his treadmill. "Better not to worry about it. Why bother our heads with things we have no say in?"

"What kind of attitude is that?" She looked at him with mock disgust.

"Colbourn's going to do whatever she's told to do with the new guy. It doesn't matter what we think. I guess the admiral already knows, and they're figuring things out now."

"Hmm."

The *Valiant* was on her way back to Earth, the *Fearless* too. The rumor was that when the vessels arrived at the rendezvous, an attack on former BA territory, now held by the EAC, would take place. Where it would be wasn't known. The likeliest area was somewhere in the Caribbean, in Taylan's opinion. That was where the cult would be the least entrenched. It was also the place where the most BA citizens still survived.

She wished the BA would try to free her homeland. She didn't think it would be long before the EAC made their push into Ireland. Her kids were there, somewhere.

"Are you sure you don't dislike this Merlin guy because he took your place?" Abacha asked, giving her a sideways look.

"Huh? You mean because he's sharing Arthur's cabin now and I'm back bunking with you guys? Why would you think that? I love listening to you snoring, and smelling Kaminski's gas all night is my idea of heaven."

He chuckled. "I'm gonna take a shower. See you after for a game of xiangqi?"

"No, I think I'll give getting my ass beat a miss this time. I might...I don't know, take a walk around the ship, or something."

"You're going to try to squeeze information out of Wright again, aren't you?"

"Yeah."

But instead of finding Wright, Taylan came across Arthur and Merlin. The two had rarely been seen since the alien had arrived. Most of the time they didn't spend with Colbourn they stayed in Arthur's cabin. She was tempted to conclude it was because the newcomer had evil designs on the someone she now considered a good friend, but it could simply be because whenever Merlin appeared, everyone gawked.

They were talking to the supply officer. The rest of the passageway was empty, and they hadn't noticed her, so she took her personal opportunity to gawk.

Merlin seemed old due to his gray hair and face as gaunt as Colbourn's, but his skin was unlined. He stood a few centimeters shorter than Arthur, and beneath his long, red robe, his figure seemed to match his face: bony yet lithe. She had to admit it would take considerable muscle power to cling to the exterior of a starship still slowing down from maximum speed.

She peered closer, trying to make out his eyes. They looked normal. No sign of the solid blackness she'd seen before.

Another thing she noticed was that he didn't breathe.

What did Arthur make of this strange creature? To him, Merlin was an old, close friend and companion who had suddenly reappeared; the only person from his former life he would ever see again. It was natural he would be happy to have him around. Did he truly understand it was impossible for Merlin to have survived in space and that he was not, in any sense of the word, human?

Taylan itched to know what had been discussed in Colbourn's office, but she couldn't figure out how to find out, unless she could get Wright to spill the beans.

~

"COME ON," she complained. "I've been involved in this since the beginning. I deserve to know what's going on!"

She'd finally tracked Wright down to his cabin. After pressing his door chime for half a minute, he'd finally appeared, looking like he'd just woken up.

"You know I could have you thrown in the brig for this?"

"But you won't," she replied, adding hopefully, "Will you?"

"Look..." he said, putting a hand on her shoulder.

He paused.

They both looked at his hand.

He removed it and rubbed a bleary eye. "If I tell you a few things that have been happening, will you leave me alone?"

"Yes! I promise. I just have to—"

He'd glanced up and down the passageway before dragging her into his cabin by her elbow.

The place was clean and sparse—worryingly so. Nothing sat on the small desk, there were no pictures on the walls, even the bed linen was standard issue. It was a lot different from Marines' bunk rooms, where personal items and general clutter gradually built up until the next snap inspection.

He pulled out a chair that had been tucked neatly under

the desk and gestured at it. Sitting on his bed, he ran his hands over his face. "What do you want to know?"

"Uhh..." Now that she had the chance she'd been seeking for days, she didn't know where to start.

"You want to know about that thing that calls itself Merlin?" Wright asked.

"I do, and other things." She was determined to extract as much information as she could. This might be her only opportunity. "Did he explain what he is? Did he come from the cloud? Is he the same thing that moved the *Fearless*?" She didn't bother asking if he was *the* Merlin. As far as she was concerned, he had to be. She also knew Wright would never admit it.

"Hold on," said the major. "One question at a time. No, he didn't explain what he is, at least not to me. I haven't been in all the meetings he's had with Colbourn. He did come from the cloud. He *is* the cloud, as far as I understand it. Is he the cause of what happened to the *Fearless*?" Wright's expression turned sour. "If he is, he hasn't admitted it. On the other hand, he's promised to do what he can to help the ship's personnel. He claims he has some way of influencing human minds, and the plan is he's going to transfer to the ship and begin treating them while we return to Earth."

"Whoa." Taylan didn't know what else to say at first. Then she blurted, "If he can help them, that's good, isn't it?"

"Is it?" Wright's lips twisted in anger and disgust. "Colbourn didn't want to let him loose on them, and I agree with her. We're basically allowing an alien entity to have access to the minds of our military personnel, assuming what he claims is true. If he *does* have some telepathic ability, who the hell knows what he might do? Do we really want a complete stranger to have mental control over an entire ship's crew? And they aren't capable of giving consent to the treatment. It's a security and ethics minefield."

"So why are we doing it?"

"Admiral Kim insists. She and the rest of the fleet commanders have reacted to Merlin's arrival like the visitation of an angel, come to save us all. And it's your Arthur's fault," he added bitterly.

"*My* Arthur?!"

"You know what I mean. It's your story about an ancient king who would return when the BI fell that's been going the rounds. And the man's so goddamn charismatic, they believe it. Did you know he's been talking to Kim via direct comm?"

She hadn't known that. She thought back to her conversation with Arthur in the mess hall and winced.

"Now Merlin's arrival is the icing on the cake," Wright continued. "The admiral and the rest of the fleet are convinced the two of them are the answer to our prayers, that all we need to do is waltz into the Caribbean, the BI, and every other territory we lost and, abracadabra, all our enemies will drop dead. They think everything will be back to how it was before the AP and EAC ever existed, by magic."

He seemed to have exhausted himself with his little speech. He passed a hand over his eyes and was silent.

He'd needed to vent. That was why he'd finally relented about telling her what had been going on in the upper ranks of the space fleet. And he wanted someone to blame. She was a handy scapegoat, considering her involvement with Arthur since the beginning. She didn't think he was being fair. The admiral's decision could hardly be *her* fault. The woman had a mind of her own as well as access to information even the major wasn't privy to. Yet Taylan decided not to argue the point with him. He looked worried and exhausted.

"Do they really think it'll be that easy?" she asked gently.

He sighed. "No. I was exaggerating. Or, at least, I hope that was an exaggeration. But they do seem to see Merlin and Arthur as devastating tactical weapons that will turn the tide for us. They don't know quite how, but they're hoping to figure it out soon. Meanwhile, the admiral has accepted Merlin's offer to help the people on the *Fearless*. He transfers there tomorrow. Colbourn wants me to go with him, and I'm happy to. I want to keep an eye on the wily bastard."

"I want to come too," said Taylan.

He rolled his eyes. "Of course you do."

He looked like he was regretting his decision to let her in his cabin.

"It makes sense," she protested. "I'm the one who was with Arthur from the beginning, before he could even speak English. And I know all the stories about him and Merlin. And...and..."

He lifted an eyebrow.

"And if we do go to the BI to attack the EAC, I know the situation on the ground there, better than anyone else aboard. So I should be working with Merlin and Arthur from now on."

"I hate to admit it, but you do have a point. About the situation in BI, I mean. You were there only a few months ago, right?"

A rush of emotion hit her. She pursed her lips and nodded, not trusting herself to speak.

"It would help to have someone familiar with what was happening on the ground," he mused. "And..." he looked at her "...you *do* know Arthur the best out of all of us. I'd be interested to hear what you think of the relationship between him and Merlin."

"Does something bother you about it?"

"*Oh yeah*," the major replied. "You know that old saying, about being under someone's spell? That's how Arthur acts when he's around his old buddy, and he's around him all the time. Merlin makes sure of it."

"No kidding."

"You miss Arthur, don't you?"

"I do," she replied simply. She wasn't ashamed of liking the old king. As a person, he was extremely likable. More than that, however, was the fact that when she was beside him she felt closer to home, her children, and her old life. Being around him brought her comfort.

An inscrutable expression passed over Wright's features, and then he said, "I'll speak to Colbourn and see if I can swing it for you."

"Thanks!" She hadn't expected him to agree so easily.

"Now can you please leave so I can get some sleep?"

14

———

Iolani was a vegan, Lorcan concluded from the absence of meat or dairy at the meal she served up. It was only to be expected of someone who had been involved in discovering, cataloging, and researching animal species for most of her life.

Personally, he loved meat and saw nothing wrong with eating animals raised as livestock. It was part of the natural order of things, and he included all the usual domesticated species in his lists of living creatures and gametes to be brought aboard his ships.

He lifted a forkful of the nut-based concoction Iolani had cooked up to his mouth and stoically chewed and swallowed it.

Beyond the windows of his host's home, a blanket of darkness was closing over the jungle, and nocturnal insects and frogs were beginning their night-long chants. Iolani's dogs sat obediently near the table, not begging, but their eyes were following every movement of food from plate to lips.

"What do you think?" Iolani asked. "It's a new recipe I'm trying out."

"It's delicious," he replied, sticking his fork again in the non-descript mound before him.

She laughed. "Polite, but unconvincing. I take it you'd rather be eating a corpse?"

He winced. So she wanted to have *that* conversation.

"Ms Hale, I can see this was a bad idea, so..." He pushed back his chair and prepared to stand.

She lifted a hand. "No, sit. I apologise. I shouldn't be rude to a guest. Please, if you don't like it, don't eat it. I won't be offended."

"I'm really not that hungry anyway," said Lorcan.

"It's probably because you exhausted yourself climbing up here. It has that effect on people who aren't used to it."

"Do you make the climb often?"

"I go up and down the mountain every day for my work, but from the base all the way up to here?" She shook her head. "I haven't been down there in years. Anything I need, I order, and delivery agents bring it up to me."

"And you've lived by yourself all that time? It must be a lonely life."

"There are many ways of being lonely."

He reflected on his own life. "On that, we agree."

"I don't have anything fancy like wine or spirits, but I brew my own beer. You're welcome to have some if you're feeling adventurous."

"I'd love some."

"The warm ambient temperature means it brews quickly," she said, standing up.

Now that things were better between them, he ventured, "Have you found any new species lately?"

She was crossing the room to an internal door. As her hand touched the door handle, she hesitated. "Not anything special."

"If you have, I'd love to have a look," Lorcan pushed. "Just out of curiosity."

"I suppose a little tour won't do any harm," she relented.

He got eagerly to his feet and followed her through the door she left open.

Beyond the living area was a long, narrow laboratory. The benches on each side of the wall contained microscopes, countertop refrigerators, centrifuges, thermal cyclers, and other equipment he didn't recognize.

She noticed the look of disappointment on his face.

"Were you expecting monkeys in cages?"

"I wasn't sure what you did with the animals you discover."

"I only observe new species. I don't lock them up."

"But insects, amphibians...the lower orders, surely they wouldn't notice? And they would have a safer life in captivity."

"My guiding principle is to never interfere if I can help it. It's standard ethics in my line of work. I'm surprised you don't know that. Besides, rather like quantum mechanics, the act of observation affects the findings. An animal in captivity often behaves quite differently from one in the wild. Breeding captive animals could even affect gene expression in the offspring."

"I see. I didn't really think about it like that."

"It's something you *need* to think about, then. Did you imagine you could breed generations of animals on your ships and then release them into the wild on another planet? They would almost certainly all die within weeks. They won't have learned how to hunt or forage—"

"That isn't so," Lorcan retorted. "We're creating habitats—"

A peal of laughter rang out from Hale. "Parks, you mean. Gardens for people to wander around so they don't miss nature too much."

"No. Self-sustaining biomes containing networks of appropriate species."

Her dismissive attitude was irritating him.

She walked to a cabinet of small drawers and pulled one out to show him. "This is a sample of soil I collected about ten meters from here. Hold it." She pulled out another drawer and held it up for him to see. "I collected this sample from lower down the slope, about eighty meters away. Can you see a difference?"

He couldn't. The color and texture of the two scoops of dark earth looked identical.

Before he gave his reply, she said, "Neither can I. I have to label them carefully, recording the exact position and depth I collected them. I also record the date, time, temperature, and precipitation patterns of the preceding week. I don't think I record enough information, but there's a limit to what I can do."

She took the sample he was holding and held it next to hers. "These two soils contain vastly different ranges of microorganisms, some of which are unknown to science." She replaced the drawers. "I could tell you more, about how those organisms interact with plant roots, transmit information, and their significance in the wider network, but even I only know a fraction of what there is to know. You get my point. You might think you're re-creating Earth's ecosystems, but it isn't possible to recreate something no one understands yet. These systems are so complicated, we may never fully understand them."

Lorcan was stuck for an answer. He was sure there was one. Something about how life sustains itself, and how they were seeding the biomes with all the known species, and that everything would sort itself out in the end, but he couldn't put it into words.

"Let's have that beer," said Hale.

～

ABOUT AN HOUR LATER, when the alcohol had relaxed the atmosphere between them, Lorcan felt emboldened to approach her again on the subject closest to his heart. Her explanation of how challenging it was to create sustainable habitats and populate them with animals to be used for colonization had only convinced him further that he needed her.

"I hope you can forgive me for raising the subject again..." said Lorcan.

Iolani softly sighed and gave a little shake of her head.

"But hasn't it occurred to you how interesting it might be to live upon a world full of species unknown to humankind? An entire planet's biome to investigate and classify? As it stands, though I have many scientists among my lists of colonists, I have no one of your caliber. I could guarantee you would have free rein in your endeavors, complete freedom over what you did. It would be an honor to have you along."

Hale had been convivial up until that point. Her features turned hard. "The problem is, it wouldn't be an honor to be a part of what you're doing. Not to me, nor any other person with a shred of morality."

"Morality?" Lorcan spluttered. "It's immoral to want to save humanity from the eventual death of its home? I'm fascinated to hear your reasoning. Go on."

"I don't think I'll be successful in explaining the concept to someone in the process of destroying humanity's home, and the home of millions of other species," she retorted.

Destroying humanity's home?

They were strong words from someone Lorcan had thought he was finally getting along with. The mood in Hale's little home had suddenly darkened. Darwin and Banks looked up, their ears pricked.

"Then save your breath," he said. "Thank you for your hospitality, but I really must be going. The moon's nearly full tonight. I'm sure I can find my own way without the help of your dogs."

"No," said Iolani, rising to her feet once more. "You're not going anywhere. You're going to hear what I have to say."

"Not going anywhere?" he asked sarcastically. "Who do you think you are?" The woman weighed no more than a hundred pounds soaking wet. He, too, got up from his chair.

"Banks! Darwin! Guard."

The two huge dogs leapt from their sitting positions to within a few centimeters of Lorcan's toes. Growling, saliva dripping from their bared fangs, they inched closer to him, as if hoping for the signal that would allow them to make him their evening meal.

"Sit down!" Iolani ordered.

Somehow, the dogs knew the command wasn't directed at them. Lorcan slowly lowered himself into his seat, his gaze never leaving the two threatening animals. "This is ridiculous," he muttered. He was deeply regretting not bringing his men with him. He was also unarmed, but even if he'd been carrying a weapon, by the time he killed one of the dogs the other one would be upon him.

Returning once more to her seat, Iolani poured herself another glass of beer. "They won't hurt you as long as you remain still. But if you make a move out of place or try to hurt me, they *will* kill you. There are no law enforcement authorities up here, Ua Talman. It's survival of the fittest, and you aren't suited to this environment."

"Let's hear it then," said Lorcan, his jaw clenched, "and not waste more time contemplating your pets' forthcoming meals."

"Right," said Iolani. "Please tell me, what the hell is it you think you're doing?"

He gritted his teeth, outrage coursing through him. "What do you mean?"

"Your project, the vast colony ships you're building by plundering Earth's resources. Did you forget about them?"

"Of course not. Isn't the answer obvious? It's humanity's greatest endeavor. We must spread to the stars. It's our destiny. The alternative is to go the way of all species that have ever existed and face our eventual extinction. Is the latter preferable to you?" he spat.

"That's the story you tell everyone. I'm interested in your real reason."

"Are you mad? That is my real reason. What other reason could I have?"

"No, you're lying. If not to me, then to yourself."

"I am not lying! This is insane. Bring your dogs to heel and let me go."

"You're forgetting something," said Hale. "I'm not an ordinary member of the public you can hoodwink with your stories of galactic adventures. I'm a scientist. My specialism is zoology, but my interests are wide ranging. I've also studied geology and astronomy in my time. And I can't believe that you also don't know enough about those subjects to be aware that what you're doing is unnecessary."

Lorcan shifted in his seat, suddenly uncomfortable. "Call off your dogs now, or I'll take my chances."

"You won't make it to the door, believe me. Then the world will be rid of you, and, without you to lead it, your project will collapse. Is that what you want?"

He became still.

"You know as well as I do you could mine asteroids for most of the materials you're ripping out of the ground here on Earth, at massive environmental cost. You might be able to make an argument for gathering species and genomes, but nearly everything else? It would be easier and cheaper for you to get it out in space. You've chosen not to do that. I want to know why."

"I wasn't aware I owed you any explanation for my choices."

She stalked over to him, leaned close to his face, and hissed, "But you do, Ua Talman, you do. You owe us *all* an explanation. I want you to think about that." She stood upright. "Darwin, Banks, here."

Instantly, the two animals were at her side, looking up at her eagerly for praise.

Lorcan didn't hang around. He ran for the door, wrenched it open, and sped out into the darkness. Stumbling and tripping over tree roots, he dashed down the track and didn't stop until he found his men's encampment.

That night, nightmares of slavering dogs bursting through the walls of his tent disturbed his sleep.

15

As soon as Kala woke, her stomach forced its way up her throat. She barely had time to turn her head to one side before its meager contents erupted from her mouth. When her stomach was empty, she continued to retch. She couldn't stop. Bile came up, and then nothing, and, finally, blood.

Eventually, the spasms eased. She flopped onto her back, only now becoming aware of Jon's bed and room. She was shaking, her head was a swollen mass of pounding pain, and her limbs were locked with cramps.

Fingers were pushing something into her mouth—a paste of some kind with a sickly-sweet taste.

"Just swallow it," Jon said. "You don't have to chew."

She worked her dry mouth around the substance, easing it toward her throat. The bolus slipped down and hit her still-churning stomach. She swallowed hard, trying to avoid bringing up the substance.

"Good," said Jon. "Now, drink."

He slid his hand behind her head and lifted it till her chin touched her chest. A cup appeared at her lips. Plain water. She managed to take a sip.

"A little more. Try," he urged.

She *was* trying. Her lips were not under her control. Water slopped out of her mouth, dribbling down her neck.

Jon relented. He lowered her head to the pillow. "Just rest. You should begin to feel better soon."

Just rest? She didn't have a lot of choice. She couldn't move. Everything hurt. She hadn't thought it possible for fingernails and eyeballs to hurt, but they did.

Worse still, the memory of her encounter with the hidden woman was already slipping away. She concentrated, trying to hold onto it, to hold on to everything she'd been told, but already some parts were becoming fuzzy. The woman had explained why the BA soldier had been able to hurt her, or had she? Kala now knew there was a way for it to be possible, but she couldn't recall why. What did seem certain was only this person and the man from the myths who might do her harm.

She could live with that. Before, she'd been afraid the woman had lied to her, that she wasn't sacred and inviolable. But, according to what she'd been told, only those two presented a threat to herself and Perran.

It was something to hold on to. Her life's choices had been founded upon the encounters she'd had with the strange, imprisoned figure. The things the woman had done, the assertions and promises she'd made, had formed Kala's beliefs and behavior.

Could she trust her?

There was no point in speculating. She'd given her answer about the BA soldier, and it seemed reasonable. Besides, Kala decided, she was too far in. She had no choice.

"How are you feeling?"

Some of her pain had lessened. Her arms and legs felt

looser, and her head no longer hammered. "Better," she murmured.

"Good. I knew the herb physic would help. I've been working on it while you were out."

The room was in semi-darkness. Was it evening already?

"How long?" she asked.

"Um, about thirty-eight hours. Your disappearance caused quite a kerfuffle, I heard, till the cook told them she'd sent you here. They came knocking at my door, but I made them all go away."

With effort, she managed to turn her head toward the old man. "Thirty-eight hours?"

"Yes, your longest episode ever."

How had so much time passed? She'd only seemed to be in the cave an hour or so. Even as the estimation passed through her mind, it became hazy. Suddenly, she had no idea how long she'd spent there.

"I thought it might be your last time," said Jon quietly. "I was cursing myself for giving in and preparing the formula for you."

"If I'd died, you would have been wrong to blame yourself. You were only doing as you were instructed. I am your Dwyr."

"Maybe. But to me, you're still the little street urchin who crept in my window and drank my latest concoction. Tell me you'll never do this again, Kala. Nothing is worth your life, especially not your appearance."

Especially not...?

It was an odd remark.

Despite the danger, Kala knew if she needed to return to the imprisoned woman, she would. But she hadn't gone there to discover a cure for her scars. She'd nearly died at another's hands. The experience had shaken her to her core and made her question all she believed in. It had been worth the risk. She had rediscovered her confidence in the path she'd chosen.

Jon had left her side. She could hear him foraging amongst his clutter, apparently searching for something. He muttered, "I'm sure it's here somewhere. At my time of life, I don't have much use for them, but I think I still have one. Ah! Here it is."

He approached, carrying a mirror.

A deep-seated fear hit her. "No! Take it away."

She'd seen enough of the burns on her body. The red, stretched, corrugated skin that remained of her face horrified her. She never wanted to see it again.

"Look."

"No, I can't," she whispered.

"You don't understand," said Jon. He took her hand and wrapped her fingers around the mirror's handle. "*Look*." He pushed her hand, forcing her to move the mirror opposite her face.

She inhaled in a great whoop and gripped the handle, staring at her reflection in the silvered surface. She looked awful. Her eyes were riven with blood-filled capillaries and sunk into deep, bruise-colored pits. Her skin had faded from its usual pale olive to chalk. Her cheeks and temples were shadowed hollows.

But she looked normal.

No burns, no scarring, nothing except what she might expect from her most recent experiences.

Dropping the mirror onto the bed, she touched her face, marveling at how soft and smooth it felt.

She tried to sit up. Instantly, the room surged and retreated around her. Her stomach heaved again.

"Lie down," said Jon gently pushing her shoulders down. "Have more of the herb paste." He picked up the mortar and scooped out some of the mixture in a spoon.

"She's taken away my scars," said Kala before accepting another spoonful of the sweet paste.

Jon nodded. "It was interesting to watch them fade and your

skin heal. This person who you've told me you see while you're gone is impressive. Over the years, I've been tempted to try to see her myself. But I never thought the downsides were worth it. Now, though... Seeing what she did for you got me wondering. Could she make me young again, do you think?"

"She says time doesn't exist."

"My rheumatism begs to differ." He chuckled. "Seriously, though. If she could give me another ten or twenty years, it might be worth the risk. There's still so much I want to learn, so many experiments to do."

Kala closed her eyes. Something about what Jon was saying had sparked a memory. What was it? Had the woman said something about a return visit, or bringing someone with her? She doubted Jon would survive the horrible effects of his formula.

That was it!

"You may be able to meet her in person," she said.

"I don't see how," he replied. "In fact, until I saw what happened to your body, I'd half believed she didn't exist and you had imagined her. I wondered if my formula only allowed you to access your subconscious. I suppose it's still possible. You could have healed your scars yourself. Scientists don't know everything yet. Take placebos, for—"

"No, she's real. I sometimes doubted that myself, but no longer. She's as real as you and I." Kala closed her eyes. "She told me she's near us now, and she wants me to go to her and release her from her prison. But...oh!"

"What's the matter?"

"I don't know where she is. 'Near' could mean anything. I think she's in a cave, but that doesn't tell me much. There must be hundreds of caves around here."

"Didn't she tell you anything else? What about a place name? Or directions?" Jon seemed excited, possibly hoping the woman could reverse aging.

"No. She doesn't know where *I* am. She could only sense I was close by. But I have to find her soon, before she's moved again."

"I don't see how that's possible," said Jon. "Not even if you have the entire local population searching. They need *something* to go on. What about a description of the place?"

"It's underground and inaccessible. No one would recognize it."

He appeared to have nothing else to offer. They sat in silence.

Suddenly, Kala sat bolt upright.

"I remembered something."

The herb physic had done its work. The room no longer rocked or swam. But she barely noticed she was feeling better.

Hesitantly, she moved her hand to her other arm. Slowly, she pulled up her sleeve, exposing her lower arm to her elbow.

There they were: Faint numbers, etched out in silvery lines, her only remaining scars.

Coordinates.

16

———

The morning after Iolani's threatening behavior and assault on his character, Lorcan was fuming. He sat in the shade, watching Bourke and Jeffries break camp, ruminating. He'd expected to find it hard to persuade her to join the Project. He'd harbored hope that his description of her new life on a colony world, and his promise she would have complete control over her research, might sway her, but he'd been prepared for a final rejection. His comment that he was one of her greatest admirers had been genuine. Simply meeting her would have made the journey worth it, and he might have come away with some rare genetic material. He'd been prepared to pay handsomely for it.

What he *hadn't* expected was to be humiliated and treated as if he wasn't fit to be in her presence; to be threatened with *dogs*, as though he were a low-class burglar or thief, come to steal her precious treasures!

His cheeks burned at the memory. He would never forget the look of revulsion on her face when she'd finally allowed him to depart.

Who did she think she was?!

Every day, he received tens of thousands of applications for a place on one of his ships. Over the years, he'd turned down hundreds of thousands, probably millions. And he'd offered *her* a spot free of charge. *He'd* asked *her* to come along, and she'd had the audacity to refuse him. Not only that, she'd refused him in the most haughty, arrogant manner possible, as if he'd been asking her to step into a cesspit with him.

As to her assertion that he was responsible for the problems on Earth, that his operations were one of the reasons so many people wanted to leave... *Pfft.* He shook his head. Didn't the woman understand the nature of human progress? Was it his fault he was the facilitator of humanity's destiny? If he didn't do it, someone else would, eventually.

Hale should have been thanking him for all that he'd done, all the money he'd paid over the years to make the dreams of so many come true.

"Nearly finished, sir," said Jeffries, approaching him under the gigantic fig tree. "Bourke is packing the rations. Would you like something to eat before we leave?"

Lorcan had refused breakfast earlier when he'd woken, anger over the events of the previous evening taking away his appetite.

"Yes," he replied. "Bring me some biscuits. And then find somewhere to wait a while. I need to think."

"Yes, sir."

He watched Jeffries return to the glade where Bourke knelt, packing one of the backpacks. At a word from Jeffries, Bourke glanced at Lorcan, and then rummaged in the pack before drawing out a packet.

Lorcan wiped his neck with a cloth. The temperature had barely dipped overnight, and today promised to be the hottest of the trip so far. The thought of returning empty-handed after so much effort in difficult conditions, as well as so much time and expense, galled him.

He took the biscuits Jeffries handed over and munched on one while also mentally chewing on his problem.

Iolani Hale's face seemed to float up in front of him, mocking him with her smile. She'd only invited him to stay for dinner in order to criticize and castigate him. She'd said she'd been expecting him, and as she waited she'd clearly been preparing her diatribe, anticipating her opportunity to tear him down.

Hmm...

Hale reminded him of Dwyr Orr: Manipulative and deceitful.

He'd had his fill of that kind of behavior, and he wasn't going to put up with it any longer. He couldn't let Hale get away with what she'd done. What if she went bragging to a vidnews channel about setting her dogs on him and chasing Lorcan Ua Talman away like a beggar at her door?

He narrowed his eyes.

What if she had security cameras recording during their encounter? He hadn't seen any, but that didn't mean anything. You could buy devices the size of a pinhead these days. And she'd been very hot on security with those two brutish dogs. He couldn't take the risk of her releasing the films in the public domain. He had an image to uphold. If people saw him in his exhausted state when he'd reached her house, or with those two dogs threatening him, it could ruin the entire Project. The participants had to have faith in him, look up to him, or it would never succeed.

He simply couldn't take the risk.

He stood up, brushing off crumbs that clung to his clothes.

"Jeffries, Bourke, come here. There's been a change of plan."

In the heat of midday, the jungle was quiet. Birds rustled dead leaves on the forest floor, looking for bugs and worms, and flies buzzed, but the rest of the wildlife was silent. Even the cicadas' striations had stopped.

Lorcan slowly lifted his water container to his lips and sucked on the protruding straw thirstily. Just as slowly, he lowered the container. His back ached from crouching, but he didn't dare move.

The open ground in front of Hale's home was a bright patch of gold in the tropical sunlight.

Lorcan checked the time.

One minute to go.

He tensed, waiting for the seconds to count down.

Thirty. Fifteen. Ten. Five, four, three...

At the end of the glade, farthest from the house, something moved. The vegetation parted, and a man staggered into the clearing.

"Help!" he screamed. "Please help me! I've been bitten by a snake. God, it hurts!"

The front door flew open and banged against the wall. Hale burst out from it and leapt down the steps.

Just as quickly, Lorcan launched himself from his hiding place and raced onto the veranda. He heard dogs' paws clattering on the wooden floor inside the house. The door, which had swung closed, began to open.

He threw himself at it and slammed it shut. There was a whine as it presumably hit a questing canine nose. Then the door bucked with the impact of two large, muscly bodies. Lorcan held his back against it, his feet firmly braced on the veranda floor. Still, it took all the strength he had to keep it closed against the combined strength of the animals, who scrabbled, scratched, and jumped at it.

Meanwhile, in front of the house, all was going as planned.

Jeffries, who had faked the snake bite, had Hale down on

the ground. He was kneeling on her and grasping her wrists with one hand. The small woman was no match for him. Bourke was preparing the pressure hypodermic.

He pushed it into her bare bicep, and Hale's struggles ceased.

"Hey," Lorcan called out, "give me a hand with this door. If these dogs get out, we'll regret it."

They were going wild and alternating between barks and whines as they desperately tried to reach their mistress. While Lorcan and Bourke kept them confined, Jeffries cut a long, smooth branch. They managed to run it between slats in the veranda roof, the door handle, and then in between planks on the floor. With some apprehension, Lorcan and Bourke stepped away from the door.

It held.

The three men exhaled with relief.

Lorcan asked Bourke and Jeffries to check the exterior of the house and secure any other exits before the dogs could remember them.

Hale remained face down on the ground, unconscious. He'd never imagined he would be using the sedative he'd brought along on Hale herself, but he was not one to ignore serendipity. They would have to reapply the drug whenever she began to come around during the long journey down the mountain, but they had brought a plentiful supply.

It was a shame he would have to leave behind all that precious genetic material in her house, but he daren't risk the wrath of Darwin and Banks. Lorcan silently decided that, when they reached civilization, he would send someone to her house to take care of the dogs.

After all, he wasn't a monster.

17

Merlin held the sergeant's face in his hands and gazed into the man's eyes. The sergeant gazed back at him, but without any intelligence in his features. He stared blankly at the alien. A thin dribble of saliva ran from the corner of his open mouth.

"Another one," Merlin muttered. "So many."

He seemed more irritated than dismayed by the numbers of people on the *Fearless* who had been affected by their transportation with the black cloud. And he still hadn't denied responsibility, Wright reminded himself.

There was so much the alien hadn't told them—what he was, where he was from, and why he was involving himself in human affairs, presumably for the second time.

It wasn't through want of asking. Wright had attended several meetings where Colbourn had quizzed the newcomer, and at each one the interviewee had given vague answers or avoided questions entirely by changing the subject or asking a question in return. The brigadier was no pushover, but even she had failed to penetrate the constant obfuscation. And she couldn't press him any harder. The admiral and most of the rest of the fleet believed Merlin was a gift horse and they shouldn't inspect his mouth too closely.

The 'treatment' the alien provided for the sergeant was the same as he'd provided for all the men and women he'd seen so far: he removed his hands from the sergeant's head, folded his arms, and closed his eyes. A line appeared between his brows as he concentrated.

Everyone in the *Fearless's* sick bay watched and waited, Arthur included. He didn't seem to get bored by witnessing the same thing over and over again. He stuck to Merlin like glue and appeared endlessly impressed by the alien's feats.

Wright hated to admit it, but he couldn't deny any longer that Ellis had probably been correct about the identity of the man he'd carried from the cave. The notion defied common sense, and he hadn't been able to bring himself to give it any credit. But that was before the black cloud condensed into human form in space and clung to the outside of a starship, asking to be let in. Now, everything he'd thought he knew about how reality worked had been brought into question.

The sergeant's blank expression was changing. He closed his mouth and his pupils constricted as he focused on Merlin, whose eyes remained closed. The floppy muscle tone of his face tightened. He straightened up and blinked.

"Wh-where…?" he murmured as he turned his attention from the alien to his surroundings. He looked confused, and then frightened.

"It's okay," said Wright, stepping up to him. "You've been sick, but you're better now."

The man focused on him and his uniform, and his face relaxed.

Merlin opened his eyes, turned toward the door, and bellowed, "Next!"

"Come with me," a medic said to the cured patient. "I'll take your details, and we can find out where you're supposed to be."

That was all that was required. After Merlin had 'fixed' them, they appeared to regain their cognitive function and memory. The men and women returned to their duties without any apparent ill effects, except general weakness and a couple of months missing from their lives.

Another patient was brought into the sick bay.

"Actually," said Merlin, grimacing, "that's enough for today. I'm tired and I have a headache."

The alien had a headache? Wright didn't buy it. He was bored. That was all.

Merlin said something to Arthur in their shared language. He replied, and they talked for a minute or two. Merlin seemed to be persuading Arthur about something. Eventually, the old king told Wright they would be back later, and the two of them left together.

"Are you just going to let them go?" asked the medic who had brought in the next patient. She was a familiar face from the *Valiant*.

"I don't have a choice," he replied. "They aren't military, let alone under my command. Hell, one of them isn't even human."

"Then they can just do whatever they like?" the medic asked. "They don't answer to anyone?"

"Technically, no. Admiral Kim has given them guest status. That means they have to obey commands intended to protect them from harm, but it doesn't mean I can order them around. They're free to do what they want providing they don't enter restricted areas or put anyone in danger."

"Well, isn't that just great?" She pulled off her gloves and mask and threw them into the sanitation chute. The other medical personnel were doing the same.

Wright felt their frustration. They had a ship full of people requiring basic care just to stay alive, and the only person who could help them couldn't be arsed. But, as he'd told the medic, there wasn't anything he could do about it except complain to Colbourn, who only maintained her hands were tied.

As he left the sick bay, a possible solution hit him. He'd been asking the brigadier for weeks to transfer Ellis to the *Fearless*, but she'd refused, saying the *Valiant* couldn't afford to spare any more personnel to feed the flagship's incapacitated crew. However, Colbourn knew Ellis's special relationship with Arthur, a relationship Wright suspected was more than platonic. What if he told her the corporal might be able to reach Merlin through Arthur and persuade him to work harder at treating people? It might work.

The possibility turned his annoyance to optimism, but then he suddenly felt bad. After weeks of waiting, word had come through that the BA military leaders had finally settled on the place to try to free from EAC control. It was not to be the Britannic Isles, as Ellis hoped. They were going to Jamaica.

18

———————

Life among the Jamaicans was hard. Hans had been given the job of fetching water every day from the nearest mountain stream, which lay about half a kilometer from the cave. The distance wasn't great, but the terrain made the journey arduous. However, that wasn't a problem. He didn't mind the work. Now he had access to sufficient food and room to move around his sores had healed and physical condition had improved. His problem was he was lonely.

The Resistance members spoke to each other in Patois. He understood a little of the language, but he would quickly become lost when listening to long conversations. And since their discussion when she'd let him out of his cage, Mariya had gone back to mostly ignoring him, so he had no one to talk to.

The other locals could speak English, but most of the time they didn't. They only used it to speak to him, and their communications usually consisted of orders or instructions. *We're running out of water. Fetch some more. Get out of the way.* They called him 'backra'. Mariya had explained the word meant white person, but Hans had a feeling it meant more, due to the disdain in their voices when they used it.

He spent a lot of time alone when he wasn't helping with manual tasks, sitting on the fringes of the gatherings around the fire in the evenings or sleeping in a quiet, out-of-the-way spot in the cave. In these quiet moments, he would think over all that had happened and everything he'd done and try to make peace with his current situation.

He knew he was lucky to be alive. If Mariya hadn't decided to take her sister's place after her death, someone else would have been his assistant, and, after the EAC invasion, the Dwyr would have hunted him down and put him to a horrible, grisly death, as she had with most of the BA government.

Then again, if Mariya hadn't taken Josephine's place, the Dwyr might not have received advance notice of the military coup, and she wouldn't have been able to time her attack so perfectly. Nevertheless, regardless of the actions of Dwyr Orr's agents, he had a feeling the writing had been on the wall for the Britannic Alliance for a long time. Only he'd been too close to the situation to see it.

And there was the fact he'd actively schemed for years to weaken the government's grip and divide its members. He couldn't deny his own hand in its downfall, though his intentions had been noble.

Mariya's words that day of his release still stung. How many had died due to his schemes and machinations? Did he regret all he'd done? His greatest regret was that now it was too late to change anything. With hindsight, he might have done some things differently.

One of the reasons he kept to himself was Mariya's warning that some of her companions had only agreed to spare his life because they thought he might be a useful hostage, not because they thought he deserved to live. His weeks of quiet hard work and unobtrusive behavior seemed to have paid off. Whereas in the early days of his release he'd attracted dark looks and lips curled in snarls of disapproval, now, apart from the occasional command, he was mostly ignored.

It would take a lot of work and time to build acceptance and trust among these people, but he knew that was the only route to his survival.

Over time, his goal renewed itself in his mind.

His attempt had failed, but that didn't mean all was lost. The BA could rise again, perhaps in a better state, perhaps even as the republic he'd long dreamed of. He'd hated the Establishment, but he'd never hated the entity itself. He'd believed in what it professed to stand for: Tolerance, courage, the protection of the weak and vulnerable, excellence through honest endeavor, a fair chance for all. That was why he'd tried so hard to oust the BA's leaders, who made a mockery of these values.

But before the Republic could arise, the EAC had to be defeated.

One evening, he decided to tell Mariya about his thoughts and feelings, hoping she could help him.

He waited until the daily gathering at dinner was breaking up and approached her as she was returning to the cave, wrapping a shawl around her shoulders.

"Mariya," he said softly, "could I speak to you for a moment?"

She told the people she was with to go on in. "What is it, Hans?"

"I want..." He paused, gathering his resolve. There was a good chance she wouldn't want to listen to him, and he was keenly aware of how tenuous his position was in the group. "I want to discuss my future. Could we...?" He gestured at the fire. It was dying down. Only a few people remained sitting around it, and they were preparing to leave.

She nodded, conveying the attitude she was allowing him a concession.

They sat on the far side of the fire, the dark forest at their backs, alive with the noises of nocturnal creatures.

"Mariya, the last few weeks have been an eye-opening and painful experience for me..."

She tutted, irritated.

"What's wrong? I wasn't looking for sympathy, only to introduce what I am about to tell you."

"Get to the point, Hans. You aren't in a governmental meeting. Your oratory has no place here. We speak plainly. If you don't do the same, you will never earn our respect."

He digested this tidbit of advice. Taking another breath of the warm, humid, fire-scented air, he said, "I'll try. I do want your respect. It's important to me."

She regarded him impassively, as if she didn't have the remotest interest in what was important to him.

"I want to help the cause," he said. "I want to fight the EAC. I know collecting water has a small value, but I can be more useful than that. As the head of SIS, I was privy to many governmental secrets."

She looked more interested, however, she replied, "So was I. Are you forgetting I worked for you?"

He acknowledged her comment with a nod. "It's clear you used your time wisely. But I know more than you. Information that's useful, even now after the BA has fallen. I'm confident of it. For years, anything and everything categorized high security passed across my desk. And I have a very good memory."

She didn't reply for a moment, only held his gaze. "I'll be frank. Your presence here is only tolerated. People don't like you, and, more importantly, they don't trust you. For some, that will never change. They learned hatred of the backra at their mother's knee. It is burned into their souls. They will either disbelieve whatever information you give them, or they will think you're setting a trap for us. Others are more reasonable and pragmatic. If you want to play a part in the Resistance, it's these people whose trust you must earn. It will be hard, but I don't see a way around it." She picked up a stick and poked the dying embers of the fire, sending sparks up into the night.

"I'll do everything I can," said Hans, "but I need your help. I need to know what I must do. I'm accustomed to dealing with very different people. For example, your advice to speak plainly...that's useful to know." For most of his adult life, he'd worked on understanding and influencing the privileged elite. He knew their weaknesses so well: Vanity, pride, snobbery, avarice. He knew what buttons to press, and they had been easy to manipulate and exploit. Though he'd spent only a comparatively short time among the people of the Jamaican Resistance, he knew they didn't have these weaknesses. He was all at sea with them.

"I know you speak three languages as well as English," Mariya said. "Can you learn Patois?"

"I already know a little. I can try to learn more."

"You don't need to speak it, only understand. My friends don't like using English. It reminds them of the past. And we don't have translators. The local net is still down."

"I'm sure I can do that."

"That will help," said Mariya. "I'll talk to some people and tell them what you've told me. I can't guarantee anything, but I'll talk to them."

"Thank you. But, if we're being honest with each other, I have to say, I'm confused. You know who I was within the BA. You must have known I would have useful information. Why didn't you ask me about it?"

"I was waiting for you to make the offer. This way, it's more likely you're telling the truth. I can't risk you leading the Resistance into a trap. It would be natural to want revenge for the way we treated you."

"I would never do that."

He wasn't sure if she believed him. She'd turned her gaze

toward the remains of the fire. The red-gold, cooling brands were reflected in her eyes.

"Mariya, which are you?"

She turned to him. "What do you mean?"

"Is hatred of the backra burned into your soul, or are you more reasonable and pragmatic?"

Without answering, she stood up and began to walk away from him, heading toward the cave entrance.

"How are things in the rest of the island?" he called out.

"Bad, Hans. Very bad. But we're fighting back."

19

———

Standing in the dank, dark entry chamber to the ancient mine, Kala closed the interface she'd been reading with an angry flick of her fingers. Things were not going well in Jamaica.

The latest expansion was presenting unforeseen challenges. It was a problem of terrain and climate, Commander Novak had reported. The mountainous topography of some areas made moving large numbers of troops difficult while at the same time it provided plenty of hiding places for guerrillas. Also, the clement weather meant the rebels could live rough indefinitely, raiding the turbulent cities and towns for food. Prior to the assault on the Caribbean, the EAC armed forces' experience of warfare had been in colder countries of the northern hemisphere, where winters were hard.

Kala mentally pushed the problem aside. She had more urgent business to attend to.

"I've been waiting for over an hour," she snapped. "I was informed the lift was operational."

"It was, ma'am," the engineering supervisor replied deferentially. "We'll have it working again soon."

He'd said the same thing when she'd arrived.

Her legs ached from standing so long in the cold, humid atmosphere. "You," she barked at another worker, "find me something to sit on."

The woman scurried away.

Kala watched the man fixing the mechanism, noticing he bore a close resemblance to the supervisor.

A few moments later, the other worker returned with a chair that looked as old as the mine. Hastily rubbing dust from the seat, she placed it behind Kala.

The EAC leader lowered herself onto it distastefully. The entire expedition was turning out to be far more unpleasant than she'd anticipated, even setting aside the news from Jamaica. She only hoped the effort and her discomfort would be worth it.

The lift machinery sprang to life with loud clanking and whirring. The large car, which had been stuck somewhere below, was rising to ground floor level.

"There!" the supervisor exclaimed. "I knew we'd do it eventually. They built things to last in those days. Not like today, when everything falls apart after you've used it a few times." Apparently realizing Kala didn't appreciate his opinions, the man cleared his throat and went on, "Ready when you are, Dwyr."

She rose to her feet. "You're sure it's working properly now?"

He hesitated. "As sure as I can be. The equipment is very old. I can't say for certain it won't break down again, but don't let that worry you. We'll fix it and have you up out of there as soon as we can."

The supervisor's words weren't particularly reassuring, but she guessed he was only being honest.

"I suppose that's reasonable," she replied. "However, I'd like your son to accompany me."

"My-my son?" he asked. He stared from the man who had worked on the lift to Kala and back.

"He *is* your son, isn't he?"

"Yes, but..."

"He's clearly familiar with the functioning of the mechanism. I want someone who knows what they're doing by my side."

Looking crestfallen, the supervisor nodded and said, "Go with her, Peter."

She'd brought a small buggy for driving the considerable distances in the vast tunnels of the mine. Two members of her household guard sat in it. Kala told the driver to drive into the lift car, then she joined them and waited for the young man. His work boots clunked as he walked across the metal floor.

She had dressed appropriately for the situation, wearing thick woolen pants, a heavy overcoat, hat, and gloves. Yet the chill of the old mine had gradually worked its way in. She shivered as they descended.

1500 meters below the surface, the tunnels stretched for hundreds of kilometers under the sea to the north. The mine had once been a global supplier of polyhalite, an inorganic fertilizer. After excavating billions of tonnes of the mineral, it had finally exhausted the supply and closed down two centuries ago. From what information Kala had been able to glean, the underground roads were labyrinthine, but she doubted they would get lost. She could already feel the pull, directing her to her target.

As they waited while the lift made its deep descent, she looked at the supervisor's son more closely. He was in his mid-to-late twenties. He remained respectfully silent, his mop-haired head hanging down. Kala took in his strong hands, fingernails begrimed with oil, and dirty boiler suit. A simple, plain man, skilled at his craft. Such were the EAC's followers.

They felt the connection with Earth. They understood their position in the universe.

One day, perhaps very soon, she would be able to show them what else the universe had to offer.

The lift stopped.

A shudder passed through the carriage as the metal doors retracted.

Utter darkness confronted them.

Even in the deepest oceanic trenches, bioluminescent life forms provided some light. Here, nothing lived except rare microscopic flora and fauna, invisible to the naked eye. Nothing gave the minutest ray of illumination to relieve the optical sense. If it were not for the lift's light, they would not have been able to see their hands in front of their faces.

Kala turned her attention inward, focusing on the pull.

She pointed. "That way."

The buggy driver started up the engine, and the headlights turned on.

When she had first looked up the coordinates the dream woman had scratched into her skin, she'd been confused. The spot lay in the Northern Sea, kilometers from the BI shore. Yet the woman had seemed confident Kala could go to her.

It was only through long investigation she'd discovered the history of the old, vast mine. Now that she was here, it was clear she was on the right track.

The buggy's headlights revealed a dusty road cut into the rock. Dust filled the atmosphere too. The beams were thick with hazy fragments.

What a barren, dreary place.

They drove kilometers, each identical to the last. Time seemed to slow down, but suddenly Kala saw twenty-five minutes had passed since they'd driven out of the lift. In that time, she'd instructed the driver to make three turns, responding to the sensation in her gut.

She could not imagine being imprisoned for decades in a place like this, though she seemed to remember the woman had said she was regularly moved. How had she survived without food or water? It was one of many mysteries Kala hoped would be revealed soon. The feat of the woman's survival heartened her. It was evidence that what she'd said was true: There was a deeper level than what humans perceived as reality, a wondrous plane of existence, where the impossible was commonplace.

"We must go left at the next turn," she said to the driver.

As if on cue, a black rectangle opened up on the left-hand side of the road. They swung around the corner, the vehicle's tires skidding a little.

"Not so fast," said Kala. "We're nearly there."

The pull was strong now. It felt as if a rope led out from her naval, and someone was hauling on it, hand over hand, drawing her closer. The sensation was unpleasant and nauseating, but it promised to be over soon.

"Stop!" she blurted.

They'd passed the place.

The tug was insistent, angry.

"Go back."

The driver put the vehicle into reverse and rested an arm over the seat, looking out through the rear view window as he guided the buggy backward.

A narrow opening appeared in the wall.

"That's it," said Kala. "Stop."

The opening was too narrow even for the small car. She told everyone to get out and come with her. The guards produced the flashlights she'd told them to bring and lit the way.

The channel seemed to be a trial dig, seeking out a new seam of polyhalite. But none had been found, and the passage was abandoned. The tunneling machine had cut regular grooves about half a meter apart. Kala stepped from ridge to ridge, lightly touching the wall to keep her balance.

Relieved only by the breaths and footsteps of her companions, a profound silence pressed in. She became aware of the millions of tonnes of rock above her, and the cold, rough sea above that, separating her from the surface. If she didn't make it out of there, she would never be heard from again.

The pull on her stomach became a vicious wrench.

"Here," she gasped.

They'd reached a dead end.

20

———

Lorcan had been uneasy about keeping Iolani Hale sedated for the entire journey back to the *Bres*. He wasn't a doctor and didn't have a medical professional accompanying him. But he also didn't think it wise to approach anyone Earthside. He employed medical personnel at his mines, refineries, smelting plants, and factories, but he couldn't trust them. They hadn't been vetted, and he didn't know their affiliations.

He was aware he'd done something many would find unconscionable, and he needed to be confident of the loyalty of everyone who knew about it.

As soon as they reached the shuttle, he ceased topping up Hale's sedation. When she came around, Bourke and Jeffries had tied her up so securely she couldn't move or cry out.

But her eyes told him everything.

If looks could kill, he would have suffered the kind of death Dwyr Orr enjoyed inflicting. Of that, he had no doubt.

Ignoring the furious woman, Lorcan focused on the scene beyond the shuttle window. The *Bres* had been slowly growing bigger as they neared her, the vast corkscrew reflecting the sun's light. Her outer shell had been completed years ago. It was building her internal structure that was the mammoth task, although, thanks to his short alliance with the EAC, it was now ahead of schedule. Free of interference from the BA, his mines and manufacturing plants were producing at unanticipated capacities.

He estimated the *Bres* and her sister ships would depart the Solar System in three years or less.

A small wrinkle in his plan sat on the opposite side of the shuttle aisle. Nowhere in his massive scheme had he factored in kidnapping a world-famous scientist.

Had he been right to do it? He'd acted in haste. It was out of character for him, and for good reason. His best ideas had always come from long consideration. But he hadn't had time to weigh up all the risks and potential repercussions. He wasn't worried about the Republic of Suriname's authorities coming after him. The country was far too poor for that kind of thing. Did Hale have any important friends? He didn't know.

Suddenly, his view of the *Bres* split into fragments. The outer pane of the shuttle window had cracked. He drew back in shock, realizing he'd seen something hit the window a second ago.

The pilot said over the intercom, "The sensors registered contact with a foreign object. Everyone okay back there?"

Lorcan inspected the damage. It didn't appear to be spreading. He told the pilot what he'd seen.

"The impact isn't currently threatening hull integrity," said the pilot, "but I'd feel better if you all suited up, just in case."

EVA suits had been stocked aboard the shuttle for just such an emergency. Lorcan told Bourke and Jeffries to put one on. Then he regarded Hale, who was glaring at him with venom. He marveled at her ability to maintain her rage at its maximum level for so long.

She needed to be put into a suit too, but that would necessitate untying her. He waited until Bourke and Jeffries had donned theirs, and then put one on himself. Explaining to the two men what had to happen, he waited at the rear of the cabin while they did their jobs.

As soon as her bindings were removed, she fought like a demon.

As he watched Bourke and Jeffries struggle with her, he wondered what it had been that had hit the shuttle. Had it been something from the *Bres*? The danger of an impact from space debris was well known. He'd put stringent safety protocols in place to minimize the risks of tools, materials, or waste being lost during the shipbuilding process. Had a piece of random space rock hit them?

Or had it been something else?

He'd been writing and releasing letters to Grace almost daily for years. He knew it was madness, but he felt as though somehow, somewhere, she was reading them. He'd known he was contravening his own safety rules, but he'd told himself that if anyone should be able to break the rules, it was the boss.

Had one of his letters hit the shuttle?

He felt guilty and ashamed. He'd done something stupid, and he could have killed not only himself, but everyone else aboard. He would have to find another way of talking to his deceased wife.

Hale was finally in her suit and tied up once more. Her gagged visage was wet with sweat from her efforts, and her bangs hung in her eyes. The rest of her journey would be uncomfortable, but they only had another half an hour to go.

～

THE SHUTTLE DOCKED, and Jeffries and Bourke had to perform the reverse procedure to remove Hale from her suit and then tie her up again.

"Where to now, sir?" asked Jeffries.

"Deck three."

That was where the cryopreservation chambers and treatment centers were situated. Lorcan hadn't visited them for a while, but he knew they were nearing completion.

They took the elevator down. Iolani seemed to be finally giving up her fight. She hung her head, and tears slid from her eyes.

Lorcan turned away.

His sense of guilt hadn't improved since the impact incident. If anything, he felt worse. Regret about his impulsive act of kidnapping the woman was beginning to bite. Whether or not it had been one of his letters that had hit the shuttle, he couldn't help feeling as though Grace was trying to tell him he'd done something very wrong.

If she'd been around, he would never have gone through with it. In fact, now he thought about it, his behavior had changed a lot since she'd died. She'd brought out the best in him. Before he met her, ambition had caused him to overlook considerations of morality and ethics. She'd moderated his excesses.

But what could he do now? He could hardly take Hale all the way back to Earth, and, besides, his reason for wanting her to join the Project remained true—she would be a massive asset to the new colony. He was confident that, with time, she would grow to love her new life. What scientist wouldn't relish the prospect of an entirely new planet to explore?

He consoled himself with the knowledge that, soon, agonizing over the wisdom of his action would be moot. Iolani Hale would be the first of the colonists to enter cryopreservation. He would schedule their respites from the life suspension state during the journey so they were never awake at the same time. It would be many years before he would have to face her ire.

The elevator stopped and the doors slid open. Holding her by her upper arms, Jeffries and Bourke forced Hale out and pushed her in the direction of the cryo lab. She stumbled. They hauled her to her feet.

"Gentler," Lorcan remonstrated. "She's no threat."

They reached the lab. The lead cryo tech, Xiao, stared at Hale, and then Jeffries and Bourke, and finally Lorcan, taking in the scene.

"How can I help you, Ua Talman?" he asked uncertainly.

"Meet your first subject for suspension," Lorcan replied. "I would like you to prepare a chamber for Ms Hale's preservation. I want it ready as soon as possible."

"I see." Xiao paused and regarded the scientist, alarm in his features. "I'm afraid I can't do that, sir."

"What?! I think you're forgetting your place. You don't have the luxury of questioning my decisions. I order you to prepare a chamber immediately."

"Sir," Xiao replied respectfully, "you misunderstand me. We've experienced a setback in the creation of the chambers. We have structures in place, but the nutrient supply system was configured incorrectly. We're removing and replacing the entire network. I sent you a report several days ago, but it appears you haven't read it yet. I take full responsibility."

It was devastating news. The cryo subjects were cooled to well below freezing, but they were not frozen. Doing so would cause their cells walls to burst, which would kill them. Instead, the water in their bodies was replaced by a solution that had similar properties but a much lower freezing point. The solution also supplied nutrients to the barely alive individuals. Without it, if they tried to suspend Hale's life functions, she would simply die.

"You...I..." Lorcan didn't know what to say. "How long will it be until you have a chamber ready?"

"I estimate it will take us twenty-six days to fix the problem. I'm very sorry."

Twenty-six days?

Nearly a month before he could put Hale on ice and forget about her?

He would have to keep her locked up somewhere. A month of the living, breathing woman as a prisoner on his ship, a thorn pricking his conscience.

21

———

"How much farther?" asked Mariya.

She sounded tired.

Hans was tired too. A ten-kilometer hike over rough ground under a hot sun quickly sapped your energy.

"We're nearly there," he replied. "Another half a klick or so." His reply was more confident than he felt. His memory of the location of the site was vague. As the head of SIS, it hadn't been his job to remember minor details like exact locations, and the actual coordinates would be encoded and buried deep within the BA's top-level secure-access files.

The path through the vegetation was a thin line of bare soil bordered by thick grass. It was barely a path at all, and Hans wasn't sure humans had made it. The narrowness of the track meant the islanders were forced to walk in single file. He trudged near the end of the line, only two others walking behind him: Mariya and a man whose name he didn't know. He was sure they weren't there to prevent him from running off. Up until a few days ago, many of the group would have been happier if he had. They'd made it clear they considered him a waste of food. Now, thanks to Mariya's support, he had a chance to prove his worth.

He only hoped no one died in the process.

Mariya called for a halt in Patois. She walked past him and the others, heading toward the leader at the front, twenty or so people away. Hans and the rest waited, sweating in the sun, as presumably some kind of consultation went on.

When she returned she pulled him to one side. Meanwhile, an instruction went out. The others were to gather off the track with the leader, a man named Devon.

"We're splitting into two groups," Mariya explained. "Devon will lead one. I'll lead the other, with you."

"Me?" Hans's vision of what would happen hadn't included him taking an active role.

She glared. "Think about it. How is it going to look if you sit to one side while everyone else takes all the risks? You want them to see you being the boss man, giving orders like those clowns, Hennessy and Montague?"

"No... But I don't have any training or experience at this kind of thing. I've been a diplomat all my life. I've never even held a gun."

"You don't need to worry about that. We don't have enough weapons to go around anyway."

Hans felt his eyes pop. "You want me to approach a potentially guarded military depot without a weapon?!"

"Make up your mind. A minute ago you were telling me you didn't want a gun."

"I didn't say that! I said I'd never held one before."

"Do you want one or not?"

"If I'm going to be in the front line, yes, I do!"

She took her backpack off her shoulders and dropped it to her feet.

He'd been tricked. A moment ago, he'd imagined he'd be

sitting in the background while others did the fighting, now here he was asking for a gun.

She was a wily one.

She handed him an old-fashioned weapon that fired rounds.

It felt reassuringly heavy and solid, but he had no idea how to use it. Apparently noticing his clueless look, Mariya snatched it back and pushed a beamer into his hands. He felt better. To use this, he only had to point and press the trigger. There was also a dial to control the intensity of the beam. He understood the principle: The lower the intensity, the shorter the range and the less damage caused to the target, but the power pack would last longer. The higher the intensity, the opposite applied. That was it.

"Happy?" Mariya asked sarcastically.

"Thanks," he replied. "I'm less likely to shoot the wrong person now, or myself."

She gave him a dark look. "You have a lot riding on this, Hans. You'll be watched."

"I know. You don't need to explain."

Nevertheless, she seemed to feel she did.

"Some of your haters are saying you only brought us here so you can cross over to the EAC," she said. "Their theory is you didn't want to walk in the forest alone, lose your way and die, so you made up a story to get us to bring you to Port Lorenzo, where you can steal food and survive by yourself."

He had to admit, it was a plausible explanation for his actions. But they didn't know him. They didn't know how fervently he believed in his political ideals. The EAC was the antithesis of all he held dear. Plus, they were forgetting the fact that he didn't want to be roasted like a chicken in a wicker basket.

"I haven't made this up," he said. "If there's nothing there, it'll be because the EAC already found it and moved everything to a new location."

"Let's hope they haven't."

It was time to move on.

Two men and three women came over to Mariya and Hans while the rest of the group continued down the trail. She led them out at a tangent, over trackless ground, aiming to approach the site from another direction.

Port Lorenzo sat on Jamaica's north coast. An ancient settlement, it had once been an active port, but in 2187 a landslide had blocked the harbor. After that, the town had become a tourist destination, but over recent decades interest in the place had waned. Now it was a sleepy backwater that few had heard about, let alone visited.

After the BI had fallen and its government had relocated to the Caribbean, a channel had been excavated through the blockage to the harbor and concrete bunkers had been sunk into the hillside. The idea had been that Royal Navy ships would bring in armaments to be deposited in a secret cache—a backup in case of invasion. The first shipment of arms had arrived just days prior to the coup, and only a few senior officials knew about it.

The EAC attack, at the height of the government takeover, when all was in confusion, had been swift and devastating. Hans felt confident no one would have had time to reach the stash, and it should be easy for the Jamaican Resistance to liberate, if they were lucky.

They were not lucky.

As he and Mariya crested a rise and looked down on the road leading to the harbor, a line of EAC military vehicles could be seen approaching the site. Hans saw jeeps, personnel carriers, and trucks. They'd learned about the cache, probably from torturing a BA official, and were going to seize it.

Hans swallowed. It could have been him.

"Damn," Mariya muttered. "They want to retrieve the arms and move them to another location."

Hans had come to the same conclusion. "Don't give up yet. We might still be able to get them."

"I wasn't giving up. Besides, we can't. Devon won't back out. We desperately need weapons. I'm going to speak to him." Crouching so she wouldn't be seen by anyone looking up from below, Mariya moved away from Hans and began communicating with the other resistance leader via two-way radio.

Other members of her team came up beside him to peer downward.

Mariya returned. "We have to move fast. Devon's group already reached the road. The vehicles just passed them. It's up to us to make them stop, then Devon will attack from behind."

"How are we going to do that?"

"I don't know. I hope to think of something by the time we get there." She announced to the rest they were moving in.

There was no easy way to get down to the road. They were forced to push through the undergrowth. Hans was quickly pierced by thorns and covered in scratches. He could also barely keep up with Mariya's team. He still hadn't fully recovered from his incarceration.

Through gaps in the bushes, he saw the gray line of the road not far ahead. What was Mariya planning? Was she just going to run out and try to attack a convoy of armed soldiers inside armored vehicles with her two-hundred-year-old gun?

Perhaps she was.

He put on a spurt of speed and caught up to her. Grabbing her shoulder, he hissed, "Wait a minute. I have an idea."

She stopped, panting. Something had cut her forehead above her eye. A trickle of blood ran down the side of her face.

"What?" she asked.

"Hold this." He handed over the beamer. "Stay here and

watch me. You'll understand and see the right time to make your move."

He could hear the crunch of tires on dirt road and feel the vibrations of heavy vehicles approaching.

In case he didn't look sufficiently disheveled already, he rubbed his hands through his hair, roughening it. Then, motioning the others to stay back, he climbed the steep bank that led to the road surface. The first vehicle in the line was only tens of meters away. He stumbled out onto the road. It didn't take much effort to fake exhaustion and near collapse. After raising an arm weakly over his head, he collapsed.

The first vehicle rumbled onward and only stopped a couple of meters from his head. Two EAC soldiers climbed out. One aimed a pulse rifle at Hans. The other, a woman, was dressed in an officer's uniform.

Rising feebly to his knees, Hans said, "I've been hiding in the jungle for weeks, but I-I can't stand it anymore. If I stay here any longer, I'll die. I surrender. Please take me to your Dwyr."

The commander lifted her upper lip in disgust. Turning to her subordinate, she gave the order to kill him.

"No!" exclaimed Hans. "Dwyr Orr will want to see me. I used to be very important in the BA Government."

"Hmm. Who are you?"

"My name is Hans Jonte. I used to be head of the Secret Intelligence Service."

The woman was silent, her gaze fixed on him.

Where was Mariya? He'd stopped the convoy. Now she and Devon were supposed to attack it. Wasn't it obvious the moment was passing?

Or had the Jamaicans decided to give up on the plan as too dangerous? Were they going to abandon him? Was he going to be taken to the maniacal leader of the EAC, to be barbecued?

"Put him in the back."

The soldier pushed the barrel of his rifle into Hans's chest and told him to stand up.

A deafening bang rang out, and the officer's forehead collapsed into bone fragments, blood, and brain matter. Before her body had hit the ground, the soldier's torso lit up with pulse fire. He dropped to one side, his rifle falling from his loosening grip.

Hans grabbed it.

Resistance fighters burst from the undergrowth, both from behind Hans and farther down the road, at the end of the convoy.

Pulse fire burst from the first vehicle. Hans fired at the soldier leaning out but missed. Another loud bang came from behind him. Blood spurted from the man's leg, and he crumpled. Mariya ran past Hans, firing again but this time with the beamer she held in her other hand. She hit the EAC soldier in the chest.

Hans's ears were ringing and his heart thumped. Time seemed to slow. Shouts and cries of pain were coming at him from a distance. Somewhere down the road, a truck exploded. A body flew into the air and landed among the trees.

Hans wasn't sure what to do. He had a rifle, but he was no fighter.

Perhaps his part was already over.

22

———

Boots could transfer to *The Fearless*, but Abacha could not. Colbourn was standing firm. Taylan didn't know why, though she suspected the brigadier was simply rehashing her former habit of being a Grade A bitch.

She hugged Abacha goodbye outside the shuttle bay.

"Take it easy, little chick," he said.

Her throat tightened, and she couldn't reply. It was the first time he'd called her that since rescuing her when she'd lain dying in Dwyr Orr's mansion in Jamaica.

After she'd finished Basic and earned everyone else's resentment by being too good at everything, he'd been the only Marine who would give her the time of day. Later, as a fellow insomniac, their friendship had grown over countless late-night games of xiangqi.

Boots miaowed in the duffle bag at her feet. She had her kit bag over her shoulders, but the cat needed a conveyance all of his own due to his unreliable toilet habits.

"You'd better not miss the shuttle," said Abacha. "Wright won't like it."

"Ugh, I don't care what he thinks. I thought he was okay, but he's turned all stuck up again. He's back to being Major By-the-book."

"That's why Colbourn likes him."

"Exactly." She sighed. "I'd better go."

"Yeah, you'd better."

The thing that was keeping her from running to catch the shuttle was her memory of the Battle of the *Bres*. That was what people were calling it, though the BA fleet hadn't come within striking distance of the colony ship. The personnel of entire ships had been wiped out in an instant, including those aboard the *Daisy*, where she'd begun her service. She hadn't been close to those men and women, but they'd been her comrades in arms.

What if the same thing were to happen to Abacha and the *Valiant*?

They were only a week from Earth and the BA counteroffensive.

Was this the last time she would see her friend?

She hugged him again.

"Whoa, not so tight," he said. "We aren't sparring now."

Summoning her willpower, she released him and picked up the bag containing Boots. Without looking back, she walked through the shuttle bay doors.

"I hope you find your kid, Tay," he called after her.

She'd never told him about her missing children, and he'd never asked her why she wore a child's necklace or what was in the vids she watched over and over again.

She lost it.

Rubbing her sleeve furiously over her eyes, she crossed the bay to the shuttle. The hatch was closing.

"Hey!" she yelled. "Wait for me!"

She began to run.

~

HALF AN HOUR LATER, as she left the *Fearless's* shuttle bay carrying her kit bag and Boots's, Major Wright approached her.

"I realized I didn't explain the situation properly earlier, Ellis," he said. "You should know, the *Fearless* is a Royal Navy ship. As the Space Fleet's flagship, she'll be captained by Admiral Kim as soon as she arrives, in about an hour. You and I are the only Marines aboard, but we'll be taking our orders from her, the same as the rest of the ship's personnel. Understood?"

"Understood, sir," she replied.

Why did he always have to be so goddamned formal?

"Good. Have you developed a plan for bringing Merlin into line?"

Couldn't he give her five minutes to settle in? Just because she was awake, it didn't mean she was on duty.

"Yes," she replied, lifting the duffle bag.

From inside it came Boots's complaint about being confined.

The major's eyebrows rose. "The *Valiant's* cat?"

Boots wasn't the *Valiant's* cat. If he belonged to anyone, he was hers. She'd smuggled him aboard the *Daisy* after a planet-side battle and brought him with her when she transferred.

But Wright didn't know that.

"Arthur used to spend a lot of time with Boots before Merlin turned up," she explained.

"Hm, you're right. He does like the animal. So you think if we get Arthur back on our side, Merlin might be less of a loose cannon?"

"Something like that."

"Well, you're welcome to try whatever strategy you think might work."

"Okay, I guess I should get started right away. Where do I stow my stuff?"

The major took her to a regular ten-bunk cabin. The only

free rack was a lower one, next to the door to the restroom. Naturally. She threw her kit bag on the bed.

"So where are Arthur and Merlin?" she asked.

"Follow me."

The *Fearless* was about double the size of the *Valiant*. A dreadnought, she carried many heavy caliber weapons for space warfare, including pulse cannon, plasma cannon, a particle lance, and distortor torpedoes. The torpedoes would have been used to destroy Ua Talman's colony ship, the *Bres*, if the *Fearless* had managed to get within range. They didn't only damage the area of impact, their warheads created a field that distorted the space between atomic particles, breaking molecular bonds in a domino effect. One strike from a distortor torpedo could take out an entire heavy class battleship. The worst thing about the weapon was that it worked slowly but inexorably, often only stopping when it hit the vacuum of space.

All Earth's powers had agreed to outlaw their use on or near the planet.

The *Fearless* also carried thirty-five Swifts, the single-seater spacecraft designed for close space combat, and twelve shuttles. Altogether, the flagship was home to 7500 men and women at full operational status. They kept the ship and her spacecraft running, operated the torpedo launchers, repaired damage during battles, repelled boarding attempts, and completed the million other tasks required to maintain a military starship and her crew.

Wright gave Taylan all this information on the way to Arthur's cabin. He also told her more stuff, about when the *Fearless* had been commissioned, how long it had taken to build her, and the battles she'd taken part in, as well as other details. By the time they arrived at their destination, she was bored out of her head.

"Thanks," she said brightly. "I can take it from here."

"You don't even know if Arthur's in," said the major.

"If he isn't, I'll find him. Don't worry."

"I was planning on taking you to the bosun too. He has to add you to the security system."

"I'm sure I can sort that out myself. I won't take up any more of your time, Major."

"Right. Well, I know I said before we take our orders from Admiral Kim, but I want you to report directly to me about Arthur. This isn't anything to do with the admiral."

"I understand, sir."

He turned and walked away.

Taylan exhaled and relaxed.

He stopped and faced her again.

She tensed.

"In case anyone asks," he said, "your reason for being here is to assist in combat training. The crew Merlin has treated have their mental capacity restored, but they're out of practice and physically weak. For the sake of appearances, you'll have to take part in some training sessions."

Great. A chance to make some friends.

"Got it," Taylan replied. "Anything else?"

"No, that's it." But he still didn't go. "Do your best, Ellis. The closer we get to Earth, the greater the danger of an attack. We need all the *Fearless's* crew back to normal as soon as possible. A lot could be hanging on this."

"I know."

Finally, he left.

23

———

Kala stepped forward, staring into darkness. She reached out. Her fingers met resistance. Not a hard surface, but a thick layer of an invisible substance, soft and yielding yet impenetrable. She pushed—hard. It made no difference.

"What is this stuff?" she asked the engineering supervisor.

The man only shook his head, unable to answer.

So it wasn't anything one might expect to encounter within a mine.

She paused, frustrated.

Blasting through the rock wall to reach the hidden cave had taken hours. The supervisor had given her ear protectors, but she'd still chosen to wait in a place distant from the resounding explosions. Despite the strength of the pull she'd felt, it had turned out the place she was seeking was meters of solid rock from the dead end. The supervisor had approached her twice during the excavation, respectfully suggesting she might be mistaken. Twice, she'd replied that neither she nor he were ascending to the surface until the chamber was found.

After the detonations had stopped again, the supervisor

came up the passage for the third time. Irritated, she'd risen to her feet.

He raised his hands, as though to ward off her anger. "Good news, Dwyr," he called out. "We're through. We've found it."

Elation filled her. "Take me there."

'Yes, ma'am. You'll have to tread carefully. There's rubble everywhere. But the roof is safe. We've made sure of that."

Now here she was, after clambering over the jagged rock waste and breathing air thick with dust, inside the hollow space, but stymied at the final hurdle. Peering beyond the invisible barrier, she tried to discern the figure of the imprisoned woman, but she could see nothing.

"You," she said to the supervisor's son, "shine your flashlight in." Something about the barrier muffled her voice, as if she were speaking from the bottom of a well.

The blackness absorbed the flashlight's beam like blotting paper soaking up ink.

"Leave me," she said to the workers. "Wait, give me that." She pointed at a man's flashlight.

In a few moments, she was alone with only a single ray of light holding back the dark.

The cold of the mine had chilled her to her bones, and she was coated in a disgusting mixture of condensed humidity and rock dust. She found a flattish piece of rock to sit on. She would not leave without releasing the woman. She'd come too far to give up now. She had to puzzle it out.

If Jon had been here with his jars of strange ingredients, she would have made him mix another batch of formula. Then, she could have asked the woman directly what to do. But Jon and his alchemical laboratory were hundreds of kilometers away.

A sharp edge on the stone she was sitting on was digging painfully into her buttocks. She began to get up again and leaned on the transparent barrier to keep her balance. This time, her hand seemed to sink deeper in. She paused, crouching in a position halfway between sitting and standing.

Had she hit on the solution?

She stood up fully. Keeping the flashlight focused on her other hand, she slowly and gently inserted the tips of her fingers into the transparent surface. Maintaining the very slight pressure, she continued to push. This time, her hand didn't meet increasing resistance. This time, it continued to move inward.

Struggling to keep her excitement under control and not push too hard, she slid her hand farther into the barrier.

She could feel something. Not some*thing*—some things. The tips of her fingers had made contact with several points. They were not overly sharp. And they were moving.

She sucked in a breath.

Fingernails.

Suddenly, a hand gripped hers, and she was wrenched forward. A boom rang out, deafening her. At the same time, air whooshed over her. The barrier seemed to have disappeared. The darkness beyond it retracted and condensed.

Kala saw rocky surfaces in the beam from the flashlight and, in front of her, a woman.

The woman.

She looked different from how Kala remembered her. She was smaller and slighter, though her ageless appearance was the same. She also looked more fragile and human.

The two women assessed each other, not speaking.

Kala hadn't been sure what she'd been expecting after achieving her goal, but it was not this. After her strange and wonderful encounters, everything she'd learned, and all that she'd applied to her running of the EAC, she'd been expecting something more momentous. They were just two women looking at each other among the dust and rubble of a dark, cold mine. After all she done to find her, she'd also expected some gratitude. She'd released the woman from her long imprisonment. A 'thank you' wouldn't go amiss. It was the ultimate anticlimax.

"What is your name?" the woman asked.

"I am the Dwyr," Kala replied haughtily. "Dwyr Kala Orr."

"*Dwyr*," the woman mused. "I haven't heard that title in a long time. Yes, I recognize you now." She looked Kala up and down. "A little dirty, but you'll do." She looked past her, to the piles of broken rocks strewn about. Then she took the flashlight from Kala's hand—Kala was too surprised to stop her—and pointed it in the opposite direction from her former prison.

"This way," she said. "Follow me."

Kala couldn't move. Her disappointment had changed to an outrage so powerful it paralyzed her.

"How dare you," she spluttered. "I am the Dwyr. *You* obey *my* commands."

The woman, who had moved to Kala's side, smirked and said, "If you have to tell someone they must obey you, you've already lost the battle. Now, come with me."

Kala leapt at her, reaching for the flashlight. At the speed of a lunging snake, the woman seized her arm. Her hand squeezed so tightly Kala screamed. It felt like her bones were about to be sliced through. Her knees buckled and she dropped onto the rock shards.

"Let me be clear," said the woman softly. "*I* am mistress here."

She let go.

Kala collapsed. Was her arm broken? She gingerly moved her fingers.

"We will collect your workers, and then we will go to the surface. The next part is coming soon. We must be ready. We must get one step ahead."

Fearing she might be left alone in the dark, Kala quickly clambered upright and went after the departing woman.

Her mind was working fast. Could she still salvage the situation? She had to figure out a way to undo the appalling mistake she'd made. It hadn't even occurred to her that the woman would want to usurp her role. She clearly intended to take over, snatching everything she'd worked for all her life from her grasp.

It was a grave miscalculation, but, she reminded herself, the members of the EAC loved *her*, not this interloper she'd unwittingly released. She also held the reins of power over all her domain. She would not give up easily, yet she had to move carefully.

Just as she had broken the barrier by subtle means, the same strategy would be required for...who?

In all her dialogues with the woman, she'd never learned her name.

The guards' and miners' lights could be seen along the underground road, and the flashlight the woman had taken from her bobbed as she moved toward them.

"Excuse me," said Kala, forcing a deferential note into her voice. "What are you called?"

The object of the question threw her answer over her shoulder.

"I am Morgan."

24

————

When Taylan stepped into Arthur's cabin, a huge grin broke over his face. He said something in his first language to Merlin, and the two of them talked while she stood there holding Boots in his bag.

The newcomer had changed from his red robe into civilian clothes. He was no longer wearing his cap either, revealing short, gray hair that matched his beard. If Taylan had passed him on the street, she wouldn't have looked twice. He appeared to be a very ordinary, rather lean, man approaching his middle years but looking good for his age.

"Taylan," said Arthur at last, rising from his bunk and stepping over to grasp her by the hand. "Come in. Come in."

The door slid closed behind her.

Boots gave away his presence with a plaintive miaow, and the ancient king's features achieved new heights of delight. "You brought the cat?"

Taylan handed him the bag. She hadn't spoken yet. As Arthur put the bag on the floor and unzipped it, she and Merlin sized each other up.

Arthur pulled an unprotesting Boots out and held him to

his chest, stroking the animal from head to tail. A loud purring filled the room. Still, Taylan hadn't spoken.

As if suddenly noticing the awkward silence, Arthur said, "Taylan, this is my old, good friend, Merlin."

"Hello, Merlin."

"But he's survived all these years too," Arthur went on. "I never thought I would see anyone I'd known in my former life. Merlin is...different from most men."

"Oh, I know," said Taylan. "I know."

The corner of the alien's lip lifted in a sardonic smile.

It was as if a second, unspoken conversation was going on between them, to which the king was entirely oblivious.

"It was Merlin who tended me after my last battle. He saved my life."

Taylan's ears pricked up. She asked the alien, "Was it you who preserved Arthur in the cave, so if the BI fell he could live again and help us?"

"It was I," he replied. "The land of your forefathers was split along different lines in those days, but the principle is correct."

A giant piece of the puzzle regarding Arthur slid into place in Taylan's mind. When she'd argued with Wright about the mummy he'd found in the cave, he'd said it was impossible for a human being to have remained alive so long. But here was the explanation. Merlin had kept him alive via some alien technology. It also explained the alien's legendary status as a wizard. He could do things that were impossible for humans then, and now.

Arthur spoke to the alien in his own language, and another conversation started up.

She was irritated. It was rude for them to talk together knowing she couldn't understand. She resented being excluded from the dialogue, and she resented her special connection to the king being usurped by this interloper.

She was about to make a remark when Arthur said, "I was

telling Merlin you're an excellent fighter at staves. He doesn't believe me. Shall we give him a demonstration?"

"What, now?"

"Why not?"

"I thought Merlin was supposed to be treating the people who still need his help." She addressed the comment directly at him, not Arthur.

"I've finished for today," Merlin said. "The process is very taxing. There's only so much I can do before I'm exhausted."

He didn't look exhausted to Taylan.

She shrugged. "If you like."

Arthur put Boots down. The cat immediately ran to a bunk and sprang up onto it. He kneaded the pillow, getting ready to settle down for a nap.

Taylan noticed Merlin seemed thoughtful as they exited the cabin, but how could she be sure his face actually reflected his feelings? What was going through the alien's mind? What was immediately clear to her was that Wright's comment about Merlin having Arthur 'under his spell' was true. What the major had tasked her with wasn't going to be easy to fulfil.

IT TOOK HER SOME MINUTES, but she eventually located staves in the equipment store. As had been the case on the *Valiant*, they were a neglected item, relegated to the bottom of a dusty pile of rarely used martial arts weapons.

She and Arthur put on their protective gear and sparring helmets. Meanwhile, Merlin examined more dangerous weapons. The range of pulse rifles available were permanently fixed to only stun in case a new recruit was a terrible shot, but they were the real thing. She wondered what the alien made of them. Was he assessing the level of military technology humanity had achieved during his long absence?

We're not quite at the all-enveloping black cloud stage, sorry.

Taylan was in a better position than she'd been the last time she'd fought Arthur with staves. Then, she'd been out of practice, but the fight had reacquainted her mind and muscle memory with the ancient art. As she fastened her helmet, she hoped she would do better this time around.

They faced each other, each holding their staff horizontally, across their chests. Arthur had about fifteen centimeters of height on her, probably around eight centimeters' longer reach, and a lot more strength. Going by their specs, he already had her beat. But her dad had taught her how to use her opponent's advantages against them. Being tall made him less nimble and slower than her, being heavy made him easier to overbalance, and carrying lots of muscle reduced his stamina.

If she simply stayed out of his way long enough, he would tire before she did, and then she could move in to finish him. But Arthur was fit. One of his favorite things to do was to train. It would take hours to exhaust him, and that would be boring.

Merlin had found himself a little stool to sit on as he watched.

Arthur suddenly came at her, swiping his staff down. If she tried to counter it, he could force her to her knees. Instead, she leapt sideways. Inertia kept him going forward. She moved behind him and landed a blow on his back. His vest protected him, but the *thunk* was satisfying. Remembering his go-to move from their previous fight, she jumped. He'd turned, and his staff swept through the place where her legs had just been.

He was side-on to her now and unstable due to leaning in to strike low. She kicked his shoulder with the sole of her foot, unbalancing him just that little bit more. It was all that was required to make him stumble down. She brought up her staff, preparing to strike the back of his head, but he managed to draw back.

His next strike caught her across her shin bone, though not

very painfully. The awkwardness of his position sapped his strength, but he occupied her long enough to give him time to rise.

He was coming at her again. She ducked beneath him and simultaneously jabbed his stomach with the end of her staff. Again, his protective vest saved him from the worst of the impact. She jumped backward and then she jumped again. Once more, his staff passed below her feet.

Really, he was too predictable.

They fought on.

Arthur was beginning to pant, Taylan noticed, while she was barely out of breath. A good sign. Tiredness would slow him down. She got in another couple of blows across his broad back and one to his thigh, and he managed a side blow to her ribs that made her gasp. Mostly, however, she was too fast and agile for him, and she was careful to always avoid a trial of brute strength.

Just as she was thinking she might win this time, sudden clapping distracted her. Reflexively, she halted and turned her head in the direction of the noise.

Arthur hit her square in the face in the exact spot where her helmet gave her no protection.

Pain exploded in her nose and upper lip.

He gave a cry of dismay, and his staff thunked onto the mat.

"Taylan, I'm sorry!"

A river of blood seemed to be running down her face. He grabbed her and leaned in, inspecting the result of his handiwork. She couldn't do anything except try to breathe and endure the waves of agony. Her nose was broken. There was no question about that. She was only wondering if she still had her front teeth.

"I apologise, too," said a smooth voice at her side. Merlin had come over. "This is my fault. My clapping broke your concentration."

Yes, it is your fucking fault.

But she couldn't tell him that. Her mouth wasn't working. And, she had to admit to herself, she shouldn't have allowed herself to be distracted.

Now Merlin had his hands on her. He turned her to face him. "Well, well, well. So it *is* you. I never imagined it would be a female."

She had no idea what he was talking about, and she didn't want to know. "I ha' to ge' to 'ick 'ay," she muttered, extracting herself from his grasp.

"What?" said Merlin, followed by, "Oh, I see. Sick bay. No need for that. Come here, I can—" He grabbed her again.

"Ge' your 'ands o' 'ee!"

"Taylan, you don't understand," said Arthur. "Merlin wants to help you."

But she was already walking away from the pair. She needed to get her injury fixed. Dealing with the alien's hold on her friend would have to wait for another time.

The gym intercom kicked into life.

"Battle stations! Crew to battle stations. Enemy ships approaching."

Oh, brother.

25

T he celebration party after the successful attack on the EAC convoy was loud and—to Hans's eyes—almost frantic with happiness. The Jamaicans drank a home-fermented brew, powerful and heady. He tried some, but it turned his stomach. They sang and danced around the fire. Forest chickens were brought out in cages, smaller versions of the one Hans had suffered in for so long. Holding the birds upside-down by their feet, someone cut their necks over the fire so the blood gushed into the flames. Their wings flapped wildly, and then they were still, hanging limply, giving off the stink of burning feathers. The chickens were removed for prepping to be cooked.

Hans could see why joining the EAC had been so appealing to the Caribbean islanders. The rituals and beliefs had similarities. He couldn't imagine the BA or the AP imprisoning him in such cruel conditions, but it would be exactly the kind of thing Dwyr Orr would do.

Mariya walked over to him where he sat on a fallen log, beyond the light of the fire. She was weaving slightly as she walked, and her smile was unusually broad. She sat down heavily by his side. The dancing and singing had left her sweaty and out of breath.

"Not celebrating, Hans?"

"I'm celebrating in my own quiet way, Mariya. On the inside."

She seemed to take his comment as a hilarious joke, pushing him roughly with her elbow and chortling. "Always so smart. You're a clever guy."

"Not smart enough to outwit you, my dear."

This was also apparently hilarious. After her laughter subsided, she said, "I got you good, didn't I?"

"You certainly did."

He decided to take advantage of her inebriated state. When sober, she was always cagey about giving him details on the Resistance, as if she didn't fully trust him yet. Her caution was wise. Though he was allied with them, Mariya had been right when she'd implied it would take him a long time to forget his ordeal at their hands.

"What will happen to the weaponry and armaments we liberated?" he asked.

They had only brought what they could carry back to the camp. Pulse rifles, rocket launchers, and grenades had been hidden in the cave, but they'd left behind plenty of the same plus heavier items.

"Gone to Kingston, Portmore, and Spanish Town. And to St. George's and Bridgetown."

So the Resistance was maintaining a network across the islands, and they were traveling by sea. That made a lot of sense. Boats would be hard for the EAC to track, and the island fishermen would know the tides and currents like the backs of their hands, as well as all the hidden coves where one could sneak ashore at night.

Mariya's head suddenly flopped to the side and came to rest on Hans's shoulder.

"I miss Josie," she said sadly.

He put a comforting arm around her shoulders. "It must be hard to lose your twin."

He felt her nod.

"What would she have made of all this, I wonder?" he asked.

"She wouldn't like it," Mariya replied, slightly slurring her words. "The Dwyr betrayed us."

"Yes. I expect she must be the main target for the Resistance. Cut off the snake's head, and the rest of the animal dies soon after."

"'Cept we can't."

"Why's that?"

"She's gone back to the BI. She got burned, and she left the next day."

"She got burned, did she?" Hans smiled grimly. After what she did to Hennessy and Montague, it was poetic justice. What a shame she didn't burn to death. Perhaps she would succumb to her wounds with time. The EAC's haste to eschew modern technology could be her downfall. "That's one point scored for the Resistance at least."

Mariya lifted her head from his shoulder and sank it into her hands. "It wasn't us."

"It wasn't? Then who?"

"I don't feel so great," she said before turning to lean over the log and vomiting.

Hans awkwardly patted her back. It seemed the right thing to do, but he was unused to caring for others. For most of his life, others had cared for him.

A large figure strode toward them, a black silhouette against the bright fire. Hans looked up at the man in alarm. Had he outstayed his welcome at the party? Was he suspected of taking advantage of Mariya in her drunken state?

Stopping directly in front of Hans, the man's hand shot out.

Hans ducked, expecting a blow.

But when he looked again, the hand remained before him, open.

He laughed awkwardly at his mistake and shook it. The proffered paw gripped his tightly, squeezing his knuckles together. A deep guffaw sounded from above. He squinted upward. Devon was grinning down at him.

"The man of the hour!" the Jamaican shouted, directing his comment to those partying behind him.

Meanwhile, Mariya who had finished expelling the contents of her stomach, had wound her arms around Hans's waist and rested her head on his shoulder once more.

Devon's shout had brought Hans to the Resistance fighters' general attention. They were making their way over from the fire and had soon gathered behind the leader in a half circle.

The attention made him squirm. These people had watched him come close to death and done nothing. Hell, they'd been the ones who had brought him near death. He would never feel safe in their company again.

"Stand up," ordered Devon.

Hans replied, "Sorry, but..." He looked at the top of Mariya's head.

Devon squatted down and cupped her face in one of his large hands, squeezing her cheeks and saying something in Patois. Hans translated it as roughly, "Wake up, darling. You're sleeping too long."

She didn't respond.

Another man approached from the crowd, picked her up, and hoisted her over his shoulder before walking unsteadily in the direction of the cave.

Hans rose to his feet and put his hands in his pockets, hoping he could leave too. But Devon grabbed his shoulders, pulled him forward, and turned to the watchers as if displaying Hans to them.

"This man!" he yelled. "This man ran in front of the EAC trucks. This man risked his life! For us! For Jamaica!"

It wasn't exactly what had happened. Devon hadn't been on the road at the time. He'd been out of sight, tens of meters away. Clearly, the story had grown in the telling. But Hans wasn't about to quibble about details. He was thankful they didn't appear to be about to put him back in the cage.

Devon's little speech brought hollers, whoops, and whistles from the onlookers.

"This man is our friend!" he announced, whacking Hans so hard on his back he lurched forward.

Shouts and cheers went up.

Then, just as quickly as it had begun, his moment in the limelight was over. Devon strode into the crowd and they all went back to partying.

He sat down on the log, pleased his flash of inspiration on the road to Port Lorenzo had led to a measure of acceptance among the fighters. He was also pleased to have discovered the Resistance appeared to be quite well organized. These men and women were different from the people he was used to working with, but he was learning their triggers and desires.

He was back in his element.

26

It was a sticky situation on the bridge. What Wright hadn't had a chance to tell Ellis was that when the BA Space Fleet admiral, Kim, arrived she would have to face the previous admiral, a man named Yorkson, who had been treated by Merlin and expected to resume control.

Everyone on the *Fearless's* bridge except Kim and Yorkson looked like they wished a black hole would swallow them. Kim had her back to the captain's seat, refusing to relinquish it, and Yorkson faced her, his hands clenching and unclenching at his sides. He was a short man, shorter even than Kim, who no one would call tall, but Wright had always thought he made up for his stature in self-assurance and dignity—up until this moment. The original admiral looked apoplectic with rage.

"This is a discussion to be had in private," said Kim coolly. "Return to sick bay for a full medical evaluation, and we will discuss the matter further. Until then, *I* am admiral of this fleet."

"I am perfectly healthy and fit to command," Yorkson retorted. "For the last time, move aside."

"I'm sure you're aware if I suspect your mental capacity, I could have you thrown in the brig."

Kim's threat caused the bridge crew to shrink deeper into their seats.

"You wouldn't dare!" exclaimed Yorkson.

Kim leaned in and narrowed her eyes. "Try me."

Wright gave a loud cough.

All gazes turned to him.

"Can I make a suggestion, admirals?"

"I'm all ears," Kim replied sardonically, while Yorkson only glared.

"Perhaps you could talk with the heads of armed forces on Earth via comm to settle the matter, or at least find a way forward." He added, "By yourselves. In a cabin. I'll take command of the bridge while you're gone."

"I'm willing if *he* is," said Kim.

Yorkson hesitated. His eyes flicked toward the captain's seat, as if he were planning to jump into it the minute Kim moved away.

She placed a protective hand on the armrest.

Yorkson gave an exasperated huff. "All right. I agree. Let's do that."

But he didn't move, and neither did Admiral Kim.

Wright had to walk over and slide into the seat before Kim would step away from it. Tutting and shaking his head, perhaps trying to make Kim out to be the childish one, Yorkson stepped to the door, jutting his chin.

Kim followed him. As they disappeared, an audible sigh of relief sounded around the bridge, and the crew visibly relaxed.

"Thanks, Major," someone murmured.

He wondered what Colbourn would have made of the two warring admirals. She probably would have knocked their heads together and thrown them *both* in the brig.

Some BA military leaders were still commanding sizable

forces on Earth. The army, navy, and air force stationed in Oceania were the most intact, though even they wouldn't last long, in Wright's estimation. Supply chains that routed through the Caribbean had only recently been solidly established after the fall of the Britannic Isles. Now that centers like Jamaica and Barbados were lost to the EAC, Oceania's military would already be feeling the lack of support.

Wright hoped the remaining military leaders could keep Kim and Yorkson from each other's throats.

They were a week from Earth. By the time they reached the rest of the fleet, Merlin needed to finish bringing the rest of the *Fearless's* personnel back to normality. Regaining the lost territories was going to be a long, hard slog for the BA, but with their flagship back in their possession, the Space Fleet could back up initiatives on the surface. It could also keep the EAC's space vessels occupied.

He'd read the official reports on Jamaica yesterday. Contact had been lost with the Resistance, or, perhaps, deliberately severed. Some said the group didn't want the BA's help, that they wanted to be entirely independent once they'd driven out the EAC. He didn't condemn their aspiration, but he doubted it was realistic. Jamaica might be hard to conquer, but the Crusade would do it eventually. The Resistance only stood a chance if it had a helping hand.

After twenty minutes or so of musing over what the future might bring, Wright's thoughts were interrupted.

"Sir," said the sensor officer, Buchanan, "we're picking up readings of two large starships heading our way."

"I take it they aren't ours," Wright replied.

'No, sir." The man's gaze was intent on his screen. "Still gathering data."

"Hail them," he told the comm officer.

He guessed they were enemy vessels on the trail of the trace of the corvette that had brought Admiral Kim. He began mentally running through the logistics of an engagement. The *Valiant* and *Fearless* were powerful vessels, but both were seriously undermanned.

"One is a battlecruiser," said Buchanan.

Great.

"She's flanked by a Class 2 frigate."

Ugh.

"EAC?" he asked.

"They aren't answering our hails," the comm officer said.

Wright inwardly groaned.

"Sound battle stations," he told the comm officer.

Then he remembered that half of the *Fearless's* personnel were barely able to feed themselves, let alone fight.

"Brigadier Colbourn would like to speak to you, sir."

"Put her through."

Colbourn's voice sounded loud and distinct in his head. *What's Admiral Kim's plan? She hasn't replied to my comm.*

She's probably too busy arguing with Admiral Yorkson about who's in charge.

Oh, him! I'd forgotten about him. Find them, Wright. Tell them to pull their fingers out, or—

Kim burst onto the bridge, Yorkson at her heels.

They're here, Brigadier.

About time.

The link cut out. Colbourn had cleared the connection to await Kim or Yorkson's comm.

"Thank you, Major," said Kim. "We'll take over from here."

Wright looked from one to the other. Could he trust them to put their bickering aside for the duration of the battle? He had little choice.

"Should I coordinate the boarding repulse teams?" he asked.

"Yes," Yorkson replied.

Neither sat in the captain's seat. Wright guessed it was by

mutual agreement. That was something to be said in their favor. He'd feared the problems in the BA were continuing the same as before.

He could organize the teams that would defend the airlocks from the bridge via comm, so he started doing that, but the list of men and women in full health was depressingly short. Many of them would still be weak, and some of them would be caring for the remaining crew who hadn't received treatment yet. The sick ones would just have to look after themselves for the duration of the battle.

He began sending out orders.

27

The trip back to Kala's castle was passing in silence. Morgan peered curiously out of the window of the aircraft, apparently taking in all she saw, from the towns and cities of BI passing beneath them to the sun and clouds. A day had passed while Kala had been in the cave, and the sun was setting. A few stars were already visible, and Morgan paid special attention to them.

Eventually, she relaxed in her seat and turned to Kala. "I need to know everything. Do you have a single source of knowledge about your world?"

Her brown eyes were frank. Kala had realized when they reached the surface of the mine the reason Morgan appeared more human to her now was because her eyes were normal and no longer fully black.

"What do you want to know?" she replied. "I can answer your questions." She wanted to restrict the woman's access to information. The less she knew, the more control Kala could exert over her.

"No." Morgan returned her attention to the view from the

window. "You must show me how to conduct my own research when we arrive at your home."

Kala's hands were already balled into fists on her lap. At this response, she clenched her hands tighter. Inwardly, she was fighting a battle. Ever since releasing Morgan from her prison, she'd been tempted to tell one of her guards to kill her. The threat she posed to Kala's position was clear. Preventing her from ordering the woman's execution was the fact that she had to hold secrets Kala hadn't even imagined. She was the key to everything Kala believed in and hoped to make happen on Earth.

She was also more than a little afraid that ordinary pulse fire wouldn't kill her, and she would exact a terrible revenge for the attempt.

She decided all she could do was to allow events to unfold and not do anything hasty until she had a better understanding of the situation. It would be impossible to withhold the existence of interfaces from Morgan. She took hers out from the seat pocket and handed it over.

The woman's face brightened. "Ah, I see." She opened the screen. "Primitive, but it will suffice."

Kala watched out of the corners of her eyes while Morgan searched for and read information. She seemed particularly interested in technology, especially starships. Next, she focused on recent world events, looking up news of wars and conflicts. She read a report on the situation in the Caribbean. It was from a global news channel, so it was biased against the EAC.

"This is your group, yes?" Morgan asked, slanting the interface toward Kala.

"Yes. Would you explain something?"

"Hmm," she replied absent-mindedly. "What?"

"How did you survive so long, cut off from everything? You had no food or water in that place I released you from."

"I do not need food or water. Though it is pleasant to enjoy them again." She picked up a cup from its holder and took a drink, smiling at Kala before replacing it.

"Then you aren't human?"

"Your questions are boring me," Morgan replied. "Please be quiet."

THEY DIDN'T GO DIRECTLY to Kala's castle. Before they reached their destination, Morgan asked her again about the man she had warned her about—the man the BA had snatched from her grasp in the mountains of West BI. She insisted on being taken to the place.

There was nowhere close to the cave where the aircraft could land. The pilot was forced to set them down in a sloping, stubbly field hundreds of meters away.

"We can come back here later," Kala protested as the exit door opened and a cool wind swept in. She was still begrimed from the mine as well as exhausted. All she wanted was a hot bath and a warm bed. "There's nothing there. The cave is empty. Why do you need to see it now?"

Ignoring her, Morgan stepped down the stairs that extended from the opening. The breeze whipped her robe around her slim form and lifted her black hair.

Kala heaved a sigh and told her guards to accompany her before following.

She'd never bothered to go to the cave herself. That night, when her soldiers had closed in on the spot she'd finally identified after long years of searching, all she'd cared about was finding the man and having him killed. When she'd learned the BA had beaten her to him, that was all that mattered. How could an empty cave possibly be important?

Morgan was striding over the field toward the lower slopes of the mountain. The ground was weedy. No crop had been planted that year. Most of the local inhabitants had been executed or had fled to Ireland. The country was next on her list to be conquered.

For someone who had spent decades imprisoned, Morgan could move surprisingly fast. Kala struggled to keep up.

The sun had set. The mountain loomed up darkly in the moonless night. Morgan was among the boulders now, climbing confidently higher, somehow unimpeded by her long skirt. Kala was sweating with effort. Her anger was compounded by tiredness and frustration. With her guards near her in that quiet, lonely place, would it be so hard to tell one of them to take Morgan out, there and then?

She would miss out on what the woman could offer her, but it would put a decisive end to the threat to her position as leader of the EAC.

Kala stopped to catch her breath. The two armed men at her sides halted with her. Morgan climbed onward, oblivious.

Kala could see the cave entrance now—a crooked slit in the rock surrounded by fragments of stone. She recalled a soldier's report that the BA had been forced to blast open the mountainside.

With Morgan distracted, it was the perfect time to execute her.

Was it the right thing to do?

Jon would certainly never approve of killing an unarmed woman. But Jon's moral compass wasn't Kala's concern. He didn't understand the necessities entailed in holding a position of power, and he never would. She was more concerned about what was most beneficial and expedient.

She made her decision and gave the order.

Her guards continued their climb, and she went after them more slowly, allowing them to get ahead of her. Morgan had reached the cleft. She disappeared inside.

Kala moved between the boulders, often forced to use her

hands as well as her feet, gradually ascending. Above her, the first of her guards reached the cave. She saw the man enter it, and a couple of seconds later his companion joined him. Continuing to climb, Kala watched the dark space for the flash of pulse fire that would signal the end to her rival's life.

But though she watched all the way until she reached the place herself, the flash never came.

Confused, she stepped through the opening. Her guards were there, and so was Morgan. She had her back to them and was bending over a raised platform hewn from the natural stone. She ran her hands across it, and Kala thought she heard her whisper, "Yes, he was here."

Why hadn't one of the guards shot her?

Kala turned to one man and then the other, glaring at them, but they didn't seem to understand the meaning of her look. Yet her order had been clear.

Morgan spun around to face them. "Someone hurt you," she said to Kala. "Who was it? One of the force that extracted Arthur?"

"Yes, it was one of the BA. But he was just a soldier. I don't know who."

"You must find out."

"I would love to, and I'm trying. But I've—"

"You must find him," Morgan reiterated.

She swept across the cave and pushed past Kala to leave it.

Kala waited until she was out of earshot, and then said quietly to her guards, "I ordered you to kill her. Why didn't you?"

The men looked puzzled. They glanced at each other before one replied, "I'm sorry, Dwyr. I-I must have forgotten."

"What about you?" she asked the other guard. "Did you forget too?"

He cast his gaze downward. "I'm very sorry, Dwyr."

"Never mind," Kala said bitterly. "Let's go."

Every visit Kala had made to Morgan via Jon's formula, the woman had impressed upon her that she was special, and part of her uniqueness was that she was inviolable. Kala had never discovered how or why, and she'd never exactly put the assertion to the test, but she'd believed her.

It made sense that Morgan was inviolable too.

28

Tension on the *Fearless's* bridge wound tighter as the ships closed the distance between them, each waiting to reach firing range. The teams to repulse boarders were in place, and Kim and Yorkson seemed to have made an uneasy truce. Wright had little else to do except wait, so he decided to try to find Ellis. She clearly hadn't been to see the bosun as she wasn't contactable via comm. He wanted to assign her to a team. Though she was only one individual, she was good at her job, and with the scarcity of fit crew they would need everyone they had.

The obvious place to look for her was Arthur's cabin. He comm'd the interface there. Neither Arthur nor Merlin had personal comms. Arthur hadn't gotten over his fear of them, and Merlin hadn't been assigned one.

The comm was answered by Arthur.

"Major Wright," he said warmly. "How can I help you?"

"I'm looking for Corporal Ellis. Is she there?"

"No. She might be in the sick bay."

"In sick bay? What's wrong with her?"

Arthur seemed about to reply, but Merlin said something in

the background, and then his face replaced Arthur's on the screen.

"There was an unfortunate accident during a sparring session," said the alien.

Ellis got hurt in training? That was a first.

"Is she okay?"

"I assume so," Merlin replied. "I offered to treat her myself, but she refused."

"Okay. Stay in your cabin." Wright closed the comm and opened another to sick bay. He told the medic who answered to put Ellis on if she was there.

When she appeared, he reared back a little and blurted, "Whoa."

If he hadn't known who she was, there's no way he would have recognized her. Her eyes were surrounded by purple/black rings like a panda in negative, her lips were puffed as if a hive of bees attacked her but also split and bloody, and her nose, her nose...

"Tanks, ma'or," she said.

"What?"

"I said, tanks 'or 'er ym'athy."

He only understood a couple of words, but he got the gist. "Sorry, I got a shock. What the hell happened to you?"

Ellis rolled her puffed eyes. She tapped her screen. At Wright's end, text appeared.

It's kinda hard for me to talk right now. What do you want?

After a brief pause, another word appeared.

Sir.

"It doesn't matter. Stay where you are until the battle's over."

No, I want to fight. Get me security access to the nearest armory. Which airlock should I go to?

"No way. You're not in any state to fight."

I discovered a long time ago the BA has some really good drugs.

Which airlock?

If her injuries did only extend to her face and she wasn't in any pain, she was probably okay to take part in the battle. Plus, as a last resort, she could remove her helmet. Her appearance alone was a deadly weapon.

"Okay, wait a minute for your clearance to activate. Aft Airlock 4."

The screen went dead.

"Thanks, Major Wright," he said.

Then an idea hit. *Merlin!*

"Admiral Kim, Admiral Yorkson, have you considered asking for Merlin's help in the battle?"

The alien had never confirmed or denied that, in his other manifestation, he'd been responsible for what happened to the *Fearless*. But if he could fling one starship across space, surely he could just as easily fling another.

The admirals stared at each other, and then both nodded.

Kim replied, "Ask him, Major. You know him best."

He contacted Arthur's cabin again.

This time, the alien answered, with a knowing smile on his face. "I was wondering when it would occur to you."

Before Wright could ask the question, however, Merlin said, "I can't help you, sorry."

The major found himself looking at a blank screen for the second time in the space of less than a minute.

He told Kim and Yorkson the alien's answer.

"Can't, or won't?" Yorkson asked.

"It doesn't matter," said Kim. "We can't order him to help us."

"Isn't there a way?"

"We have about fifteen minutes to think of one."

"It shouldn't be that hard," Yorkson mused. "It isn't in his interest for the *Fearless* to be defeated."

"What does he care?" Kim asked bitterly. "If the ship's destroyed he can poof into a cloud and float away."

Wright wondered about what the admiral had said. What she hadn't considered was that Merlin was clearly here for Arthur, a regular human being who couldn't puff into a cloud and fly away. Even as a mummy, he'd needed air.

FIFTEEN MINUTES HAD PASSED, and no one had thought of a way to make Merlin pull his magic cloud trick out of his ass. What was more, no other BA space fleet vessels were within a day's travel of the *Fearless* and the *Valiant*. Aside from the *Cornflower* and Admiral Kim's corvette transportation, the *Buttercup*, they were on their own.

The EAC battlecruiser fired her pulse cannon. The bolts sped across space.

"Return fire," snapped Kim. "All pulse cannon."

On the holo displaying the ships' positions, the frigate began to peel away from the battlecruiser. Wright wondered what instructions the admirals had given Colbourn regarding the *Valiant's* deployment. She was low on manpower, too, due to so many of her crew being transferred to care for the injured on the *Fearless*.

The pulses from the battlecruiser had impacted harmlessly with the flagship's force shield, and the return fire had a similar minimal effect. It was when the ships drew closer the real damage would be done. Plasma cannon and particle lances were only effective at short range, and disruptor torpedoes, though deadly, were slow across the vast distances of space warfare. The *Fearless* would have to get in very close for the EAC ships to not have time to destroy them with pulse rounds before they reached their target.

The frigate was firing at the *Cornflower*, which had gotten ahead of the larger, slower ships. Yorkson barked an order to her captain to pull back and wait to engage Scorpions, the EAC's close space combat craft, should any launch.

The *Valiant* began to maneuver away from the flagship, mirroring the movement of the frigate.

"*Come on,*" muttered Yorkson. The *Fearless's* acceleration was already pushing Wright hard into his seat. The battlecruiser was also piling on speed, her heading dead on. The two ships were playing chicken.

"Power up the particle lance," ordered Kim. A short burst of explosive ray from the lance could penetrate so deeply into a starship it would cleave her in two.

Meanwhile, the *Valiant* and the frigate were drawing closer.

Pulses from the battlecruiser continued to impact the *Fearless's* force shield, and the flagship's pulses flew out with equal regularity. Eventually, one or both ships' shields would collapse, and the pulses would hit their hulls directly. That was why Kim had begun to slowly build up power in the lance—the ship couldn't spare much energy from her shields.

The frigate began to fire at the *Valiant*.

29

———

In the *Bres's* control center, Lorcan was absent-mindedly juggling, standing in front of the display screen, watching the ever-scrolling images of the vessel's construction sites. He'd realized he'd become too unfocused, allowing daydreams and nostalgia to invade his thinking. He needed to get back on task and concentrate on the here and now, before he did something else that might jeopardize the shiny future he had planned.

Iolani Hale was confined to her suite. It was the best on the ship, aside from his own. Spacious, luxuriously furnished, fully equipped with its own spa, gym, and sim room, it contained everything anyone could desire for a pleasant stay. The suite had also contained its own printer, but he'd had that removed. He didn't want Hale to create something to help her escape.

Guards stood outside the door round the clock, but she was a smart woman. He wouldn't put it past her to fashion a club or similar item to take them out.

It was true that she would then have to somehow get aboard a shuttle and pilot it all the way back to Earth, but unlikely though that was, he couldn't take any chances. If she went around spreading her story of her kidnapping, she could ruin everything.

He hadn't told any of his workers on the *Bres* what he'd done, but Bourke, Jeffries, Xiao, and now the guards he'd directed to watch Hale knew. It was inevitable the news would get out.

From the coolness of the people he worked with directly, it already had. Kekoa seemed especially affected. Her expression as she sat at her console was sullen. Jurrah and Steadman were also quiet, though they seemed more afraid than angry.

Lorcan walked to his seat, placed the juggling balls on the armrest, and sat down. He was in a difficult position, and he didn't know how to get out of it. If only he'd been able to place Hale in cryo. Then, he might have been able to keep Jeffries, Bourke, and Xiao quiet. He had much he could offer in exchange for their silence. But to keep Hale's presence a secret while she was living aboard the ship was impossible.

"Sir," Kekoa suddenly blurted, swiveling around to face him. "Could I please speak to you outside?"

His stomach sank. He had a feeling he knew what was coming.

"Can't it wait until the end of the day?" he asked. "I'm sure you must be very busy."

"No, it can't."

"Very well," he replied tetchily.

She followed him into the passageway.

"I want to tender my resignation," she said as soon as the doors closed. She glared up at him, looking as though she was about to cry, though with rage, not sadness. "I don't have anything to give you in writing, but my letter will arrive in your inbox today."

"Hmpf. You know you have three months' notice to serve?"

"I know, but I'm breaking my contract. I'll be leaving on the next cargo transport."

"If you break your contract, I'll sue. You're a vital part of the management team. Many of the habitats are unfinished. To get someone in to take over your role will be expensive and time-consuming, and set the Project back weeks. If I win in court—and I will—you'll be ruined."

"I don't care!" Kekoa exclaimed, clenching her hands into fists and leaning in to glare at him. "I *refuse* to be a part of this. I've put up with so much over the years. Your moods, your arrogance, your petty, nasty vindictiveness, your stupid *fucking* juggling. You like to think you're the big boss who can throw his weight around and do anything he likes. But you aren't. We're all here of our own free will, we can all leave, and there's nothing you can do about it.

"I will *not* tolerate you imprisoning an innocent woman. Let me guess, she stood up to you, right? She didn't want to join the Project, so you decided you were going to force her. Who the *fuck* do you think you are? God?"

Lorcan saw red. *Who did he think he was?* Who did *she* think *she* was, that she could insult him? He was the originator, owner, and leader of the Antarctic Project, humanity's greatest endeavor. She was just an engineer, one of many he could have hired to do her job.

"Fine!" he spat. "Do it! I don't owe you any explanations. You don't like the way I run things? Leave. I'll find someone to replace you. It probably won't be that hard. In fact, I'm sure I'll be able to find someone better, someone who actually knows what they're doing and doesn't cock things up half the time. Go! We'll all be better off without you."

Kekoa spun on her heel and strode away.

Lorcan watched her go, still seething over her slurs. He knew what he'd done was questionable, but it didn't give her the right to talk to him like that. If she'd approached him more reasonably to discuss the matter, he would have explained the necessity of Hale's temporary imprisonment. He would have made her understand, but she was deliberately choosing to cast what he'd done in the worst possible light before learning all the facts.

He marched into the control room and threw himself into his seat, offense and rage consuming him. Picking up one ball at a time, he flung them at the display screen. They hit and slid to the floor.

For the next few hours, he stewed over Kekoa's resignation and impending departure, not leaving his chair.

A comm from Admiral Bujold arrived.

"Sir, there appears to be a battle going on between the EAC and BA."

"Details?" he asked.

"It's about two hours from our current position. The BA ships were heading for Earth, and the EAC has intercepted them. The fighting's just begun."

His military starships were patrolling a region of space roughly equidistant between Earth and the colony ship-building site. After successfully defending the vessels from the EAC not too long ago, he was wary of a second attack.

"And why are you telling me this?" Bitterness and spite from Kekoa's act of disloyalty edged his question.

"I-I wondered, in light of our recent defense of the BA's ship, the *Valiant*, if you wanted to do anything."

He recalled the ship's commander, Colbourn, refusing to offer him anything in return for his help.

"Thank you for your consideration," he replied sarcastically. "But our ties with BA are severed. They're on their own."

"Right, sir," said Bujold sadly. "It's probably moot at this stage anyway. By the time we arrived, we would only be searching for survivors."

"As I've learned today," Lorcan said, "we must all look out for ourselves."

He closed the comm.

Toward the end of the day, his ire had begun to cool and he was wondering if he'd been too harsh with Kekoa. Perhaps it was natural she would be uncomfortable with what he'd done to Hale. She didn't have the full facts, and he hadn't taken the time to explain them to her. Perhaps it would be worth sending something out to everyone aboard to spell out the situation. If he didn't, he might see more ill-considered, snap reactions. What he'd said to Kekoa was correct. He would be able to replace her, eventually. But losing more of his team would be inconvenient and costly.

He resolved to write something that evening and broadcast it first thing in the morning.

Another comm arrived. This time, it was from the man he'd put in charge of organizing Hale's guards. His face appeared on Lorcan's interface, sweaty and fearful.

"Ua Talman, I'm sorry to report Ms Hale has gone missing from her suite. We're currently looking for her."

"She...What in damnation happened?! How did she get out?"

"I'm still not sure, sir. Both of the guards seem to have been momentarily distracted. When they returned, they immediately checked whether she was still there and discovered she wasn't. Her door was unlocked, and she was gone."

30

─────────

The *Fearless's* force shield was weakening under the barrage of pulse bolts from the EAC battlecruiser, but the ship was nearly within range to use her particle ray and plasma cannon. The battlecruiser didn't look like she was going to back down. Wright could see how destroying the BA's flagship would be a helluva victory, but it was not a foregone conclusion. The EAC commander was taking a big risk. Even poorly manned, the *Fearless* was functioning well.

The same couldn't be said for the corvettes, *Cornflower* and *Buttercup*. Both ships had taken excessive fire, and Yorkson had ordered both ships to hang back, perhaps planning to throw them at the EAC vessels as a last resort.

The *Valiant* was in a worse position. She'd already taken several direct hits to her hull. The frigate she was fighting appeared to have better defensive capability, taking out many of the *Valiant's* pulses before they even reached her.

"Estimated time to loss of force shield?" Yorkson asked the weapons officers, Daintree and Pascal.

"A minute and a half," Pascal replied.

Yorkson and Kim looked at each other and nodded. "It's enough," said Kim.

Wright wondered how much energy had already been expended in the hundreds of pulse bolts they had unleashed on the battlecruiser. At this rate, they would have to coast the rest of the way to Earth, relying on inertia to carry them.

Assuming they won.

"Multiple impacts on the hull!" someone shouted.

Their force shield was still up, which meant the hits weren't from an energy weapon.

"Railgun," said Kim and Yorkson simultaneously.

"Launch Swifts," said Kim.

The titanium slugs from the battlecruiser's railgun could puncture the *Fearless's* skin. The resulting loss of pressure would only be a problem for personnel who didn't make it behind the automatic seals that would lock down in response. A more serious outcome would result if the slugs hit her weapons.

And there was nothing they could do about it. The *Fearless* didn't carry a railgun herself. The configuration of the weapon's design, requiring a 'rail' along the ship's spine, didn't work alongside the platform-mounted particle lance on her bow. One ship couldn't carry both, and the lance's maneuverability made it the superior choice.

The *Valiant* did carry a railgun, but the ship had to be face on to her enemy to use it, and the frigate was too fast at getting out of the way.

Tiny dots appeared on the holo as the *Fearless's* Swifts sped out. Yorkson ordered the pilots to focus their attention on the battlecruiser's railgun. Meanwhile, Kim told the helm to move out of the line of fire. But the ships were now so close and the flagship's size constrained her movement so much, the battlecruiser wouldn't have much trouble following her.

A flood of dots spilled from the EAC ship. She had launched her Scorpions to engage the Swifts.

"Thirty seconds to shield loss," said Daintree.

"We're in plasma cannon range," added Pascal.

"Let them have it," said Yorkson.

Wright felt a shudder as the cannon fired. The stream of high-energy, ionized gas would pierce the battlecruiser's force shield as the titanium slugs had plowed through the *Fearless's*. The effect would be similar to a pulse bolt—craters of burning, melted metal and explosive decompression at large hull breaches. And the plasma was harder to stop. A single pulse hit only punctuated the stream.

The *Valiant* was in trouble. Over the course of many space battles, Wright had become accustomed to reading and interpreting the minute movements of ships on the holo display. Colbourn's ship had slowed and, rather than attempting to turn face on to the frigate, she was maintaining the same course, as if to get away.

The brigadier wasn't running. She wasn't capable of it. Something was wrong with her vessel. Possibly, one of her engines had been hit.

Yorkson and Kim were in constant comm with Colbourn, and from the grave looks on their faces, Wright knew his suspicions were correct.

"Shield down." said Pascal.

"We must be able to reach them with the lance by now," declared Kim.

"Yes," Daintree agreed, "but we'll cause—"

"Fire particle lance," ordered Kim.

Yorkson looked as though he wanted to disagree but said nothing.

"Minimal damage," Daintree continued to himself.

On the holo, a thread of light shone from the *Fearless*, reaching across space to the EAC ship, a deadly strand of energy.

Then it disappeared.

"What happened?!" Kim exclaimed.

"I'm seeing…" Pascal consulted his screen. "The lance isn't responding, ma'am. It's out."

"Out?" asked Yorkson. "How?"

"It's that damned railgun," said Kim.

"That's my guess," said Pascal. "Running a diagnostic."

"It doesn't matter," Yorkson muttered. "We don't have the time or crew to fix it. We'll just have to hang on until we're close enough to launch torpedoes."

Now that the force shield was down, the *Fearless* was also taking hits from the battlecruiser's pulse bolts. Its own bolts had to be diverted to stave off the worst of their attack. Now, it was plasma cannon against railgun, each ripping the other ship's hull to pieces. Wright saw alarms going off all over the ship as the hull took a battering. And with the reduced number of personnel, each breach would take longer to patch.

"Are the torpedo crews in place?" Yorkson abruptly asked Wright.

"Yes, sir." Along with the boarding repulse teams, he'd verbally rounded up the men and women whose job it was to man the launchers. They'd been thin on the ground. The order in which Merlin had treated the *Fearless's* personnel had been random. Wright had breathed a sigh of relief when he'd finally found enough of them.

"What do you think?" Yorkson asked Kim.

She bit her lip.

Although disruptor torpedoes were devastating, they were slow. They would home in on their target, so the battlecruiser couldn't outmaneuver them, but if they were launched from too far away, they could easily be taken out by pulse bolts. Plus, they weren't energy weapons. The *Fearless* carried a fixed number that wouldn't be replenished until they were restocked. Once they were all fired, that was it.

A light flashed on Wright's interface. Deck one, containing the waste treatment, laundry, printers, and hold, had entirely depressurized. Everyone else on the bridge had seen the alert too. A silent wave of alarm and sorrow went around the room. It would have been impossible for everyone on the deck to have escaped in time.

Yorkson and Kim shared a mutual look. "Launch torpedoes," Kim said.

The holo display didn't show the solid cylinders flying toward the battlecruiser. They weren't small, but they were too small to show against the vastness of space, and the energy from their thrusters was nothing compared to the power of a pulse bolt. But the impacts of the battlecruiser's pulses as they hit them was visible. Tiny flashes lit the display, less powerful than the smashing together of pulses.

"If they do nothing," said Yorkson, "at least we will have distracted their pulse cannon for a while."

Wright tried to count the flashes. He got to thirteen, and then stopped, unsure if he'd missed some or if he'd mistaken a torpedo's destruction with a pulse bolt collision.

Tense silence reigned. All gazes were fixed on the holo.

"The *Valiant's* down," said Daintree.

Wright's chest tightened. In the strain of the battle with the EAC ship, he'd forgotten about Colbourn's plight. At Daintree's statement, he looked at the ship. She was moving in a direct line, apparently unable to turn. The frigate was closing in.

"It's a hit!" yelled Pascal, leaping from his seat. "We hit her!"

A shout of relief and joy went up.

One of the disruptors had got through. It didn't matter if the impact was dead on or glancing. The warhead would have exploded, and the battlecruiser must have begun to disintegrate.

The mood on the bridge took a fast downward turn. Officers who had jumped up and slapped each other's backs sat down, and quiet fell once more.

Wright knew what everyone was thinking because he was thinking the same. He was imagining himself on the battlecruiser, panicked and fearful, knowing within minutes the ship would be nothing but a cloud of atoms—knowing that, if he didn't get to an escape vessel in time, *he* would be nothing but atoms.

If the effect reached the escape craft, there would *be* no escape.

One second, the crew would be inside the ship, the next, the bulkhead would disappear, and they would be looking out at empty space. The very air they breathed would break down before its pressure forced it out into the vacuum.

Wright watched the mote of light that signaled the presence of the battlecruiser.

He watched it for one minute, two minutes, three minutes.

It was gone.

31

———

Hans carefully inspected his fingernails. They were grimy with soil and the nails were chipped in places.

Good.

He'd snuck out in the early morning to scrape and scratch in the dirt to achieve the right effect. There were no mirrors among the basic supplies the Resistance had gathered, but, judging from the shaggy feel of his beard and hair, he didn't need to do anything to make them look more disheveled. He checked his clothes. They were dirty and torn, and sweat patches stained his shirt.

Perfect.

"Hans," called Mariya before continuing in Patois. "We're leaving. Are you ready?"

He stepped from the semi-darkness in his spot in the cave into the light of the electric torches.

"I'm ready."

The leaders of the Resistance group—Mariya, Devon, and a man called Charles—were waiting for him at the bottom of the slope that led out of the cave.

As Hans reached them he said, "I want to thank you again for this opportunity. You can't imagine how much I appreciate it."

Mariya nodded, but the two men didn't comment.

Had he said the wrong thing? Perhaps he'd been too effusive. He was still learning how to be accepted by the Jamaicans. It was possible he might never be accepted, but he would try. At the very least, he wanted to worm his way into their confidence. He'd made a good start with the raid on the EAC convoy. Now he had to build on his success.

They emerged into the brilliant sunlight. Hans blinked and squinted. The empty bamboo cage that had held him for weeks sat open in its usual place.

He gave a shudder. When they returned, if he did well at the meeting, he might propose they burn it on the fire.

They followed the trail up the side of the hollow to Mariya's car where she'd parked it when she'd brought Hans to the hideout. It didn't look as though it had been driven since. Thick dust coated it, turning the windscreen and windows opaque, and dead leaves decorated the flat surfaces. They spent a few minutes cleaning it.

"Is it safe to drive this now?" asked Hans. He guessed they hadn't used the car because they feared it might be identified. Mariya had been employed by SIS, after all.

A look passed between Devon and Charles before the latter replied in English, "It is safer now than it was. The commander Mariya killed at Port Lorenzo...It turned out she was the de facto EAC leader on the island. They've been less organized since she died, and the Dwyr hasn't named a replacement yet. From what we hear, she's been distracted and out of touch lately."

"Ha! Good for us," exclaimed Hans.

"It's a small risk to take the car," continued Charles, "and the alternative is a twenty-kilometer hike."

Devon opened a door. "You sit in the back."

Mariya drove, though, it seemed to Hans, more expertly than she had before. She must have been faking then, maintaining her mask of ignorance and innocence.

The car rocked and shook as they traveled along the rough dirt track. As the others talked, Hans kept his mouth shut and listened. His understanding of Patois had improved, and he caught the gist of about seventy-five percent of what they said. They were discussing the situation on the island. He heard references to seven or eight more Resistance groups. The largest was based in Kingston, and it had been obstructing the EAC takeover of the city since the early days following the invasion, blowing up installations, sniping at soldiers in the streets, and organizing mass defiance of the new authority.

Some members had been caught and hanged, or worse, making an example of what would happen to others who refused to accept the new status quo. If anything, this seemed to have inflamed the Jamaicans' anger. They'd lived too long under a ruling class, as they saw it, to passively accept another, especially not one that was already carrying out mass executions.

Hans didn't see the meeting place from the road. Mariya stopped the car apparently in the middle of nowhere. They got out and continued on foot down yet another barely discernible trail.

"The other members are approaching from different directions?" asked Hans.

Mariya gave a nod.

Five minutes later they stepped into a shady clearing in front of a waterfall. The pool at its feet spilled into a wide stream that ran out between the trees. These overshadowed the clearing on all sides, protecting the wooden hut at the stream's edge from drone surveillance.

Inside the hut, several Resistance leaders were already waiting. They shook hands with and hugged Devon, Mariya, and Charles but regarded Hans with wary eyes. He heard murmured exchanges in Patois as the leaders questioned the wisdom of having a backra at the meeting, hearing their secrets. Devon assured them Hans was a friend.

The door opened, and three more Resistance fighters stepped into the hut.

"Let's begin," said a slim woman.

They sat down around a rickety table.

All except one man.

"I'm not taking a seat at the same table as him," he said in Patois, jerking his chin in Hans's direction. He folded muscular arms over his chest. The sleeves of his shirt had been torn off at the shoulders, and he wore a bandanna pulled low over one eye, which appeared to be blind.

An embarrassed pause followed.

Others present seemed to share the man's sentiment. Though they were seated, they looked to Mariya, Devon, and Charles for an explanation for Hans's presence. But his 'friends' didn't speak.

Hans grew uncomfortable in the hot, humid room, the air thick with sweat and unspoken hostility. He realized he was on his own. Mariya and the other leaders of the group at the cave would abandon him if necessary in order to remain on good terms with the rest of the Resistance.

He cleared his throat and rose hesitantly to his feet.

Everything would hang on what he said.

"I know why you might not trust me," he began, speaking slowly and carefully in Patois.

The listeners' eyes widened.

Hans went on, "And I understand. But please believe me when I say I don't want a return to the old days of the Britannic Alliance. For most of my life, I worked to make the Alliance a republic, and to put an end to the Establishment. I hated everything about it. My family were immigrants. I am not like the others, and now I've spent time with my good friends, Mariya, Devon, and Charles, I see a new side to Jamaica I never saw before. I realized my dreams were stupid. I was wrong to want to impose a new system on people I knew nothing about. Now, I want to work to undo all the wrong the Alliance did. I want to help return this island to its people: Jamaicans.

"If you choose not to accept me, I understand. I will leave and never return. But, as Mariya will tell you, I used to hold a position of power in the BA government. I know information that could help you, and I'm willing to tell you everything. I owe you all that much and more."

His little speech, given in the locals' language, had somewhat of the desired effect. The glares softened and the tension eased.

"Is this true?" the slim woman asked Mariya.

"He is my sister's former boss, head of SIS."

"He is the reason we have the military power to carry out our next task," said Devon. "I will vouch for him."

The woman took a silent vote, looking from face to face of all those present. None posed an objection. She turned to the man wearing the bandanna. He gave a grudging nod.

"Let's speak," she said.

32

———————

"Turn on the extractor!" Taylan exclaimed as a Marine exited the restroom next to her rack, letting loose a powerful stench from the open door.

"Sorry," he replied sarcastically. "Non-operational, Corporal Nose. But what do you care? Don't tell me you can smell anything through that."

Whether or not the fan was working was up for debate. The Marine was probably lying, but Taylan couldn't be bothered to take the bait. She had more important things on her mind.

She opened her interface. The bosun had said she would be cleared to access the *Fearless's* net within a few minutes, and he was right. The shipwide updates were available to her.

Quickly, she looked up reports on the status of the *Valiant*. She couldn't expect to find out much about the damage the ship had sustained, but that wasn't what she needed to know. What she was looking for was...

The KIA list popped up. The names of men and women killed in the battle with the EAC frigate was depressingly long. She began to scan them, but realized she was being stupid.

She opened the search, and said, "Emeka Abacha."

The search displayed no results.

A burden of fear and dread slipped from her heart. He wasn't dead, or at least, he wasn't known to be dead. Worry once again creeping over her, she opened the MIA list.

Starship crew who didn't answer comms were counted as missing in action until their bodies were recovered and identified. There had been cases of personnel sucked into space while wearing EVA suits, unconscious and their transmitters damaged, who had been recovered alive. It was an old Space Fleet saying that you weren't dead until you were frozen and dead.

Taylan spoke Abacha's name again into the search.

The hit turned green in the line of black names.

She turned numb. She was holding the interface, but she couldn't feel it. The chatter in the cabin became distant and indistinct.

Abacha was missing.

Her friend had been hurt, possibly killed. Or he could be dying out in space somewhere, right now, alone and afraid. He'd helped her when she'd been dying, but there wasn't a thing she could do to help him.

She dropped the interface onto her rack as if it were red hot and put a hand over her mouth.

"Corporal Ellis, come to my office."

Wright's order had arrived via her implant. She touched the place behind her ear where the device sat, just under her skull. If only she could turn the damned thing off. She didn't want to talk to Wright. She didn't want to talk to anyone.

With hands of lead, she pulled on her boots. Avoiding her bunk mate's legs, which were hanging down from above, she got up and walked out of the cabin.

Taylan had been too busy in the aftermath of the battle to see Arthur and Merlin and try to stick a wedge between them, as Wright had asked her. She supposed that was what the major wanted to talk to her about, but she didn't have anything to tell him. Like every other able-bodied, mentally sound person aboard the *Fearless*, she'd been assisting with repairs. The flagship would be limping to her rendezvous with the rest of the fleet, but she would make it.

Unless the EAC intercepted them again.

She didn't know if the same could be said of the *Valiant*.

But she couldn't think about that now. All she could think about was Abacha.

When the door to Wright's office opened, the major's eyes popped. "Haven't you had your face fixed yet? Strike that. Sit down, corporal."

She did as he ordered.

"Why haven't you had your injury treated yet?"

"I haven't had time, and sick bay is overloaded anyway." She sighed. "And they gave me plenty of medication. I'll be okay until they have time to see me."

"Right, well, at least you can speak now."

"Yeah," she said. "My lips have gone down quite a bit and my mouth stopped bleeding."

He frowned as if something puzzled him. "Is there another problem, Ellis?"

"No, sir. Can I ask why you want to see me?"

"What happened to your face? I don't think you told me."

"It was Arthur. We were sparring. I know it looks bad, but it wasn't his fault. It was Merlin's."

"Merlin hit you?"

"No, I already told you. Arthur did it. Is this what you wanted to talk about? It isn't important now."

"Is that what's bothering you?"

"No, sir." Taylan was struggling not to lose control of her emotions. She was sick with worry about Abacha. "I'm sorry, Major, but do you think you could get to the point?"

He'd been leaning over his desk, peering at her. After she

asked her question, he straightened up and knit his fingers. "All right. If you're sure you don't have anything you want to tell me. When we get to Earth, you're to take part in a special operation. You, me, and a handful of others. I'll brief you properly on the shuttle. I just wanted to give you a heads up and check you were fit for duty. Now I've seen you, I'm glad I did. I'll comm sick bay and see if they can move you up the priority list."

"Thanks for letting me know, sir. Am I dismissed?"

Wright gave her another puzzled look.

"Yes. Dismissed."

She left him and returned to her cabin.

While she'd been gone, the rest of her bunkmates had been called away. The room was empty. Taylan was thankful for the solitude, however brief it might be. She was heartsore in a way she hadn't been for a while.

Lying down, she pulled out her interface again and checked the KIA list. Relieved to see Abacha's name hadn't been added to it, she brought up the MIA list. He remained on it.

Her head flopped to her pillow. She rested the interface on her chest. She recalled her friend's last words to her: *I hope you find your kid, Tay.*

He'd known or guessed the source of her abiding sorrow, yet he'd also had the sensitivity to know she didn't want to talk about it. He hadn't needed her to explain a word to him about Kayla and Patrin. He'd respected her silence. He'd been a good friend.

Her nose stung as tears overflowed her eyes and ran into it as well as down from the corners of her eyes onto her pillow. She lifted the interface once more and opened the screen. The bosun had said he'd transferred all her files from the *Valiant*. She wanted to see her kids again. It wouldn't make her feel any better, but she needed to see them.

She followed the oft-trodden digital path that led to her vids.

At the end of it, there was nothing.

None of her files were there.

Alarmed, she tried again, with the same result. The place that should have stored her personal data was empty. She sat up and comm'd the bosun.

He took half a minute to answer.

"You said you'd transferred all my files. Some are missing."

"I transferred all that was there."

"Can you check?"

"I transferred everything on the *Valiant's* database that belonged to you, Corporal Ellis."

The screen went black.

Taylan comm'd him again. He had to have made a mistake. The vids had definitely been in her files when she'd left the *Valiant*. Unless...

The bosun answered, looking irate. "I have more important things to deal with than this, Ellis. I already told you—"

"Was the *Valiant's* database damaged in the battle?"

"Nope. It's intact, unlike the rest of the ship. Don't comm me again, or I'll report you for wasting my time."

33

Kala put her interface down on her desk. The news of Commander Novak's death was disappointing. She had liked the commander, who had accompanied her when she first set foot on Jamaican soil following her successful invasion. The report said Novak had been investigating intel obtained from a BA captive of a secret BA arms cache, when she'd been caught in an ambush by insurgents. The fighters were popping up all over the country, killing soldiers on guard duty, sneaking into barracks and setting them on fire, and planting homemade bombs.

She needed to address the problem, but she needed to address the problem of Morgan first.

The woman had wandered off into Kala's castle, saying she didn't need or want a guide to show her around. It was one more instance of her acting as a law unto herself, and Kala felt powerless to stop her.

Did Morgan know she'd ordered her death? Kala had feared the woman would want to punish her or get revenge, but she hadn't mentioned the murder attempt. Either the effect that caused the guards to forget their intention to kill her was automatic, or Morgan had a reason for not letting on she knew about Kala's order.

There was so much she didn't know, and so much she needed to know.

Perhaps the information lay somewhere in her books.

Morgan.

She'd read the name before in tales about Arthur, the man of the myths Morgan had told her to find. But *that* Morgan had lived at the same time as Arthur. Was it possible they were the same person? Arthur had somehow survived thousands of years, so the Morgan of the present day could have done the same.

Thousands of years, trapped underground alone in the darkness, with no chance of escape. How had she not gone mad?

But Morgan was not human. She didn't have the same needs as human beings. She was an enigma, but others had written about her in the centuries after her and Arthur's time.

Kala rose and went to her bookcase. She ran her fingertips across the leather spines. The titles and decorations had worn away, but she knew each book like a mother knows her children, by touch alone.

When she found the relevant volume, she pulled it carefully from the shelf.

Footsteps sounded outside her door, which stood open.

Morgan walked in.

She appraised the room with her gaze. "Delightful. Cozy and warm. What are you doing?" She gave the book in Kala's hands a suspicious look.

Kala slid it back onto the shelf. "Have you finished your tour of my home?"

"I have." Morgan rested a hand on the door jamb. "I've even picked out a room for myself. I think I'm going to like it here."

Was she planning on taking Kala's room as her own? It wouldn't be surprising.

Morgan gave a small smile and tilted her head. "What's wrong?"

"Nothing. If you tell me which room you've chosen, I'll ask the servants to light a fire and air it. The castle can get cold and damp, even in summer."

"Something *is* wrong, but you don't want to tell me." Morgan walked up to Kala and took her face in her hands. "I know this has all come as a shock to you. Having me around in your day-to-day life must seem strange. I bet you often wondered if I were only an illusion, and here I am, as real and solid as you are. Don't worry. You'll get used to me. And I have so much to teach you, so much you can learn about all those secrets I've told you over the years. Do you want to learn about those things?"

"Yes," Kala replied fervently. "Yes, I do."

"Well then, things aren't so bad, are they? A little surprise, an unexpected guest, a new mistress. You'll get used to your new situation. Oh, and I nearly forgot! I found a small surprise of my own." She returned to the door and leaned out.

Kala heard her whisper, "You can come in now."

Perran walked in.

Kala froze.

"You didn't tell me you had a son," said Morgan. "And what a sweet little boy he is. He reminds me of my own dear Mordred. He grew to be a wonderful young man, and I'm sure your child will too." She ruffled Perran's hair, and he looked up at her adoringly.

What had Morgan done to him? The only person Perran had any love for was her. He held everyone except his mother in contempt, as a boy of his station should. Had Morgan affected his mind as she had the guards'?

Kala clenched her jaw, stifling a sob. She held herself rigid, resisting the urge to run to her son and snatch him away from the bitch.

"Ah, Mordred," said Morgan softly. "I miss him so much." She turned her gaze from Perran to Kala, and her expression turned steely. "Mordred died on the field of battle at Arthur's hand. It broke me. I never got over it. To lose your child is a terrible, terrible thing no parent should ever have to face." Her hand no longer ruffled Perran's hair. She let it sit on his head. "Pray nothing like that happens to you, Kala. For example, if you were to make an attempt on the life of a powerful person, someone even more powerful than yourself. You might find that, instead of coming after you, they choose to hurt the person you love. If that happened, do you think you would ever be able to forgive yourself?"

"Ouch!" Perran cried out. "You're pressing too hard."

"Am I?" Morgan said, casually removing her hand. "I'm sorry. That was clumsy of me."

She and Kala locked gazes.

No more needed to be said about Morgan's threat, but Kala wondered about the wider implications. Was Morgan vulnerable after all? Could *she* hurt her, though her guards could not? Morgan had insinuated that Kala's offspring would inherit her immunity from harm, though up until that moment she hadn't known about Perran. But she'd clearly implied she could hurt him. And Kala knew from her experience in the mine that Morgan could injure her.

Some similarity existed between the three of them, and Kala had to find out what it was. She would play Morgan's game and be the eager learner. Along the way, she would learn useful skills and knowledge, and, eventually, she would learn how to rid herself of this insufferable usurper.

34

The *Bres's* shuttle bay was locked down. Kekoa and Hale would not be escaping that way, even if one of them could pilot a shuttle, which Lorcan doubted. The cargo bay, where the massive ships carrying building materials from Earth arrived, had also been closed. It wouldn't have been hard for the two women to sneak or bribe their way aboard an empty vessel returning to the home planet. He'd never bothered to put security measures in place to prevent people from leaving in that way, never imagined a scenario where anyone would want to. Up until then, everyone on the *Bres* and her sister ships was there of their own free will, and if they wanted to leave, they could do so on the next scheduled shuttle trip.

Up until then.

Lorcan had retrieved his juggling balls from the floor of the control room and retreated to his suite. A thorough search of the ship was going on. Kekoa and Hale would be found, and... what then? Lock them *both* in a cabin? Multiply his complement of prisoners to two? The situation was getting out of hand.

He began to toss the balls from hand to hand and build up the steady rhythm that helped him think. Returning Hale to Earth at this point was out of the question. He'd feared the negative publicity she could create after their encounter in Suriname, but that would be nothing compared to the tales she could spin about her kidnapping.

What was he to do?

Damn Kekoa! She'd made everything more complicated.

The two men who had been guarding Hale reported a depressurization alarm had sounded, and they'd run to reach the next section before the automatic seal closed. They'd abandoned their prisoner to her fate, which turned out to be Kekoa letting her out of her room.

Morons! He was surrounded by them. All his life he'd been battling fools sent to plague him.

What *was* he to do?!

It would be days until Xiao had the cryo chambers ready, and even if they were working tomorrow, could he put the two women on ice now? Hale and Kekoa were different animals when it came to the reactions of his employees. Hale was a stranger, but Kekoa had been working for him for years, since the inception of the Project. She was a well-known face, and, though he didn't concern himself with the interpersonal relationships of his staff, he had the impression she was well liked.

Dammit!

The juggling balls fell from his hands. He couldn't concentrate. He sat down and pulled out a pen and paper from the shelf in his coffee table.

D*EAR* G*RACE*

·   ·   ·

I F ONLY YOU were here with me now. I'm in sore need of your advice. I have done something...

W HAT? How should he describe his actions? Regrettable? He certainly did regret how things had turned out. Ill-advised? The only advice he'd taken was his own. Reckless?

For a short while, he struggled with what to write. Then, he put down his pen, picked up the paper, scrunched it into a ball, and threw it across the room.

Writing to Grace was providing him no solace.

Lorcan left his suite and walked along the passageway. Ten meters away stood a closed door, the entrance to a luxury suite similar to, though not quite as good as, his own. After another ten meters he encountered another entrance to a suite, and then, the junction at the end of the passageway. Usually, he would turn right here and walk another hundred meters or so to the control room.

He turned left.

This way led to a Maglev station. The transportation system had recently come online, but Lorcan hadn't used it yet. The engineering team were completing a month's test run of the same timetable that would apply after the *Bres* embarked on her voyage, ferrying passengers between service and entertainment areas.

The sign stated a train would be arriving in ninety seconds.

Exactly on time, the carriage slid into the station with barely a whisper. The doors opened, and Lorcan stepped aboard. Inside, the metal, plastic, and paint exuded a smell of newness. All was spotless, pristine, and perfect. And it should stay that way indefinitely. In another sector of the *Bres*, nanobot specialists were working on sanitation and repair devices. Minuscule sanobots would remove dust, sweat, oil, and anything else that could conceivably be deposited on surfaces.

Repair bots would identify and mend or replace degrading materials before a human would notice a change in appearance.

He had thought of and accounted for everything.

Everything.

Everything except human nature.

The carriage had built up speed without his noticing. Outside, lights in the tunnel walls were flashing past. He was nearing one of the agricultural zones, where crops from all over Earth would grow, maintaining a living gene supply as a backup to stored seeds, tubers, and rhizomes. When the colony ship arrived at a potential new home, the zones would serve a second function: Breeding and growing genetically engineered varieties that would thrive in the new planet's conditions.

Lorcan grimaced, remembering Hale's lecture about soil ecosystems. Had she been right?

He clicked his tongue against the roof of his mouth.

Of course she had. If anyone on Earth knew about soil microorganisms, it was Iolani Hale.

The lights in the tunnel were slowing down. The braking was so smoothly graduated, he barely felt it. The carriage stopped and the doors opened.

Without knowing where he was going or why, Lorcan stepped out onto the empty platform. The carriage whisked away, and he was alone.

He walked through to the wide, metal-floored passageway and picked a direction at random. Many sectors were unsigned as yet. He passed three doors before deciding to enter the next one he happened upon. It opened to reveal an expanse of soil. The lights on the ceiling above were for the benefit of the workers only. They were not the blazing floodlights that would mimic sunlight. He crossed the metal shelf to the edge of the field, squatted down, and picked up a handful of earth. Had it been seeded with microorganisms? He had no idea.

A horrible fear grew in his stomach, and a vision played in his mind. He was on the colony planet. The colonists had disembarked years ago. They had tried to settle the new world, but they had failed. Supplies had run out, their crops would not grow, the local flora and fauna were poisonous to humans, and the *Bres* had used up all her fuel.

People were dying. They were slowly starving to death, and there wasn't anything he could do about it. He'd vetted each of them, accepted huge sums of money or years of service in return for a place on his ship, and he'd failed them. Their futures, their lives, would be lost, and it would be all down to him.

In his dreams of the future, he'd never imagined such an outcome.

"Ua Talman."

It was Steadman comming him.

"Yes, what is it?"

"We've found them. Hale and Kekoa. They were hiding in Cargo Bay 3. They're being brought to the control center. Unless you would like them to be taken somewhere else?"

"No, the control center is fine. I'm on my way."

35

———————

Hans's palms were so slippery with sweat, he could barely maintain a grip on the heavy pulse rifle. He guessed it was an old model, perhaps one of the first to be developed. The power pack was large and stuck out so his arm sat uncomfortably over the stock. His mouth was bone dry and his heart raced. Sweat coated his face, stinging his eyes.

"Don't worry," Devon said softly in the darkness. "We're going in fast. It'll be over before you know it. And the EAC are easy to identify by their uniforms. You're not in danger of killing anyone from the Resistance."

The last possibility compounded Hans's fears. He'd feared he was about to die, but until then it hadn't occurred to him he might accidentally kill someone he shouldn't. He would be surprised if he killed anyone at all, but if he did, it had better *not* be a Resistance fighter. His position was insecure as it was. He couldn't afford to be anything other than squeaky clean.

Hennessy and Montague's military coup had wrecked the governmental building the BA had used to house the temporary Parliament, so the EAC had taken over a different place from which to conduct their operations. It used to be the home of a wealthy local family, but they'd donated it to the nation decades ago. From the point of view of the Resistance, it was a fortunate choice. The large stately home was surrounded by grounds even though it sat in the heart of the capital. Guards patrolled the perimeter, but the locals who had grown up in the area knew of a secret way in, through a sluice gate in the foundations of the wall. The gate allowed excess rain to drain from the grounds into a waterway, preventing flooding during tropical rainstorms.

It hadn't rained for weeks. The waterway and drainage channel were dry, and the old gate's bars had been easily sawn through in between guard patrols.

Hans waited with Devon, Charles, and the man with the bandanna, who Hans had learned was named Bunny. He didn't think he'd ever seen anyone who looked less like a fluffy rabbit. The four men crouched next to the wall of a large fountain. The pump had been turned off, and the water had turned stagnant and stinking. They were waiting for the signal.

Bunny leaned into Hans. "What's the matter? Feelin' scared?"

Hans couldn't deny it. If he could smell his own fear, so could the others.

"I bet this wasn't what you were thinking of when you said you wanted to help us, right? So smart. So fine. Speaking Patois like a born Jamaican."

"Shut up, Bunny," whispered Devon.

He took no notice. "Why are you really here, Mr Hans Jonte, head of SIS?"

The final 's' sound hissed between his teeth.

"Is it Mariya? You fancy some 'o that sweet—*Ooof!*"

Hans had driven the stock of his rifle into Bunny's side.

"Hey!" Charles whispered fiercely. "Cut it out, or you'll get us killed."

"Yeah, shut your face," said Devon. "You had that coming, Bunny. Don't disrespect Mariya."

Bunny's healthy eye narrowed, and he edged away from Hans. In the quiet of the night, his mutterings were barely audible: *Return the island to its people. Jamaica for Jamaicans.* Bunny spat in the dust.

When Hans had offered his services to the Resistance, he thought he'd made it clear he anticipated working in an advisory capacity. If not in terms of the group's strategy, then as a source of valuable intelligence. He hadn't anticipated being required to take part in attacks, yet here he was. Were they testing him to prove his loyalty? Or was it a cultural thing, that they expected every able-bodied adult to lend a hand? It could be either, or both. It didn't matter. When it came down to it, they'd assumed he would fight alongside them, and he couldn't refuse without losing all credibility.

Boom!

The sound wave hit Hans's eardrums like a sledgehammer. Simultaneously, the ground shuddered and the sky winked to daylight and then back to darkness. Stone fragments rained down in a crackling hail.

It was the signal.

More by reflexively copying the others than under his own willpower, Hans leapt from his hiding place and sped toward the building. Half of the west wing had crumbled away. Flames spurted from the wreckage. In a tiny corner of Hans's mind, a part not taken over by utter panic, he rued the destruction of the beautiful, ancient building. It was irreplaceable, and who knew how many precious antiques it had housed?

The three other men were ahead of him. Hans tried to run faster, not due to eagerness to fight, but out of fear of being left behind and forced to face the EAC defense alone. Pulse fire was already blazing from the windows and doors of the house. Hans saw more Resistance fighters running in from the left and right. Some were hit by the pulses and fell, their bodies smoldering.

A light passed his head, briefly blinding him. He'd nearly been hit.

What was it the soldiers in the sims did? He began zigzagging, trying to move erratically so the enemy couldn't get a fix on him. But now he was falling behind. His three fellow fighters were nearly at the mansion's main doors. They were firing as they ran, and the EAC soldiers were ducking into and out of sight to return fire.

Fire his pulse rifle! That's what he should do.

He lifted the heavy weapon and tried to aim it, but it was hopeless. The muzzle jerked up and down and swung from side to side. He was more likely to hit a Jamaican than an EAC soldier. And if he ran to the side to clear his view, he risked being left even farther behind.

One of the three men ahead of him suddenly fell flat on his back. As Hans passed him, he looked down and caught a glimpse of Charles, still alive and grimacing, the side of his torso a burnt, bloody mess.

Hans ran on.

He had only another thirty meters of ground to cover before he reached the house. And then what? Would he be shot dead at the door? Resistance fighters were swarming the house, climbing in the windows. But the EAC were still holding the main doors. Regular pulse bolts flew from the entrance.

Then Bunny fired at exactly the right time, and one of the soldiers toppled from the side of the doorway and hit the floor face downward.

The scent of smoke and burning wood hit Hans's nostrils. And something else—a horrible stench of barbecued human flesh.

Almost before he knew it, he was at the feet of the stairs

that rose to the entrance. Devon and Bunny were bounding up them.

A flash. A gargling scream.

Bunny came sliding down the stone steps on his back. His head hit Hans's boot. He'd been shot in the neck.

Paralyzed, Hans stared at the dying man. Bunny's good eye roved wildly. He choked up blood. Then he was still.

Hans looked up.

Devon was gone.

A pulse bolt flew past his shoulder. It had come from behind him. Hans turned. EAC soldiers were running at him out of the shadowy grounds. The guards from the perimeter were responding to the attack. Reinforcements would no doubt be on their way too.

Now, the danger was from the rear.

Hans ascended the steps two at a time and ran through the open double doorway.

Inside was carnage.

EAC and Resistance fighters lay in the lobby, dead or injured and groaning in agony. On the stairs, hand-to-hand fighting was going on. The beautiful, ancient walls were scorched and pitted. Blood congealed on the marble floor.

Hans swung about, uncertain what to do or where to go. Devon was nowhere to be seen. He supposed he should try to mount the stairs, or maybe search for EAC soldiers on the ground floor. If he came upon one, would he be able to kill him? He'd never killed anyone. He would have to try if he wanted to live.

He jogged toward an opening beneath one set of stairs, but as he neared a fallen Resistance fighter, a feeling of familiarity slowed his steps.

"*Mariya!*"

He dropped to his knees.

She was hurt. A pulse round had hit her hip and blood was

running from the wound, a tiny fountain gushing up at each heartbeat.

He clamped his hands on it, pressing down hard.

Her head turned toward him.

"You're going to be okay," said Hans. He cast about for a medic. Did the Resistance even have them?

"Mr Jonte," she said. "You're so kind. Would you like a coffee?"

"Don't joke, Mariya. Mariya, don't..." A vise had fastened around his throat. He couldn't breathe. Where were the medics?

It felt like someone had rammed a knife, hilt deep, into his heart. The pain was unbearable.

He'd thought Mariya hadn't meant anything to him. He'd thought she was only another tool to be used to achieve his aims. But as her life leaked away beneath his hands, he understood she was more to him. So very much more. And he hadn't realized it until it was too late.

She smiled her lazy smile. "It's okay, Hans. Don't cry for me. I'm going to see Josie again."

"No."

But he had never been in control of what Mariya did, even when he'd been her boss. She breathed heavily, and then her smile froze and her eyes became fixed.

"*No.*"

He kept his hands on her, unable to move.

EAC soldiers burst into the lobby.

Fear sparking him to life, Hans did the only thing he could think of—he slid down next to Mariya's body. He was already covered in her blood. Perhaps the troops would think he was dead. In the fight for the building, he might be able to slink away without being noticed. One thing he knew for sure: If he drew attention to himself, he was dead.

Mariya was still warm as he pressed against her. God, he missed her already.

His ploy seemed to be working. The soldiers were ignoring him as they pounded past, heading into the building. They were running up the stairs too, dispatching Resistance fighters on the way. Hans suppressed a shudder as a man hit the floor near his head.

Pulse fire hissed, boots stamped overhead, shouts rang out.

Hans waited until he could hear no movement or voices nearby, and then cautiously lifted his head a fraction, just enough to get a view of the lobby. It was empty of living, uninjured soldiers, though in the darkness visible through the doorway, helmet lights moved and occasional pulses flashed.

He began to inch his way toward the exit, remaining in a prone position so he could freeze and try to look dead if anyone came in.

The EAC seemed to be winning. The Resistance fighters had begun to take control of the headquarters, but enemy reinforcements had arrived and swung the tide of the battle in the opposite direction. The attempt to take the building had failed.

Now, he had to get out of here alive and find out who else had survived. It was a big blow to the struggle to retake Jamaica, but he wouldn't give up. He would continue to work with the remaining Resistance to help them regroup and continue to fight. Though he doubted he would ever get over Mariya's death, he would never give up on his vision.

A deep rumble like thunder came from outside.

Hans heard a shout from the garden.

"Get in the house! That's a BA corvette!"

36
____

Ellis's face looked better, but her mood didn't seem to have improved. Wright couldn't figure out what was wrong with her. Before the battle with the EAC ships, she'd been her usual disrespectful self. Then, when he'd seen her to tell her about the spec op, she'd transformed into this quiet, deferential Marine, remembering to say sir and not speaking out of turn.

Something serious must have happened.

The pilot comm'd the dropship cabin. "Prepare for liftoff."

Wright fastened his harness and snapped his helmet seals shut. The spec op team did the same. All except Arthur and Merlin. He comm'd them one-to-two, explaining what they had to do. The two of them looked distinctly odd in Marine EVA suits. Did Merlin even need one? The point of wearing them was in case they were attacked and the cabin depressurized. The alien had put one on anyway.

Who was he to argue with a shape-shifting extra-terrestrial?

The ship's thrusters fired. She rose from the launch pad and flew out from the *Fearless's* bay into space. Wright estimated they had an hour before they reached their destination. Plenty of time to brief the team.

He switched his comm to wide broadcast, only excluding the pilot. The fewer people who knew about the operation, the better. He went through the usual preliminaries, and then said, "The aim of this mission is to assassinate Dwyr Kala Orr."

He paused to allow the fact to sink in. Arthur and Merlin gave no reaction because they already knew why they were there. Three of the Marines' eyebrows rose behind their visors. The features of the fourth, Ellis, remained downcast.

Huh. He'd definitely expected that little tidbit to perk her up.

"Awesome," said Wilson, a burly Marine Wright had included due to his close-combat prowess. He wasn't as good as Ellis, but he was good.

"We get to take out the bitch queen herself!" Wilson went on.

The corner of Merlin's mouth rose in a half smile.

"Quieten down and listen," said Wright. "I have a lot to tell you, and you're gonna have to remember it all without anything written down."

Ellis wasn't even looking at him. She seemed lost in her thoughts. Whatever her problem was, he needed her to get over it.

"Ellis."

She still didn't look at him.

"Ellis," he barked. "Pay attention."

"What's a matter, corporal?" Wilson teased. "Missing your vids?"

Her head snapped up.

Her hands flew to her harness clasps and tore them open. In another second she was on Wilson and ripping off his helmet. She managed to get in two punches before Wright reached her and hauled her off the shocked Marine.

But he couldn't hold her. She broke free from his grasp and launched herself at Wilson again. The first two punches had left him dazed. The third knocked him out cold. He hadn't had the chance to raise a hand to defend himself.

Thankfully, the two other Marines in the cabin had the good sense to come to Wright's aid without being asked. Together, the three of them succeeded in restraining Ellis as she raged. Her helmet comm was off, so no one could hear what she was yelling behind her visor.

What had Wilson said? Something about vids? Whatever it meant, it had something to do with the corporal's mood. Until Wilson woke up or Ellis calmed down, Wright had no way of knowing. He comm'd her, one to one.

"Corporal!" he shouted. "Sit down!"

With the help of the other two Marines, he hauled the struggling woman back to her seat, forced her into it, and fastened her harness. "You get up again and you're going straight out the airlock," he warned. "You understand me? You're a danger to everyone on the ship right now. Calm the hell down. That's an order."

Something of what he'd said must have got through because she stayed in her seat, though the look she was giving Wilson implied *he* would be the one going out the airlock the next opportunity she had.

The burly Marine was beginning to come around. He moved his lips, and blood ran from between them. His right eye was already beginning to swell.

Great.

He was on probably the most important mission in the history of the war between the BA and the EAC, and he had a Marine who hated another's guts, had already injured him, and planned on finishing the job.

Just great.

"Everyone take five," he said.

Wilson removed his glove and stuck a finger in his mouth to probe his gums. Then he opened and closed his mouth a few times, experimentally. He didn't seem badly hurt. When he'd completed his self-assessment, he picked his helmet up from where Ellis had thrown it and replaced it on his head. All the while, he didn't meet the gaze of the corporal glaring at him.

Even though her face was partially obscured by the tint of her visor, she looked angrier than Wright had ever seen her, and he'd seen her angry plenty of times.

Over some vids?

He opened a one-to-one comm again. "Ellis, I don't know what your beef with Wilson is, and I don't want to know. We have a mission ahead of us that's vital to the future of the Alliance. If we're successful, it could mean the end of the war. You're going to keep a lid on your emotions until we're done. You understand?"

She didn't reply.

"Ellis, answer me, or goddammit, I'll—"

"Understood, sir."

As he'd been speaking, she hadn't taken her eyes off Wilson for a second.

Wright checked on Arthur and Merlin. The ancient king appeared confused and alarmed, while the alien was smiling scornfully.

He switched his comm to include all the cabin passengers. "We'll be landing in Ireland in about forty-five minutes. From the drop site—"

"Ireland?!" Ellis blurted.

"Yes, Ireland," he patiently replied. "From the drop site, we're—"

"But you said we were going to assassinate the Dwyr," Ellis interrupted again. "She's in Jamaica."

Wright sighed and prayed to a deity for help. "According to

our intel, the Dwyr returned to BI several weeks ago. She's taken up residence in a castle in West BI."

"West BI?!"

"Corporal Ellis, set your comm to receive only. That way, no one except you has to hear your inane remarks."

His words had been transforming. The woman had lost interest in Wilson and was now sitting up straight and looking eager. Wright silently thanked the deity who had come to his rescue.

One of the main reasons he'd wanted Ellis to come along was her knowledge of the local terrain. That, and her skill at all combat. The three other Marines were also the pick of those available. Arthur and Merlin were there because the entire mission was Merlin's idea. He'd claimed the BA could be successful in the attempt, but only if it acted quickly and with his and Arthur's help. Merlin had also explicitly asked for Ellis too, though he'd offered no explanation as to why she was important.

Wright began to explain the mission details.

37

Taylan stowed her EVA suit and returned to her seat on the dropship. Once they landed, they would only have time to grab their packs and weapons before leaving the ship. Though Ireland wasn't enemy territory yet, they needed to keep their arrival secret if possible. EAC agents were probably already operating there, passing intel across the Irish Sea as Kala Orr prepared her attack.

The ship swayed and juddered, buffeted by turbulence.

The burly Marine, Wilson, hadn't met her gaze the entire ride from the *Fearless*. His eye had puffed up satisfyingly and a purple bruise had bloomed on his jaw, but she wasn't done yet.

The minute he had stepped into the dropship, she'd recognized him as the guy who'd stormed out of the training session after she'd put him on the mat. She'd thought that was the total of their history. He was an immature jerk, but she could still have worked with him for the mission's duration. That was before his remark about her vids.

He'd taken them, or probably deleted them. When he'd done it, she didn't know. She hadn't felt the need to watch them for weeks. But at some point before he'd transferred from the

Valiant to the *Fearless*, he'd bribed or coerced a data tech to find her personal files and mess with them as revenge. The manchild couldn't get over being beaten, especially not in front of an audience.

Aside from Kayla's necklace, the recordings were all she had left of her children. Just the notion they were most likely gone forever cut into her so deeply she could hardly breathe when she thought about it. The loss of the vids coupled with Abacha being missing were more than she could bear. When Wilson had made his remark, all she'd been able to think about was making him pay for what he'd done. Then Wright had stated they were going to Ireland.

Ireland!

Her kids had probably been taken there on one of the boats ferrying refugees from West BI, though she'd searched the camps for months and not been able to find them.

Then the major had said they would progress to her homeland to assassinate Dwyr Orr. Her heart swelled at the thought of seeing the beautiful mountains and valleys again.

The dropship was descending fast, too fast for Taylan's stomach. She closed her eyes and waited for the descent to end.

The cabin jumped as the ship hit solid ground. Instantly, the hatch opened and fresh, cool air swept in.

"Move out," ordered Wright.

Taylan undid her harness, grabbed her pack and rifle, and ran from the ship, down the ramp, and into long grass. The dropship shone no external lights, the pilot navigating on night vision. As soon as the hatch closed, they were in darkness.

"This way," said the major.

He'd explained they wouldn't be wearing armor for the mission. They had to blend in with the locals, so the only military gear they would bring was their pulse rifles. Everything else they carried was civilian. Consequently, they were operating without the benefit of helmet lights, HUDs, or any other helpful devices.

Wright was already disappearing into the gloom. It was a starless, damp night. Taylan followed him across the rough, open ground. A minute later, she heard the dropship's thrusters fire. Their noise grew quieter until it disappeared and the only sounds were the wind in the grass and the footfalls and breathing of her companions.

Wright had said they would hike cross country to a safe house near a port town. In the morning, they would cross to West BI. The Dwyr was now living in a castle on the coast, near the forces she was gathering for the push into Ireland.

Taylan knew the port town well. It was where her children were supposed to have gone. She had searched every inch of the place and the camps of thousands surrounding it.

"Taylan," said a deep voice close to her ear. Arthur had caught up to her. "I am glad you're with us. Can I ask why you were so angry with the man called Wilson?"

"It's a long story and too hard to explain. Sorry."

"It's important to put aside our differences so we can fight well."

"I know that, but…"

Shit.

Arthur had a real talent for making people feel guilty, or, Taylan reluctantly admitted, bringing out the best in them.

She couldn't lie to him. "I'm not even sure I'll be taking part in the assassination attempt."

He didn't reply immediately. His heavy footsteps crunched next to hers for several paces. "Why, Taylan?"

"I just feel like this battle with the EAC isn't my problem. I enlisted with the BA to try to help in the fight, but I'm just one person and I don't think I'm really needed anymore. The Alliance has you and Merlin now. My part is over, and I should concentrate on what's important to *me*."

Again, the ancient monarch didn't answer straight away. When he did speak, all he said was, "You must do whatever you feel is right and just."

He slowed his pace and dropped back in the line.

THEY ARRIVED at the safe house about three in the morning. It had begun raining halfway through their hike. By the time they reached their destination, streams were running down the streets that sloped toward the harbor and the downpour was creating a cacophony on the pavement. After climbing several fences, they huddled outside the back door of the property. Wright rapped on the door with one knuckle. It opened, and they slipped inside.

"Through here," said their host in a heavy accent. The woman was young and slight with shoulder-length brown hair that hung forward, obscuring her face. She opened a door, revealing steps leading downward.

At the bottom was a bare cellar of old brick walls, lit by a single bulb.

"The boat to West BI leaves in two and a half hours at first light," said Wright as everyone was easing packs from tired shoulders and dumping them on the cold, concrete floor. "Make the most of the time and get some sleep. We'll eat in two hours, and then we won't be resting again until the job's done."

Taylan took off her rain-soaked jacket and spread it out to dry. She unrolled the thin mat in her pack, leaned the pack against the wall, and lay down. Putting her arm under her head for a pillow and drawing up her knees, she closed her eyes.

She listened: Rustling, whispered words, people stepping quietly past. The noises faded away. The light went out. The breaths of her companions grew slower, deeper, and more regular.

Taylan opened her eyes.

Arthur's words had been playing on her mind.

You must do whatever you feel is right and just.

She'd planned on doing something debilitating to Wilson, something to remember her by. But, even if she was fast, unless she actually killed him, he would be bound to wake the others up. Then she wouldn't be able to carry out the next part of her plan.

And Arthur's words nagged at her. Would hurting Wilson be *just*? Would it be *right*? The Marine was an asshole, but he probably hadn't known how much her vids meant to her. He might have thought he was only inconveniencing her. She didn't know for sure he understood the impact of what he'd done. And even if he did, was her desire to hurt him justice or the need to take out her anger on someone? Nothing she could do would bring those vids back. If she did get her revenge, wouldn't she be stooping to his level?

Everyone seemed to be sleeping. Taylan slowly sat up.

Light shone through the gap under the closed door at the top of the stairs. She was surrounded by the humped forms of her companions and Arthur's somewhat larger hump.

Which one was Wright? She couldn't tell. She felt bad about leaving without saying goodbye to him. Despite having a stick up his ass half the time, he was a good guy. She would miss him.

Ah, well. It couldn't be helped.

She turned onto all fours and reached for her jacket. As she did so, she caught sight of Merlin, sitting in the corner, his back against the wall.

The light from the gap under the door lit up the whites of his eyes and faintly illuminated his face.

Taylan froze.

Aliens didn't sleep, of course.

Would he give her away?

Her fingertips contacted the neck of her jacket. She grasped it and slowly dragged it toward her. In a silent conference she didn't understand, she and Merlin held eye contact as she pulled her jacket over her shoulders.

The alien smiled his small, closed-lipped smile that didn't reach his eyes.

Taylan rose halfway to her feet, turned away from Merlin, and tiptoed to the staircase, stepping over her prone comrades.

She climbed the steps quietly, eased the door open, and stepped out.

38

———————

Hale and Kekoa stood in the center of the *Bres's* control room. Lorcan had expected them to be cowed, afraid of what he might do to them, but their expressions were defiant. For some reason, the room was empty apart from the two women, and Steadman and Jurrah.

Putting aside his confusion about why only four people were there, he decided to get straight to the point. On his journey over, he'd come up with a solution to his problem. He'd berated himself for not thinking of it earlier.

"Right, now your foolish little escapade is over, I have a proposal to make both of you. Step into my office, please." He began to walk toward the small room adjoining the control center that he used for private conversations and work that required deep concentration.

"No," said Hale.

He halted. "What?"

"We're not going in there," said Kekoa, clasping her hands behind her back and tilting her chin up.

"Anything you have to say to us," said Hale, "you can say in front of Jurrah and Steadman."

"We want witnesses," Kekoa added.

What a pair of upstarts.

"So that's how it is, is it?"

"That's exactly how it is," said Hale.

"Hmpf." The difficulty they were creating was easily remedied. "Steadman, Jurrah, please leave."

Jurrah made a circle with his fist and gave a small cough into it. Steadman looked embarrassed before saying, "We would rather remain here, sir."

Jurrah jabbed him with his elbow.

Steadman said, more confidently, "We're staying here."

Lorcan paused, momentarily flummoxed. He'd encountered workers who had grown too big for their boots several times over the years. At every encounter, he'd sacked the person concerned immediately. He wasn't about to allow an employee to dictate to *him*. But he'd never been confronted by four of them at once. Technically, Hale wasn't his employee, but he'd wanted to make her one of his team.

She stepped forward. "I can see that, perhaps for the first time in your entire life, you're at a loss for words, Ua Talman. Perhaps it will help if I take over from here?"

"No, it would not!" Lorcan spat. "You and Kekoa might have managed to get a few of my staff temporarily on your side, but I am the owner of this enterprise. *I* call the shots around here, not some jumped up researcher."

Hale shrugged. "Go ahead and say whatever it is you want to say."

"Thank you so much for your permission! Fine. If Jurrah and Steadman are to hear this too, the same applies to them. Remember that, gentlemen." He took a breath and composed himself. "I will admit I acted recklessly when I took you from your home in Suriname, Iolani. I apologize for—"

"Recklessly?" Hale scoffed. "More like outrageously and completely illegally."

Lorcan continued, raising his voice, "As I said, I apologize for my hasty action. It was a mistake, and I regret it." He didn't bother to say sorry for attempting to put her in cryo or imprisoning her. If she wasn't going to be gracious in accepting his apology, he saw no point. "Obviously, my behavior has put me in a difficult position. I cannot allow you to jeopardize the future of the Project, Hale, which you would assuredly do if I were to allow you to return to Earth. As to you, Kekoa, I have no doubt you would also blab to a vidnews channel the minute you stepped off the shuttle.

"Therefore, I would like to propose a large cash settlement in exchange for your silence. I can have a lawyer create contracts today, and you must sign them before you leave. If either of you breaches your contract, I will personally see to it that you're bankrupted by lawsuits and the rest of your days are spent living in misery. I don't think I need to convince you I have the money and influence to do it."

Hale turned to Kekoa and raised her eyebrows. "Have you finished?" she asked him.

"I think I've covered the gist, yes."

"Good. Speaking on behalf of your three employees present in this room and myself, the answer is no. We do not accept your proposal."

"A stupid reply, but nonetheless expected. All I have to say in that case is, I'll see you all in court. Or, rather, my lawyers will." He turned on his heel, about to march out and leave the nincompoops to their Pyrrhic victory.

"Lorcan, please stay," said Kekoa.

There was a note in her voice, a gentleness, that made him pause. He hadn't heard that soft, female tone in a very long time. He stood a moment, his back facing them, before he mastered himself and turned around. "Do you have something to add to your refusal?"

"I...We have a proposal of our own," said Hale. "Would you like to hear it?"

"Fire away."

"First of all, what's happened with my dogs? Did you leave them to starve?"

"Certainly not. They're being well cared for."

"Good. That was a wise decision. A lot hinged on your reply."

Pfft. He gave a slight shake of his head. The woman's arrogance was unbelievable.

Hale put an arm around Kekoa's shoulders. "Since this good woman broke me out of my prison, I've had a chance to talk with her about exactly what you're doing here. I mean aside from all the lord and master stuff. The plans for the colony ships, especially the habitats. I have to say, what I heard deeply concerned me."

"Really," said Lorcan flatly.

"Really," Hale replied in earnest. "I mean, I can see what you're attempting, and I'm sure it looks good on an interface screen. But, honestly, I think if you carry on as things are, you're heading for trouble. Maybe not in the few years after you leave, maybe not even for decades, but eventually, you could end up engineering a catastrophe the likes of which has never been seen in the history of humanity.

"Kekoa has done as good a job as anyone could expect in the circumstances, and I'm sure the rest of your staff is just as smart and hard working, but what you're attempting is nigh on impossible. And no one, least of all you, seems to understand that."

"I see," he replied. "Thank you for your pearls of wisdom." Despite the acid sarcasm of his words, a sliver of self-doubt was beginning to pierce his confidence. He'd imagined exactly the scenario Hale described only a short while ago in the agricultural zone.

What if she was right?

He'd come so far, worked so hard, spent so much money and made so many promises. The Antarctic Project had taken on an impetus of its own. He didn't see how it would be possible to stop it now, or even alter course to a less ambitious aim.

Hale stepped closer to him. "How long do you have before your planned departure date?"

"The Project is on track to complete in about three years. Once all the ships are finished and provisioned, it's up to me when we actually start out, but I imagine it would be soon after."

The scientist said, "I don't like you, Ua Talman. I didn't like you before I met you, and I certainly don't now. That isn't going to change. However, you have some good people working for you. They, at least, know the difference between right and wrong. Even more importantly, millions are putting their lives in your hands. I take those lives seriously. I feel a duty, a moral obligation, to try to save them if I can.

"Your threats don't mean anything to me. Do you honestly think I care about money? Or that you could tarnish my reputation with lies? Horseshit. You can't hurt me. But I know how desperate people are to leave the planet you've helped to destroy. I could go home and talk to the media, tell them everything you did to me, and people wouldn't care. You're offering them a dream, an escape. You could kidnap, rape, and murder a hundred famous scientists, and they would still be lining up for a place on one of your ships."

She sighed. "So, though I hate to say it, my proposal is that I act as an adviser to the Project. But I want to be clear. I don't mean adviser as in I give you advice and you choose whether or not to take it. I mean when it comes to plans for supporting human life on other planets, you do exactly what I say."

Lorcan snorted derisively. Hale was a piss poor negotiator.

She'd just told him she had no power over him. On the other hand, the other things she'd said had made an impression. He didn't like the part about having to do whatever she said, but he did want the benefit of her knowledge. He'd never been in any doubt that the Project needed the best of the best if it were to succeed.

He held out his hand.

"Oh no," said Hale, putting her own behind her back. "I want everything in writing, signed and sealed. So you can't go back on your word."

"Are you saying you don't trust me?" he asked.

She rolled her eyes.

39

———

"You may have already noticed you have an ability to influence the thoughts and feelings of others," said Morgan.

"I remember you telling me I could once," Kala replied, "on one of my visits when I was younger. I have tried since then, with some success, I think. It's hard to tell."

"You can only tell by the actions of the person you're trying to influence. If they behave as you want them to, for instance. Some minds are easier to control than others."

They were sitting in Kala's study, which overlooked the river that nearly encircled the castle. The river led down to the sea and the harbor where her naval ships were preparing to launch an attack on Ireland.

She was busy. Her attention had returned to her armed forces. Not only had the situation in Jamaica worsened, she'd lost one of her starships in a battle with the BA. She'd realized she couldn't afford to be neglectful. Her military needed her input and guidance.

But she also thirsted to learn whatever Morgan was willing to teach her.

"What makes a mind easy to control?" she asked.

"A good question," replied Morgan. "It isn't what you might think. Intelligent people can be just as easy to control as stupid ones. Susceptibility is more to do with thinking habits. Are they the type of person who is curious and open to new ideas? This makes them vulnerable to external influence. They're less likely to notice they're thinking something out of the ordinary or that doesn't fit with the situation. While people who are used to trains of thought that always head in the same direction become alarmed if they think something new and different."

"So I suppose it's hard to tell when you meet someone how easy it will be to bend their will to yours."

"Exactly."

Morgan reached out to touch Kala's hair. Kala became still, loathing the contact but not wanting to offend the powerful creature. She'd told Perran to stay away from their visitor. Whether he would obey her or not was another question.

Could Morgan read her mind?

"You're a quick learner."

"I've hardly learned anything yet."

"Oh, but you have. You've taken the things I told you and built...this." Morgan swept her arm wide, taking in the room and the view from the window, including the protruding castle towers. "An empire."

"Thank you. It's an empire I hope to expand soon, and I was hoping for your help."

"Naturally. That's why I'm here."

Is that so?

The previous night, when Morgan had gone to her chamber and the castle was quiet, Kala had taken down from her shelves all the books that she could recall mentioned the woman called Morgan. She'd read everything she could find on her. The stories had told of a person with mystical powers who had bewitched Arthur, her half-brother, and borne his child.

That was the man, Mordred, Morgan had mentioned yesterday. So Arthur had killed his own son in battle. Then something must have happened that resulted in her being imprisoned for thousands of years. Kala didn't know for sure who was responsible, but she had an idea.

Morgan had said her son's death broke her.

If anyone hurt a hair on Perran's head, Kala would have them flayed and disemboweled alive. She couldn't imagine the pain Morgan must have felt. But the information made her suspicious. Morgan had insisted over and over again how important it was that Kala found Arthur. Was her visitor really here only to get her revenge?

"Do you remember this place?" Kala asked.

"This castle?" Morgan stood up and walked to the window. She leaned out into the sunlight and peered at long lines of ancient walls. "No. It was built after my time. The castles were smaller and rougher then, often built only of timber. This world was a different place."

"You aren't from this planet, are you?" Kala asked.

Morgan faced her and frowned. "So many questions. You're getting boring. Perhaps I should teach your son instead."

"No, please teach me. Perran is too young. And he's probably off somewhere, playing. You were telling me about mind control."

"Yes, I was, wasn't I?" She returned to her seat. "It's a matter of projection. You have the rudiments already, but we can refine them."

"Tell me how. And I want to know what else I can learn."

"One step at a time, Kala. One step at a time."

40

The rain hadn't stopped. Taylan let herself out the back door of the safe house and paused to put on her jacket. She'd left her pulse rifle and pack behind. Carrying them around town would draw attention. But she was already regretting her decision to not bring her backpack. All she had was the clothes she stood up in, no food or any other supplies.

She couldn't risk going back. She would be bound to wake someone up, or Merlin might change his mind about giving her away.

Why hadn't he said anything or alerted Wright?

She gave up trying to figure out what was going on in the alien's mind and stepped out into the night. Retracing the route that had brought them to the safe house, she made her way back to the road, climbing fences and trudging through muddy yards.

From memory, the refugee camp had sat on the town's northern outskirts. It was as good a place as any to begin her search, and she might be able to scrounge a little food.

She set off.

It was still hours until dawn. No one was about and no street lights shone—probably in anticipation of the feared EAC attack. The rain fell in a steady stream.

Taylan remembered the last time she'd been here, nearly a year ago. She recalled her growing desperation when she couldn't find Kayla or Patrin. The town had been the destination of the ferry from West BI, one of the last to get out as she understood. When she'd finally arrived, she'd been confident it would only be a matter of days before she found her children. Then days had dragged into weeks, and she had broadened her search to surrounding camps, villages, and towns, only to come up empty handed.

This time, she wouldn't give up. She would keep going until she found them, even if it took the last breath in her body.

Footsteps pounded behind her, wet and heavy on the sodden sidewalk.

Someone was in a hurry.

Taylan turned and looked back. It was hard to see in the dark, but the person running toward her seemed to be a man. She moved to the side of the street to get out of his way, but as she watched and waited, recognition flashed in her mind.

It was Major Wright.

At first, she shrank into a doorway, hoping he wouldn't see her. But of course he'd seen her. That was why he was running.

She leapt from her hiding place and sprinted up the road. Despite the delay, she still had a head start on him. If she could reach the town center she might be able to lose him in the maze of streets. After a minute's running, she risked a glance over her shoulder. He was gaining on her. She mentally cursed and tried to speed up, but she was already going as fast as she could. She was panting, and her lungs were beginning to ache.

Then it hit her. Why was she running? What could he do to make her go back? Threaten to shoot her? He wasn't carrying his rifle. Beat her up? She'd like to see him try.

She halted.

They weren't aboard the *Fearless* anymore. They weren't even in BA territory. There wasn't anything he could do to force her to take part in the mission.

He reached her in a few seconds. By the time she realized he wasn't going to stop, it was too late to get out of his way. He barreled into her, and they both hit the ground.

He was on top of her, his face centimeters from hers, wet from sweat and rain.

"What the fuck do you think you're doing, Ellis?!" he yelled.

She gave a mighty heave and pushed him off. Clambering to her feet, she exclaimed, "Get away from me! I'm not a Marine now. I resign."

He also stood up. They faced each other, panting.

"I told you once, you don't get to leave whenever you want. You don't get to choose your departure date!"

"Well I *am* choosing," said Taylan. "I'm staying here."

"Goddammit!" He leaned in, glaring at her.

She'd never seen him this angry, not even when he'd broken up the fight with her cabin mates on the *Valiant*.

"Don't you understand you're risking the future of the BA?! Perhaps the future of the planet?"

"You have Merlin and the others," she replied. "You don't need me."

"If I didn't need you I wouldn't have assigned you to the mission. I can't believe you're walking out. How can you be so irresponsible?"

"I'm not being irresponsible. It was irresponsible of me to enlist. I should never have left Ireland. I have to find my kids and get them away from here. Everyone's saying the EAC are going to invade soon. I have to get them to safety. I *am* being responsible. My first responsibility is to my family, not to you and *not* to the BA!"

She strode away from him. Her part in their conversation

was over. If he'd wanted an explanation for her behavior, he had it.

Somewhat to her surprise, he didn't come after her. She continued walking, not looking back.

"Taylan," he called out, "wait a minute."

She walked another few steps, and then halted, deciding to give him the chance for his say. He seemed to have given up on trying to force her to go back. She didn't want to part on bad terms. None of what had happened was his fault.

His voice sounded again, close to her ear. "Let's get out of this rain."

The front door of a nearby house had an awning overhanging the street. They moved beneath it.

"I thought it might be something like that," said the major. "The vids...They were of your children, right?"

She swallowed. "They were all I had of them, apart from this." She touched her necklace.

"And Wilson deleted them or something? I understand now." He looked out into the rain. "It's true. The EAC are about to make a push across the Irish Sea. All the signs are there. It's only a matter of days, we think. That's why it's vital we try to take the Dwyr out now. If we leave it too long, she's going to embark on another genocide."

Looking her in the eyes, he went on, "I picked you for the operation because of your relationship with Arthur. Merlin maintains we'll never do it without both of them, but I don't trust that alien as far as I could toss him at 10 Gs. I do trust Arthur, and I know he'll listen to you. I have to keep a grip on the situation, and I need you to achieve that. I didn't only bring you because you're handy in a fight."

"You're right not to trust Merlin," she replied. "He saw me leave, and he didn't try to stop me."

"No kidding? I'm not surprised, but I'm confused. He was

the one who woke me to tell me you'd gone. He must have waited a few minutes to give you a start."

"Maybe he just likes drama."

Wright considered for a moment, and then said, "If we succeed in assassinating the Dwyr, the invasion of Ireland won't happen, and you'll have all the time in the world to find your children."

"And if we fail, I could die, and they would lose their mother and their only hope of escaping the war. Not only that, killing the Dwyr might not put an end to the EAC. Someone else might step into her shoes, and everything will carry on as before. I'm sorry. I don't want to make things even harder for you, but I have to put my kids first."

"What if you do find them and manage to escape to the States? Do you think the EAC is going to stop at Ireland? You know that woman is intent on world domination. The States will be the next place she'll go. Where will you run to then?"

She didn't have an answer. All she knew was she had to keep them safe now. Whatever happened afterward, she would deal with it then.

"Okay," said Wright. "Look at it this way. In twenty-four hours the mission will be over, for better or worse. It's only going to take a day. Your children have been missing for months. Is a day going to make that much of a difference?"

He hadn't mentioned the possibility that she wouldn't survive it, but he did have a point. Wherever Kayla and Patrin were, they probably wouldn't be moving from there anytime soon.

"Taylan," he continued, "people are dying to create this chance for us. The BA is attacking the EAC in Jamaica and in space to distract the Dwyr from what's happening on her doorstep. I know you don't consider yourself a Marine, but if you won't do this for the Alliance, do it for those men and women. Don't make their sacrifice pointless."

She drew a trembling breath. Somewhere out there, her son and daughter were missing their mother, or maybe not. Kayla at least had probably begun to forget her.

She blinked back tears. "All right," she said. "One more day. Then I'm gone."

He gripped her shoulder. "One more day."

41

———

At the end of the jetty, a rusty old fishing boat bobbed on the choppy sea. The dawn was gray, the rain relentless, and now a gusting wind whipped it sporadically into Wright's face. His contact had said the crossing would take about four hours, which meant they would arrive in West BI mid-morning.

He checked the quay was empty, and then led the team out. Waves banged the boat into the wooden piles as they jumped aboard, timing their jumps so they didn't end up in the water, at risk of being crushed between the vessel and the jetty's edge.

The captain and mate were the only crew. As soon as the last person was aboard, the mate lifted the loops of rope that tied them to the land, and they sped out to sea.

Two hours later, when the rain had finally stopped, Wright spotted Taylan heaving her guts up over the side. He waited until she was finished before taking her some water.

"Thanks," she said, grabbing the bottle. She took a drink, swirled it around her mouth, and then spat into the sea. "I was never a good traveler. Not by boat or shuttle."

She sank to the deck and rested her back against the bulkhead, putting one knee up and stretching out her other leg. Wilson and the two other Marines were huddled in the stern, keeping out of the wind. Arthur stood in the bow, Merlin beside him, looking out toward the West BI coast. The ancient king's hair hadn't been cut for a while, and as it had continued to grow at a prodigious rate, the red-gold mane and beard now was doing a lot to help him look the part of an exiled monarch returning by sea to reclaim his kingdom.

Wright sat beside Taylan, out of sight of the others.

She looked exhausted. He felt a little guilty for persuading her to stay for the mission's duration. He didn't have any kids, but he could imagine the wrench she must be feeling now she was delaying her search. On the other hand, everything he'd told her was true. He was glad she'd listened to him.

"Tell me if I'm out of line," he said, "but is it okay if I ask what happened to your kids' dad? I take it he isn't with them."

She pulled a face. "He went to Old France to join the local resistance organization years ago. His family was French. I never heard from him after that. When he left, I didn't even know I was pregnant with Kayla."

"I'm sorry."

She shrugged. "We used to fight a lot. I don't think we would have lasted much longer. Maybe that was why he went. He could see the end was coming."

"Or maybe he just wanted to fight the EAC."

"Maybe. But if that was the case, he could have stayed in the BI. The writing was on the wall by then. The invasion was inevitable. As I see it, he abandoned us. Kayla never knew him, and Patrin barely remembered him. It's in the past now. No point in dwelling on it."

Their conversation faded to silence. Wright leaned his head back and closed his eyes. The boat's motion was making him queasy too. He tried to focus on the assassination plan, such as it was. Merlin only wanted their help to get into the

Dwyr's castle. Then he and Arthur would take it from there, he said.

Suddenly, soft lips touched his own. He jerked his eyes open.

Taylan pulled away. "Sorry, I didn't mean to startle you."

"Wh-what was that?"

"I thought...because you were asking about my ex... Sorry, I'm mixed up right now. I made a dumb mistake."

"It's okay. To be honest, I'm flattered. I didn't think you saw me in that way. I thought you liked Arthur."

"Arthur?! No. I mean, I like him, but not like that. He's too perfect."

"*Too* perfect? Meaning I'm not perfect?"

She laughed and shook her head but didn't answer.

"Nothing could happen between us anyway," he said, trying to smooth the awkwardness.

"Why not?"

"Because you're a corporal and I'm a major. According to BA regulations, fraternization between ranks is strictly prohibited."

"Does fraternization mean f—"

"Yes, that's what it means," he hastily interrupted, "among other things."

"Well, that's a stupid rule."

"No, it isn't. It's meant to prevent senior officers from using their position to coerce lower ranks into improper relationships. And it means you never have to send someone you love into battle."

She thought for a moment. "Okay, it's a pretty good rule. But I bet officers do end up sending people they love into battle."

"Yeah, I'm sure they do," he conceded.

"So you can't date anyone who isn't the same rank as you? That narrows the pool quite a bit. You must live like a monk."

Before he could answer, she cut in, saying, "Wait. Don't say it." She quickly rubbed the top of her head, messing up her hair, and then announced in a deep voice, "*My love life is not your concern, Corporal Ellis.*"

He chuckled. "Is that really how I sound?"

"Uh huh." She gave him a quick smile. "I was never great at being a Marine, was I?"

"Maybe not the best, but, believe me, I've seen worse. At least you can hit a target and take a man down without too much hassle. And tie your boots and wipe your nose." A bittersweet feeling settled on him. When the mission was over, he would be sad to see her go, but he would also be happy she might finally be reunited with her kids.

Assuming they both survived.

"If I'd been able to bring Abacha along," he mused, "we might have saved all the trouble on the dropship. Wilson was my fifth choice. When I get back, I'll see to it he's disciplined for what he did to your vids."

"I think Abacha's dead," said Taylan quietly.

"Why?" Wright asked. "He's in the *Valiant's* sick bay."

"He is?!"

"He was MIA after the battle, but they found him. The doc said he was unconscious and trapped under a dislodged duct. He's going to be okay."

"Phew! That's great news. I've been worried about him."

Wright was getting cold and stiff sitting on the deck. He got to his feet and leaned on the rail, watching the gray, heaving waves. A line on the horizon implied their journey would soon be over. The hard part would come next.

"You know what, Ellis?" he said.

She looked up. "What?"

"You could act a *tad* more disappointed about the no-fraternization rule."

THE FISHING BOAT captain couldn't risk taking them into a West BI port. Instead, he piloted the boat as close to the land as he dared in a small, sandy cove.

"That's it," he said. "Any closer and I'll beach her. You'll have to wade to shore from here. I'll be back here at dawn tomorrow, and I'll wait an hour. No longer."

Wright jumped into the sea first, his rifle and pack held over his head. He was chest deep in icy water that seemed to suck the air from his lungs. A wave crashed into him, propelling him toward the shoreline. As he waded forward, he heard the splashes of the rest of the team jumping in. He reached the beach and walked up to the high tide mark. When he turned to assess the others' progress, Arthur was emerging from the churning water like a sea god.

Shivering with cold, they quickly changed into dry clothes, and then climbed the path up the side of the cliff. At the top, Kala Orr's castle was clearly visible in the distance. It was far too early to set out for it. They would have to find a place to hide and wait out the day.

42

Morgan had returned from walking the castle grounds. She went out there every morning, for exercise or to experience being outdoors after her centuries of incarceration, Kala supposed. A chill permeated the atmosphere as she entered the dining room. Kala had been too slow to send Perran away from the lunch table, and now she would have to endure Morgan's manipulation of her boy. She was sure the woman was influencing his young mind. She'd said curious and flexible minds were the easiest to control, and Perran had always been a curious child.

"The sky has cleared," said Morgan. "What do you say we take a trip to the harbor this afternoon? I'd like to see where the ceremony is to take place."

"Can I come too?" Perran asked.

"No. You have lessons, remember?"

"I'm sure missing a few hours of classes won't make any difference," Morgan said. "Perran should be involved in the planning, and he should attend. He will succeed you one day. It's important he sees these things first hand."

"What things?" Perran's eyes grew wide with excitement. "What's going to happen?"

"He's too young," Kala protested. "He won't understand, and he might be frightened."

"He will understand through experience, and then he'll lose his fear."

Kala picked up her napkin from her lap, carefully folded it, and put it down next to her plate. "If you insist." She gave Perran a tight smile. "If you're coming with us, hadn't you better go and get ready?"

"Yes!" He bounded from the table and ran out of the room.

The invasion of Ireland would begin in five days' time. Most of Kala's warships were at or near harbors along the west coast of the BI. Her soldiers were also arriving at the ports and preparing to embark. And at her military airfields, bombers and fighter planes were being put through maintenance checks.

It was at the harbor near her castle that the largest naval force had gathered, and it was here she would hold the ceremony to launch the invasion. A spectacle of a special kind was required. Ritual and custom were glues that helped to hold her empire together, and she couldn't afford to disappoint her people. At the same time, she resented Morgan's interference with her plans, especially involving Perran in them.

"Kala," Morgan said. Her expression had turned serious as Perran left. "Have you managed to discover any more information about the person who burned you?"

"No, not yet. My main source of BA intel was based in Jamaica, and since the country has fallen, my supply has been cut off. I've been trying to infiltrate their space fleet. I can sometimes turn new recruits before they leave for space, but recruits' access to useful intelligence is limited. I need someone higher up the ranks, but they're hard to reach."

"This person belongs to the space fleet?"

"Yes, I'm fairly certain of it."

"Then perhaps the problem isn't so urgent. You said Arthur is with them too?"

"He has been all along, as I understand it. He left aboard one of their corvettes."

"Hm. I may be worrying unnecessarily."

"What's your concern? I know you've explained in the past, but I could never remember clearly after my visits."

Morgan paused, as if weighing up how much to tell her. "You and Perran are of my line, which means you have inherited a measure of invulnerability from me. It's more complicated, but that's what is relevant here. Arthur has been given the ability to overcome your invulnerability. That is why he was preserved after the battle where he killed Mordred and I was imprisoned, and that is why it was important that you found him. But, from what I can tell, it was not Arthur who hurt you."

"How do you know?"

Morgan smiled condescendingly. "Arthur wouldn't have arrived looking like a BA soldier. Whoever it was who burned you, it's someone else. I suspect this person is a descendant of someone else who lived at the same time as Arthur, and who was imbued with a similar ability to hurt me and Mordred. He's inherited it in the way you inherited your protection from harm."

"Who gave them this power?"

"My enemy." Her expression turned dark as a thunder cloud.

Kala became wary of pressuring her too much and angering her.

"Does the person I'm looking for know only he and Arthur can hurt me?"

"It's impossible to say."

"I think he must. It's too much of a coincidence it was he out of all the soldiers who chased me when I escaped my house in Jamaica."

"In this matter, there are no coincidences."

Perran bounced into the room, his cheeks flushed. He'd put on his jacket. "Are we going now?"

"I'm ready," Morgan replied. "Are you, Kala?"

"It'll only take me a minute." She rose from the table.

Her short conversation with Morgan had created more questions than it had answered. Why wouldn't Arthur wear a BA soldier's armor? What was it that gave her invulnerability? If she was descended from Morgan, did that mean she wasn't entirely human herself? How could she protect herself and Perran from Arthur and the other man?

Who was Morgan's enemy?

∾

PRIDE AND PLEASURE swelled in Kala's heart as she regarded the flotilla of warships awaiting her order to set sail for Ireland. In truth, many of them would mainly be transporting troops to land. She didn't anticipate breaking through the BA's pathetic naval defenses would take much effort.

Her vantage point on a specially built platform gave her a wide view of the harbor and out to sea. Her gaze dwelt particularly long on the pride of her fleet, *Hecate*. The amphibious assault ship had been seized in the battle for the BI and repaired. The BA's name for her had been *Princess Royal*, but Kala had insisted on changing it, against the advice of her naval officers. They claimed it was bad luck to give a ship a new name, but she'd been determined to do it. She was damned if she was going to have a vessel named after the odious BI aristocracy in her fleet.

Beyond the foot of the platform, the quayside spread out widely. There was plenty of space for the crowd that would witness the ceremony. Morgan had impressed upon her the need for something a level up from the traditional smashing of a bottle of champagne, followed by a wild, no-holds-barred celebration. Kala had agreed to her suggestion, but she hadn't picked a subject yet.

Perran grabbed the railing excitedly and leaned out over it.

"Careful, dear," she said, gently touching his head.

Morgan stood on her other side. "It will be magnificent," she murmured.

43

All the windows in the castle were dark except one, high in a tower. A pair of guards had just passed by, which meant they had at least a few minutes to scale the perimeter fence and slip inside.

Dwyr Orr's security was slack. A patrol of armed guards seemed to be all she had in place. They'd seen one of the guards touch the fence, so it clearly wasn't electrified. Wright guessed the BA's strategy of attacking the EAC on two fronts had worked. The Dwyr's attention was elsewhere than her own backyard. Either that, or the woman was stupidly arrogant.

"We go in one minute," he said. "Remember," he added to his Marines, "stick to Merlin and Arthur. You're here to protect them at any cost."

Exactly what the alien's plan was, he still hadn't explained. All Wright knew was that it involved killing Kala Orr.

All were dressed in black including black woolen hats. They'd smeared their exposed areas with black skin paint. The Marines carried their pulse rifles while Arthur only had a knife. Merlin was unarmed. Quietly, they prepared to leave the patch of woodland where they'd been since darkness fell, waiting for the castle inhabitants to go to sleep.

At Wright's signal, they slipped out from their cover and ran softly, keeping low, to the fence. Ellis was the first to reach it and climb up and over, followed by Wilson. The two other Marines, Maynard and Bates, did the same. Wright waited for Merlin to scale the bars too. He wanted to make sure everyone was inside before he entered the grounds too.

But Merlin hesitated, and Arthur didn't leave his side.

"Hurry," said Wright. "More guards will be coming soon. Do you need a hand getting over?"

"There's something wrong," said Merlin.

"What?" The major looked around, trying to find the source of the alien's problem.

"Something…" Merlin held out a hand toward the fence. "There's a barrier."

"*There's a freaking fence!*" Wright hissed. He added, more calmly, "You have to climb over it if you're going to assassinate the Dwyr."

"I can't pass it. *She's* been here and created a boundary. She must have been released. We're too late."

"Who's been released? Kala Orr?"

"No, someone else. I'm sorry. You have to call off the mission."

"I can't call it off! Tens of thousands of BA military are engaged in battle right now to give us this chance. We have to see it through."

"No. Not like this. It has to happen another way, at a later time. I'm telling you, I cannot pass the boundary."

"There is no other way!" Wright exclaimed, struggling to keep his tone low.

"What's happening, Major?" Wilson asked quietly from the other side of the fence.

"Wait," he replied. He turned to Arthur. "Are you staying here with Merlin or coming with me?"

The king said gravely, "If Merlin says we must do it another way, then that's what we must do."

"We won't get a better opportunity than this," Wright argued. He suspected Merlin was up to something. His talk of boundaries and a nameless woman who'd been released made no sense. "We're going ahead. Are you coming or not?"

"I cannot," said Merlin.

Arthur didn't reply.

They were out of time. Wright began to climb the fence.

"You're making a mistake," said Merlin.

The major dropped to the ground. "We're on our own," he told the others. "Merlin and Arthur backed out."

"What?!" whispered Ellis. "Why?"

"I honestly don't know. But we're going to do this without them. Let's go."

They ran across the empty sward surrounding the castle.

Before they were even ten meters from the fence, pulse fire burst from the castle windows. Soldiers poured from the doors and seemed to rise right out of the ground. They must have been waiting in trenches, Wright guessed, invisible from a distance.

Dwyr Orr was *not* slack about her security.

"Retreat!" he yelled. "Get back!" He began to fire, laying down cover for the others, but it was hopeless. They were vastly outnumbered and not even wearing armor.

Maynard fell.

Wright grabbed him and began hauling him one-handed while continuing to fire. Ellis grabbed his other shoulder to help.

Wilson hit the ground next.

"Leave me," Maynard gasped. "Run." Both his legs had taken a hit.

"No way," said Wright. If they could just get him to the fence... It was hopeless. Merlin had been right.

Maynard was still aiming and firing as he was pulled backward. The leading EAC soldier toppled face downward as he was hit.

"Pick him up," shouted Ellis, releasing Maynard and kneeling on one knee to aim at the approaching troops. "I'll cover you."

But as Wright bent down to heft the Marine onto his shoulder, Maynard took another hit. He collapsed, lifeless. Wilson was also unmoving.

A pulse bolt flashed past Wright's head. "We're giving away our positions by firing," he said to Ellis. "We have to get out of here."

They ran.

Bates had made it to the fence. Wright saw him drop down the other side and his shadowy figure sprint for the trees.

A scream came from behind. Ellis had been hit. He ran back. Like Maynard, she'd been hit in the thighs. He stooped and got his shoulder under her midriff before lifting her up. They were only a few steps from the fence. When he reached it, Arthur was already there and leaning over the top, ready to take Ellis. He ported her over while Wright scaled the bars. By the time he touched ground, Arthur was on his way toward the woodland.

The pulse fire from behind continued as he sped to the cover of the vegetation. Underneath the trees, the noise of his companions crashing through the undergrowth was loud. They would have to run far and fast to escape the EAC soldiers who would be sent out to find them.

It was nearing dawn before Wright judged it was safe to stop. They'd come many kilometers from Dwyr Orr's abode, trekking fast across the hilly landscape, walking in streams and across stony ground to avoid leaving a trail in the damp earth. Eventually, they'd come to a place that seemed deserted, and there was no sign of pursuit. He didn't have much of an idea where they were except that they'd come inland. The Dwyr would predict they would go to the coast to escape to Ireland, so he'd gone the opposite way. He hoped the fisherman who'd brought them to West BI would spot the searching soldiers in time and stay away.

Along the way, they'd briefly halted at Merlin's request. Wright still couldn't quite believe what the alien had done. He'd seen Merlin repair the damaged minds of the men and women of the *Fearless*, but he'd never imagined what else he could do.

He'd asked Arthur to lay Ellis on the ground. He'd knelt beside her and put his hands on her wounds, and he'd closed his eyes. Within less than a minute, miraculously, he healed her burned skin.

With the EAC on their heels, there had been no time for wonder at the alien's feat. They'd run on, Arthur now unburdened.

A brook ran down from the hills. They washed the black skin paint from their hands and faces. All they had was three pulse rifles and Arthur's knife. They'd left their packs behind in the woods. Wright squatted at the water's edge, trying to figure out their next move. It would probably be best to wait for dark, and then try to work their way back to the coast. Their only hope lay in getting back to Ireland somehow. He couldn't risk trying to contact BA forces via his comm implant while in EAC territory. He could give away their position.

He focused hard on finding a solution to their plight. He

didn't want to think about what a disaster the mission had turned into, or the deaths of Maynard and Wilson.

Merlin stepped on stones to cross the brook and stood on the opposite bank, surveying the landscape. "I see. It makes sense now."

"What makes sense?" Wright asked. He rose to his feet. "Did you know the Dwyr had a whole platoon waiting for us? Is that what your 'boundary' bullshit was about?" He knew his accusation was probably unfair, but he still harbored deep suspicions about the alien's motives.

"I wasn't lying," Merlin replied haughtily. "I told you that making the assassination attempt last night was a mistake, but you ignored me. If you're looking for someone to blame, you don't have to look any farther than yourself."

"You're the one who said we could do this! The whole operation was your idea. The BA military heads would never have agreed to such a hare-brained scheme if you hadn't suggested it. We were lucky to get away with our lives. If the EAC troops had waited *one* more minute before springing their trap it would have been over for all of us. Now two men are dead and we're lost behind enemy lines with no easy way of getting out of here."

"Don't give up so easily. We can do this. I just have to figure out how. It isn't easy, you know. I admit the barrier was a surprise. I'm acting against a force I thought I'd neutralized." He looked at the hills again. The sun was beginning to edge over a distant summit. "I have to read the signs and interpret them correctly."

More gobbledygook.

"Well if you can find a sign that points us toward the coast," said Wright, "that'd be great."

Merlin scowled at him and stepped over the stream again. He walked to Arthur's side and began to talk to him in his own language.

Taylan arrived in Merlin's place. "I want to check you're going to keep to our agreement."

Wright sighed. "What agreement's that?"

"One more day, you said. So…" she squinted at the rising sun "…I guess I'm no longer a Marine."

He sighed. "Yeah, Corporal Ellis, you have an honorable discharge. Good luck with your new life in enemy territory."

"It might be enemy territory to you. To me, it's home."

"Of course it is! I'd forgotten. I don't suppose you know where we are?"

"I'm not sure. This place does look familiar, but I could be imagining it."

"Major," Bates called out. He was sitting on a flat stone a few meters from them. When Wright looked at him, he nodded toward Merlin and Arthur, who were walking away.

"Hey," yelled Wright. "Where are you going?"

"We have to get some things of mine," Arthur replied. "We'll be back soon."

44

———————

Taylan trudged behind Arthur and Merlin for a while before they finally noticed her and waited for her to catch up. Wright had asked her to go after them, citing her friendship with Arthur as the reason. She suspected it was also because he thought she was the least tired of all of them. It was true that Arthur had carried her all the way through the woods until they stopped so Merlin could heal her legs.

As she walked alongside them, she grimaced at the memory of the alien's touch. The sensation had been weird and uncomfortable. It had taken away the terrible pain of her wounds, yet she half-wished she'd been able to receive regular treatment. Who knew what Merlin had done to her?

"So where are we going?" she asked.

Arthur replied, "To retrieve my—"

"I know we're going to get your things. But where are they?"

And how could they possibly still be there after three and a half thousand years?

"I don't recall the name of the place," said Merlin, "but I

believe it's near here. I'm not certain. Landscapes change over time."

The hills couldn't have changed *that* much, Taylan thought. As she looked about, the familiarity she'd mentioned to Wright grew. She'd been here before, maybe as a child.

"I remember now!" she blurted as it came to her. "I know where we are. We're in the Preseli Hills. Carn Menyn, Foel Drygarn, and Y Frenni. I climbed them all when I was a teenager."

"You know this area?" Merlin asked. "Then maybe you can help. Do you remember a small, ancient chapel somewhere hereabouts?"

"A little church? Not off the top of my head, but I'll think about it."

If she could have conjured a church right there and then, she would have done it. She hadn't slept for two nights or eaten for a day, and they must have run twenty kilometers cross country. She was about to drop. Silently cursing Wright and his request—she wasn't a Marine anymore!—she trudged onward.

That moment on the boat when she'd kissed him had been embarrassing, but they seemed to be over it. What had she been thinking? He'd looked cute sitting there with his eyes closed and that stupid tuft of hair sticking up. And she'd been so sad about her kids. She'd screwed up, but it wasn't the end of the world.

Her subconscious must have been working on Merlin's question because the image of a derelict chapel popped into her mind. It had been little more than old stone walls. The roof must have caved in long ago. Where had it been?

"Stop," she said. "I think I might know the place you're looking for. Wait here." They were in a cleft between two hills. Picking the highest one, she wearily climbed to the top. Once she was up there, the wind hit her hard. Holding her hair away from her face with one hand, she scanned the surroundings.

Memories of her holiday returned to her. Dad and her mother bickering, though not seriously. It had been more of a habit than anything with them. Long days spent tramping up and down, up and down, until she'd thought her legs couldn't take it anymore—

There it was!

She'd spied a gray wall, almost lost among vegetation grown wild. When she'd visited the church, the locals had kept the place neat and tidy for tourists. But, naturally, that had all stopped after the EAC took over and the only way to survive was to hide.

"I found it!" she shouted down to Arthur and Merlin, and pointed.

She ran down the hill, and her companions began to walk in the direction she'd indicated.

She halted in horror. Men and women were emerging from hidden places in the hillsides and running toward them. As she went to shout a warning, someone flew into her from behind and grabbed her waist. She overbalanced, and they both tumbled down the slope, over and over, locked together. They reached the bottom and began to slow down. Taylan swung her fists at the man and kicked him, trying to break free.

They struggled on the ground. She got on top of him, pinning him with her knees, and clasped his throat in both hands. Shouts were coming from behind her. The man's eyes were popping and his face was turning red. She squeezed tighter. She might not have been able to kill Dwyr Orr, but at least there was one EAC invader who was going to die today.

Then she realized the shouts she was hearing from Arthur and Merlin's attackers were in her mother tongue.

Horrified, she snatched her hands from the man's throat.

"Wyt ti'n Gymraeg?" she asked.

Are you Welsh?

He nodded.

She leapt up. "I'm so sorry!"

He rubbed his throat, but didn't seem able to answer.

She spun around. Merlin and Arthur were standing back-to-back. Arthur had his knife out. One of the attackers was on the ground, clasping a bloody leg. The others encircled her companions.

She yelled in Welsh and waved her arms. "Hey, we're friends! Not EAC. We're not EAC!"

THE RESISTANCE GROUP had been on their tails ever since they'd entered the hills. Wary of the pulse rifles the Marines carried, they'd been waiting for the right moment to attack. Splitting up had been the catalyst. Wright and Bates were already captured, back down the track.

Without their uniforms to prove their affiliation, none of the group had believed Wright and Bates when they'd said they were from the BA, but Taylan's native Welsh convinced them. The captives were set free, and both sides apologized for the damage they'd inflicted on the other.

"Where are you heading?" asked a woman who seemed to be the leader of the group.

"The chapel over the hill," Taylan replied. It felt good to speak her first language after so long. "My friend, Arthur, has to collect some things from it."

"St. Martin's? There's nothing there but old stones, but I'll take you to it. My name is Angharad, by the way."

Taylan introduced herself, and then told Merlin and Arthur to follow them. Wright and Bates stayed behind. As they walked, she and Angharad did the usual thing of comparing localities and families. Taylan found it surreal. It was like she was out for a picnic with some new acquaintances.

The crumbling walls of the church appeared in the

distance. Taylan also couldn't imagine Arthur would find anything, but she knew Merlin wouldn't give up until they went and looked.

They had to beat down overgrown weeds and shrubs to reach the doorway. Vegetation was growing thickly inside, too, heading for the open sky above.

"This is it!" Merlin exclaimed. "This is the place." He forced his way through the greenery to the stone altar and then around it to the other side, where the priest would stand. "Arthur, come here."

Curiosity driving her, Taylan followed her large friend, benefiting from the crushing effect of his passage on the plant life. Angharad came with her.

The far side of the altar was constructed from blocks of cut stone, the gaps between them filled with mortar. Merlin asked for Arthur's knife. He slipped the blade between the blocks, freeing the crumbling remains. It was impossible to pull the stones out, so he pushed on one near the top. It didn't move.

He asked Arthur if he could kick the wall in.

It only took a couple of tries to dislodge a stone. It fell into the hollow center, and then the entire altar quickly followed, collapsing in a cloud of dust.

Everyone had jumped backward to avoid the falling stones. Merlin waved the dust away and leaned over the rubble to peer into it.

"They're here! They're still here! Arthur, help me lift the stones away."

Taylan caught a glimpse of metal. Even more remarkable than the fact that whatever Merlin had sealed in the altar all those years ago had never been found and removed, was the shine that came from it.

Arthur pulled it out and wiped off the dust. It was a helmet. Conical, with cheek and nose guards and a flap that extended to cover the neck, it looked as fresh as the day it had been made. But that wasn't all. Merlin was now picking up something else—chainmail, as long and wide as needed to fit Arthur's size, every link reflecting the sunlight.

He put it down before reaching deep into the rubble again. "I can't get it out. We need to move some more stones."

Taylan and Angharad helped to lift blocks from the pile. Gradually, they revealed a long blade.

Arthur knelt down, grabbed the hilt, and drew it out. He climbed to his feet and grasped the hilt with his other hand too. Standing with the point on the ground, the sword reached the middle of his chest.

The expression of someone meeting an old friend after long years spent apart came over his face.

45

Kala watched impassively as the BA soldier writhed and screamed. The man torturing him wasn't a professional. Up until then, she'd had no need for one. The seduction of her belief system was sufficient to persuade her people to obey and to tattle on friends and family who broke her laws. But things were moving to a new level.

She enlisted the services of the castle's butcher to carry out the task, and it had been a good decision. He'd performed well. He knew which parts of a body were vital to survival and which were most sensitive to pain.

"That's enough for now," she said.

The torturer put down his knife and the soldier's screams ceased. He only panted and moaned.

It was fortunate the soldier's comrades had left him behind. He was the solution to her quandary over who to use for the ceremony—providing he remained alive just one more day. He'd held out all this time, but she had a feeling he was about to crack. She might still learn some useful information.

"Give him some water and something to eat. Then ask him the questions again."

She leaned close to the man's bloody, sweating face. His eyes drooped and his mouth sagged, but she knew he was listening. "You can make this stop. Tell me who it was who hurt me. You know his name. He must be famous in the BA. Tell me his name and all you know about him, and you won't have to endure any more pain."

No answer came.

Straightening up, she realized she'd stepped in the man's blood, puddled on the stone flags of his cell. Wrinkling her nose, she moved away. "Wait one hour. Then start again."

The guard opened the door, and she stepped into the passage. Someone was approaching from the end. In the underground darkness, lit by torches, she couldn't make the person out at first. Then he walked into a pool of light.

"Jon," she said as the guard closed the cell door. "What are you doing here?"

The old man looked from the guard to her and replied, "Can I speak to you in private, Kala?"

They walked together to the end of the passage, where stone steps spiraled upward to the ground floor. No one else was about.

"You must call me Dwyr in front of others," Kala said. "If you're overly familiar they'll lose respect for me."

Jon grimaced. "What about *my* respect? Do you care about that anymore?"

"Of course I care. What do you mean?"

He said softly, "I heard about what you're doing in there." He indicated down the passage with his gray, bushy eyebrows. "I didn't believe the rumors, so I came to see for myself. I didn't even need to see. I heard all I needed to know. You've gone to some excesses in the past, Kala Orr, but this takes the biscuit."

She stiffened. "I wasn't aware I needed your permission to govern my realm."

"But you aren't governing. You're turning into a tyrant. Did the woman you released from the mine put this idea in your head? I hope so. I hope you didn't think it up all by yourself."

Morgan *had* made the suggestion that the BA soldier might be the key to finding out who had burned her. She hadn't explicitly mentioned torture, but it was the obvious inference. However, Kala wasn't going to tell Jon that. Morgan regularly undermined her authority. She needed to cling to her sense of control.

"Everything that happens in my domain is by my decree and my decree only. I'm sorry if you find what I'm doing distasteful, but I neither asked for nor want your opinion. Stick to your potions and experiments, Jon, and leave the management of EAC affairs to me."

She swept past him and mounted the stairs.

"Kala," Jon called out. "Kala, listen to me. You don't have to behave like this."

His voice faded as she reached the top of the staircase and walked into the main hall.

WHEN SHE AWOKE the following morning, her stomach fluttered with uncharacteristic nervousness. She wasn't sure why she felt apprehensive. She'd been looking forward to this day for so long, and now it was finally here. She should be happy, but instead she was filled with doubts.

What if something went wrong with the ceremony?

What if Morgan did or said something that would lower her status in the eyes of her people?

What if Perran was upset by what he saw?

Trying to push her fears to one side, she climbed out of bed. A servant had already been in her room while she slept to light a fire in the grate. The flames sputtered and spat fitfully as the fire struggled to get going. She picked up the poker and drove it into the coals, twisting and thrusting it to allow some air in. It didn't make any difference.

She gave up and sat on the rug in her nightdress, sudden apathy filling her. When she'd been a street rat in Berline, she would have given anything to live the life she was currently leading. In fact, she would have given anything just for the chance to sit on a rich rug in her own room in front of a fire. But somehow, everything had started to feel sour and meaningless.

It didn't take much thinking to link the change in her feelings about her life to the moment she'd released Morgan from imprisonment. Ever since then, she'd battled to maintain her grip on her position and power. But it was more than that. She never seemed to feel any positive emotions while she was in Morgan's company. Desire, yearning, dissatisfaction, jealousy, anger, yes. All these and more. But her love for Perran had been turned into fear of losing him; her pleasure from gaining new knowledge had become frustration that she didn't know more; and the triumph she'd felt about the adulation of her people had been transformed to dread that she might lose it to someone else.

The creature from the mine sucked away the joy of living wherever she went. And there could be no end to her existence. She didn't age, and she couldn't be hurt.

Except maybe she could.

She'd said she had an enemy. Who was it? Not Arthur or the other person Kala sought. Someone else. If she could expose Morgan to her enemy, that might be the end of her problems. But how to find him or her? Morgan certainly wouldn't reveal the name. Perhaps the stories from her past might shed some light.

It wouldn't hurt to look.

Feeling better, Kala went to call for someone to help her wash and dress. Donning the ceremonial robes took time, and everything had to be perfect.

While she was waiting for a servant to arrive, she heard shouts and cries coming from outside. She walked to the window and pulled back the heavy curtains. The sky was clear and the sunlight strong. She blinked as her eyes grew accustomed to the brightness.

Below, on the castle green, people were yelling and wailing. Some were running into the castle, but most stood in a group, pointing at something.

She followed the direction of their fingers with her gaze. They were looking at an open window in a tower with a bundle of rags hanging from it. Confused, she squinted at the window, trying to figure out what everyone seemed so dismayed about.

Then she recognized the white hair and beard of an old man.

The bundle of rags was a human being, swinging gently by his neck like a rag doll, wearing an ancient nightshirt. One of his feet was stuffed into a fluffy slipper. The other was bare.

46

———

"We could certainly use your help, if you're offering," said Angharad, her eyes twinkling.

She was in her late fifties or early sixties, Wright guessed. About the same age as Colbourn, but the similarities ended there. Except maybe for her caginess. It had taken him days to winkle the plans of the West BI Resistance from her. Even now, he didn't think she'd told him half of their arrangements.

He understood her reluctance. It was conceivable that Arthur, Merlin, Bates, Ellis and he were EAC spies. They made a strange crew if that were the case, but it wasn't impossible.

"I am offering," he replied. "Anything we can do, we'll do it. Except maybe for Arthur and Merlin. They seem to be making their own arrangements."

The older woman bit her lip. "Let me think about it."

The Resistance in that area of West BI were housed literally inside a hill. A boulder stood at the entrance with a narrow gap behind it. Unless you knew it was there, you would never find it. They spent their days in the damp, earthy interior and came out at night to steal sheep, forage in the fields, or, if food was especially scarce, steal from the nearby town that had been taken over by the EAC.

Their existence so long after the enemy invasion was a testament to their caution and resourcefulness. And now their patience was about to pay off. Ever since the Dwyr had moved into the castle by the coast, they'd been watching EAC movements. It wasn't too hard, Angharad had said, to pretend to be a member of the cult. They didn't look different from the people of the BI. The most intrepid among the Resistance had mixed with townsfolk and listened to the news and gossip. Some had even gone as far as to pretend to be workers at the military sites. It was risky. The biggest giveaway was their accent, so they worked hard to sound like the invaders.

Along with other groups ranging up and down the coast, they'd learned of the preparations to attack Ireland, and, in conference with those groups, they'd organized a range of acts of sabotage.

That was about as much as Wright knew. That, and the fact that the invasion would be launched tomorrow after a ceremony at the port nearest the castle.

While Angharad was pondering over what roles he, Ellis, and Bates could play in thwarting Dwyr Orr's latest genocide attempt, he decided to slip out and get some fresh air. It was fairly safe to wander the hills at night, the Resistance members said. The area had gained a reputation among the local EAC for being dangerous, as so many of them who entered it were never seen again.

He emerged onto the stony ground in front of the hideaway. The sky was clear for a change. The rain rarely seemed to stop in that part of the world. The moon was up, making it easy to see his way as he walked down the remainder of the slope to the bottom of the hill. Not paying too much attention to where he went, he set off along the dip.

As well as concern about doing all he could to foil the

launch of the invasion tomorrow, he was also bothered by worries about how he would get everyone back to Ireland. At the forefront of his thoughts, however, as she'd been ever since that moment on the boat, was Taylan Ellis.

He couldn't get the memory of those soft lips on his out of his mind. Her joke that he lived like a monk wasn't too far from the truth. He'd accepted long ago that he had to choose between his personal life and his job, and he'd thought he'd made peace with his decision to choose the latter. But Ellis had thrown him into turmoil, and he didn't think it was only his natural inclinations as a healthy man that were driving his disturbed state of mind.

The woman was irritating as all hell as a Marine, but as a person, he liked her. She was brave, smart, loyal, and funny, and, confusingly, he found her disregard for authority refreshing.

He'd begun to dread the day he would return to the *Fearless* or the *Valiant*, or wherever the Royal Marines sent him, leaving her to search for her children. The chances they would ever meet again were slim.

His heart heavy, he began to take more notice of his surroundings. He must have been wandering for half an hour. The shadowy hills still surrounded him under a star-filled sky. He was reminded of the last time he'd been in West BI when he'd taken Arthur from the cave in the mountain and carried an injured Ellis back to the *Daisy*.

But here there was no snow on the ground. It was late spring, and the night air was warm.

He'd arrived at the place where Arthur and Merlin had recovered the artifacts the alien had hidden so long ago. The chapel walls were black against the glittering sky.

A figure stood in the doorway, his back toward Wright, looking into the building.

Wright crept forward a few paces until he realized he was

looking at Merlin. He walked up to him, hoping to get a better handle on what he had planned. He'd said he hadn't given up on his scheme to assassinate the Dwyr.

When he reached Merlin, the alien put a finger to his lips and nodded toward the inside of the chapel. Wright looked in.

A space had been cleared in the vegetation in front of the debris from the altar, and Arthur was kneeling in it. The bright moonlight illuminated the altar's remains, turning them into a pile of broken silver. For the first time, Wright noticed a cross on the chapel wall.

Arthur knelt on one knee, his other raised. In his right hand he held his sword hilt, the long blade stretching tall. His other hand was clasped to his chest, and his shaggy head was bowed.

"What's he doing?" Wright whispered.

Merlin raised his eyebrows before replying equally quietly, "Praying, of course."

Praying?

Wright was not religious and in all his life he hadn't encountered many strong believers. The notion of true faith in a deity was strange to him, though he understood in Arthur's time such beliefs were common and deeply held.

"What's he praying for?" he asked. He guessed the ancient king was hoping for divine help at Dwyr Orr's ceremony.

"Forgiveness."

Wright frowned. He couldn't imagine Arthur doing *anything* that required forgiving. "For what?"

"Not for what he's done. For what he's about to do. He's asking forgiveness for the murders he will commit tomorrow."

47

———

Taylan reached the port before dawn, yet the crowd was already gathering. Small groups dotted the wide quay where Dwyr Orr's ceremony would take place, and more people were arriving, walking in from the surrounding streets, some carrying young children, others supporting an elderly relative. By the time the ceremony started, the place would be packed. Ropes had been strung along the harbor wall, probably to prevent accidental falls into the water.

A huge ship loomed tall at the quayside, some kind of amphibious craft. The harbor was huge, but the vessel took up most of the available space, a mountain of gray steel. Its main deck stood high out of the water, and heli rotor blades peeked over the edge.

When Angharad had suggested the Marines help the Resistance with an attack on the ship, Taylan hadn't understood the ambition of the plan. She kinda wished she was working with Wright and Bates. She knew that, whatever happened, after today she would never see Major Wright again, but if this was going to be the last day they both spent alive, she would have liked to spend it with him.

Except Merlin had insisted she had to help Arthur assassinate the Dwyr. They were tied, he'd said, by ancestral and arcane links. It was something to do with one of her forebears, a knight of his table, whose blood she carried. He hadn't explained how he knew or exactly what it meant. She wondered if the alien was making it all up. Ever since he'd arrived, she'd had the sense he was playing with all of them.

Whatever.

Wright had agreed it made sense for her and Arthur to handle the hit on the Dwyr. So here she was, dressed as an EAC guard in a stolen uniform, courtesy of the Resistance, and carrying a similarly purloined pulse rifle. The idea was, when an opportune moment came, she would shoot Dwyr Orr. Angharad had said they would have a boat waiting for her and Arthur when the deed was done. Escaping from the mob of outraged cult followers would be the hard part.

"You," said a voice.

An EAC soldier had come up behind her. From the double sunburst on his uniform shoulder, she guessed he was an officer.

"What are you doing here?"

Taylan didn't answer. If she spoke, her accent might give her away.

"Get over there, on the route marker."

She nodded and began to move toward a line chalked on the ground.

"What's up with you?" barked the officer. "That's no way to respond to an order."

She mentally rolled her eyes. It was just her luck to encounter an EAC version of Major Wright. She put a hand to her throat and said hoarsely, "Sorry, sir. Got a bad cold."

"That's no excuse. Now go and do your job."

She supposed her job was to keep back the crowd when the Dwyr's vehicle arrived. The platform where she would stand was already constructed. Taylan began figuring out the lines of sight. If she was to shoot the Dwyr and get away alive, she would need to slip through the crowd and fire from near the harbor's edge.

Arthur would make an attempt on the leader's life too, but it wasn't clear how. He couldn't fire a pulse rifle, and if he tried approaching with that massive sword of his, he wouldn't get two meters before he was taken down.

She was worried about him. She'd tried to spend more time with him and extract him from Merlin's influence but it was impossible. The two were thicker than thieves, especially since they'd found Arthur's sword and battle dress. And the king had changed. He'd become distant and...regal, as if he were reverting to the man he'd been before.

While Taylan had been musing, the crowd had grown bigger. Workmen came to string ropes along each side of the marked route. More guards arrived to keep the people back. Hawkers pushed carts selling snacks and drinks, and women dressed in sweeping, decorative robes approached groups and individuals to talk to them. At first, Taylan thought the women were prostitutes, but after watching their activities she realized they were fortune tellers. How predictable it was that EAC followers would believe a random stranger could tell them their future.

THE CROWD SURGED and heaved behind Taylan, forcing her into the rope barrier. It was nearly noon. The ceremony was due to begin not long after. A rush of adrenaline began to replace the tiredness from her long wait.

Whatever the outcome, it would all be over soon.

Holding her rifle across her chest, she pushed into the people nearest her, driving them back. They were jammed in with little room to move. From where she was standing all the way to the harbor's edge, she could see nothing but heads. How had no one fallen in the water yet? Or maybe they had, and nobody cared. The faces around her looked feverish and delirious. Kala Orr's people seemed to be working themselves up, ready to release a burst of frenzied adulation when their cult leader arrived.

The hum of chatter began to rise. Excitement surged. The vehicle bringing the Dwyr had been spotted. Bodies thrust against Taylan, crushing her. She curbed her urge to yell at them, only locking her knees and leaning in hard to resist the pressure.

But then, by itself, the pressure began to ease. A hush settled on the place, and the people became still. Eyes widened and mouths fell into wide gapes. She heard the whine of an approaching vehicle.

Dwyr Orr was here.

Taylan turned around.

The approach route for the EAC leader's conveyance curved, so at first she could only see the top half of the vehicle. Dwyr Orr stood at the front, wearing the strangest costume Taylan had ever seen. Two great horns draped with cloth stuck out above her head, and her face was wrapped in another cloth, covering her hair. Elaborate robes fell from her shoulders to her feet, decorated in symbols. She held both her arms out in front of her in a welcoming gesture.

What a nutcase.

Another woman, wearing a long, dark dress and smaller and slighter, stood to one side and a little behind her. A young boy stood on her other side. There were more people behind them, but Taylan couldn't make them out.

She had a clear line of sight from her position to the Dwyr. If she shot her now, she would be unlikely to miss. But she was meters and hundreds of rabid fans from her chance of escape. She would likely be ripped limb from limb, and though her death might be worth it if she put an end to a great evil in the world, she had two children who needed her.

Then light glinted on something in the area above the Dwyr's vehicle. A transparent barrier was in place to protect the leader.

Taylan exhaled.

If she'd tried to shoot her, the pulse would never have made it through the protective barrier. She would have sacrificed her life for nothing.

She turned to look at the platform where the Dwyr would stand. A barrier had been erected around that too. She quietly cursed.

They'd been naive to imagine killing the woman would be so easy. Hell, her followers were so insane she probably needed protection from *them* as well as her actual enemies.

What should she do?

There wouldn't be another opportunity as good as this for a while. Her castle was too well protected. And if the ceremony went ahead, the invasion of Ireland would begin and tens of thousands would lose their lives, maybe including Taylan's children.

Arthur would never break through the barriers with his sword even if he managed to reach them. It was down to her to do it. Perhaps there would be a moment when the woman moved from the vehicle to the platform that she would be unprotected. If she could get one shot in at the right time, she might do it.

The vehicle rounded the curve.

Taylan's heart stopped.

A man was tied to a pole attached to the front. Nearly naked, he was suspended upside down. His feet, waist, and the wrists of his outstretched arms were strapped to the pole. He'd been horribly tortured. What remained of his skin hung from him in long strips, some old and crusted with blood, some fresh and dripping.

As she watched, she saw him twitch.

The world retreated, and a piercing whine filled her head.

He was alive.

God, he was still alive.

White hot rage began to fill her. She'd heard tales of the depth of the Dwyr's evil and depravity, but she'd never seen it up close. Only the knowledge that her effort would be useless stopped her from unleashing pulse round after pulse round at the monster. She had to keep her cool. When her chance came, she would take it, even though she would certainly die. Dwyr Orr could not be allowed to live.

The place was utterly still as the crowd gazed at the tortured man. Taylan found she couldn't look away from him either.

The vehicle slowly drew closer until it was only meters from her.

No! No! No!

Wilson.

The tortured man was Wilson, the Marine who had destroyed her vids, the man they thought had died in the assault on the Dwyr's castle. He'd still been alive, and they'd left him behind. And now this had happened to him.

His eyes locked on hers.

He'd recognized her.

Pity and sorrow welled up inside her. Wilson had been an asshole, but he hadn't deserved to die like this. She couldn't tell Wright. He would never forgive himself for leaving the man behind, even though they'd both thought he was dead.

The vehicle was drawing level with her. The figures on the top remained fixed in their silent tableau.

Wilson's lips moved. He was trying to say something.

What was it?

She thought she heard the word, *Sorry*. Then he'd gone past.

48

"Now," said Angharad.

Wright looked through his binoculars. In the distance, the crowd in the harbor was transfixed on the Dwyr as she passed through them. Even the lookouts on the ships were peering at the spectacle.

The Resistance leader was correct. They had to make their move. They might never get another opportunity as good as this.

All night, Wright, Bates, and the Resistance fighters had been trying to approach the amphibious assault ship moored in the harbor, and all night the security patrols had been too extensive to penetrate. Floodlights had shone from the vessel, sweeping the water, and small, fast vessels had sailed up and down its side.

The rower dipped his oars in the water and, the boat moved out from the tall reeds that had hidden it. They rowed down the river leading to the harbor.

"Go faster," Angharad urged. "Or it'll all be over and they'll see us."

The rower sped up his pace until they were gliding along rapidly, helped by the river's current as it ran down to the sea.

Wright gave the magnetized charges a final check, to steady himself as much as for assurance. Taylan was somewhere in that crowd on the quay, among thousands of people who would kill her if they found out she wasn't one of them. And she was about to do something that would reveal that fact.

He wished he'd argued harder with Merlin about her taking part in the assassination. The alien had insisted and wouldn't budge, even though he couldn't give a sensible explanation as to why it had to be her.

It should be her where he was and him up there among the EAC followers. Or, preferably, she should be on her way to Ireland and not taking any risks at all.

"Okay," said Angharad. "Slow down and keep as close to the bank as you can."

Overhanging vegetation poked into the boat as they slowly moved along. They were nearly at the harbor. Though they were so close, strangely, no noise from the crowd reached them.

Wright wondered where Merlin and Arthur were. Was this going to be a replay of the scenario at Dwyr Orr's castle? Was the alien going to encounter another invisible 'barrier' that would prevent him and his friend from risking their lives?

Their boat slid into the harbor.

"Just a little farther," Angharad murmured.

If they'd had proper equipment, the job would have been so much easier. Even just some underwater gear. But the West BI Resistance only had what was left over from the invasion war, the things they'd managed to steal from the EAC, and their wits and courage. Luckily, they seemed to have plenty of the last two items.

"Stop," whispered Angharad.

The rower reversed the oars' direction, and the boat slowed.

"Think you can make it from here?" she asked.

Wright was not a great swimmer, despite being a Marine. Military starships generally didn't carry swimming pools. He checked the distance and knew he would never make it all the way underwater, but he could probably make it into the shadow of the ship, where he could risk surfacing to take a breath.

"Yeah," he replied.

Bates also agreed.

They climbed over the side of the boat and slipped into the chilly water. Angharad handed Wright a charge. He trod water while he got his bearings, took a breath, and then went under.

49

———

"My people!" Dwyr Orr called out. "Your love and devotion overwhelms me!"

Taylan's raging hatred of the woman hadn't faded. If anything, it had grown stronger, frustrated by powerlessness. There had been no chance to shoot her as she moved from her vehicle to the platform. The entire passage had been guarded by the transparent protective material. The only way to kill her would have been to drop a bomb on her.

The assassination attempt had failed before it had begun.

Taylan guessed their attack on her castle had triggered the additional precautions. They'd screwed up.

She would just have to wait until the ceremony was over to sneak away and hope Arthur didn't do anything stupid...wherever he was. At least there was still the possibility the Resistance might sabotage the launch of the invasion.

The Dwyr was still talking. She was spouting some rubbish about the EAC taking over the world and turning the Earth into a paradise for all who worshipped her.

Taylan grimaced and stopped listening. The woman's words hurt her head, and she hated to the depths of their souls all the people who stood around her, adoring the excuse for a human being. Didn't they understand they could one day be hanging from a pole on the Dwyr's vehicle, hurt almost beyond recognition? Or if not them, someone they loved?

Someone was walking down the route, dressed head to toe in black.

Who was this? The crowd watched him as he approached the feet of the platform.

The Dwyr must have announced something but Taylan had missed it.

The man bowed to the Dwyr and her entourage. He turned and bowed to the crowd.

He took a knife from the sheath at his hip and walked over to Wilson.

A beat of silence.

She looked away.

A roar went up from the crowd. People jostled against her.

She looked back.

Wilson was dead.

After allowing a short time for jubilation, the Dwyr held up her hands for silence.

"We are about to embark on the next stage of our great journey, and the blood sacrifice guarantees our success. Have no fear, we will win our next battle, as we have won so many battles before, to the glory of all. In a moment, I will give the signal for the launching of the *Hecate*, and as she sets sail, so will all the vessels to take part in the great invasion. Our aircraft will take to the air, and our starships are already in battle with the BA forces who might try to fight against us.

"But before I give the signal. I want to give a warning. We have enemies among us, enemies who want to destroy your Dwyr."

Shouts and echoes of *Nooo!* and *We'll stop them!* came from the crowd.

"These people have special abilities, but they can be defeated. To do it, I need your help. Will you help me?"

The cry went up. *Yes!!*

"One of them is called Taylan Ellis."

Everything around Taylan seemed to come to a grinding halt. *What the f—*

"But she won't give you her name," said Kala Orr.

Painfully aware of the audience behind her, Taylan wished she could turn invisible. Did the Dwyr know what she looked like? If she did and she told her followers, how would she make it out of the place alive?

"She may even be here today," said the Dwyr. "Actually, I hope she is. I have a special surprise for her." She said something to someone in the group of people clustered behind her.

The group parted, and two children walked forward.

Kayla and Patrin.

Her legs nearly collapsed beneath her.

Her kids! How the hell did Dwyr Orr have her kids?

"If you're here, Taylan," she said, "I want to make a bargain with you. Step forward now, give yourself up, and your children will live. I'll give you one minute. Then I will kill one of them. I haven't decided which one yet. Maybe the girl. I prefer boys myself."

Wilson. Wilson had seen her vids. He must have described Kayla and Patrin to her, or maybe she'd found them after he'd given the Dwyr her name.

What choice did she have? Dwyr Orr might not keep her word. She might kill her children anyway. But she had to give them at least a chance of survival.

She raised her hand.

At the same time, a scream burst out. More screams and more came in quick succession.

It was Arthur.

Towering over the heads of the crowd, clad in his chainmail

and helmet, the king was approaching, wielding his sword like a scythe.

Blood flicked from it as it swept through the air, slicing through skulls as if they were gossamer, severing necks, carving into arms and torsos. The people directly in his path fell like wheat before a harvester, and the ones not directly within his reach struggled to get away. As terror and panic spread, the crowd heaved. Shrieks, cries, and splashes came from the harbor's edge.

A guard near Taylan took aim. She sprang at him, sending him to the ground and his shot wild, disappearing into the air.

But more rifles were aimed at Arthur. One pulse flew out and missed.

The next did not.

The bolt hit him square in the face.

It had no effect.

The raw energy broke over him harmlessly. Arthur blinked and moved on, Death in a sea of people whose time had come.

Taylan gawped, unable to believe what she was seeing. Pulse bolts impacted him from all around, but he was impervious to them. A soldier reached the towering man after forcing himself against the stampede. He raised the stock of his weapon. Arthur cleaved both his arms at the biceps, leaving him staring stupidly as arterial blood spurted from his stumps.

Unstoppable, he marched onward in the direction of the Dwyr's platform.

Taylan swung around to see what the woman was doing in reaction to the nemesis heading her way. Could Arthur's sword cut through the barrier protecting her? From what she'd seen so far, anything was possible.

Dwyr Orr was holding a knife to Kayla's throat.

The Dwyr's meaning was clear: If Arthur threatened her life, she would kill the child.

Taylan screamed.

She leapt into the crowd, fighting through the churning bodies.

"Arthur!" she bellowed. "Stop! Wait!"

But the ancient king seemed to be moving on automatic, unaware of what was happening around him. His staring eyes were focused only on the Dwyr as his sword rose and fell.

The people standing behind her were pouring off the platform and scattering into the crowd. Only the woman in the dark gown, Patrin, the other boy, and Kayla remained with the Dwyr.

"Arthur!!" Taylan cried out. "No! Please! My daughter. She has my daughter!"

Despair drove her forward against the flood of bodies moving in the opposite direction. She had to reach him. She had to stop him.

A man fell in front of her. She trod on his back. More people were falling. She hauled them out of her way. Arthur was passing her. A trail of bloody corpses lay in his wake.

"Stop! No!"

The Dwyr raised her knife, preparing to strike.

A crush of the fallen appeared at Taylan's feet. She vaulted over them.

She'd reached him.

She grabbed his left arm, saturated with blood.

He pivoted.

The great blade swung toward her.

She caught a glimpse of reddened, wet steel. The blade sliced into her throat.

It stopped.

Arthur had halted. His gaze held hers. They were still, frozen, her hand on his arm, his other hand holding the sword that was centimeters from killing her.

His eyes were the eyes of a crazed man. They'd lost all their warmth and humanity. But deep in their depths sat a spark of recognition.

Boom!

An explosion rent the atmosphere, and the harbor jerked beneath her feet. Taylan was deafened.

A second explosion must have occurred, but she didn't hear it. She only felt a shockwave.

Though she would have said it was impossible a minute ago, the crowd's panic doubled. Someone crashed into her and she fell. She fought to get up, but only managed to raise herself halfway off the ground.

Arthur had moved on, but when Taylan turned to look at the platform, things had changed there. The Dwyr was climbing down the back of it, her headdress discarded.

And the woman who had accompanied her...

Taylan's mouth fell open.

The woman was disintegrating. She was turning into a dark mist. The mist grew thicker and darker, and soon that was all that was left of her. The darkness floated upward and dispersed into the clouds.

Something else was rising behind her. A small shuttle was taking off. Dwyr Orr was getting away.

A foot pressed on Taylan's hip, and then another landed on her shoulder. Another person fell on top of her. She couldn't get up. The weight grew heavier as more people seemed to add to the pile. Her lungs were being crushed. She was suffocating. She tried to yell, but she couldn't take a breath.

Then, just as blackness was overcoming her, the weight eased. She could breathe again. Pulling in her knees and elbows, she managed to move the person on top of her and get out.

The quayside was a scene of terrible destruction. Bodies lay in a line, marking the path Arthur had traveled. More of the injured and dead from the stampede littered the place. The gigantic ship was listing, and...

She turned toward the platform. Arthur stood in front of it, red from head to toe, resting on his sword. The platform itself was empty except for two children.

Her children!

She sped over the ground separating her from them. Within seconds she was at the base and running around the back to find the stairs. She leapt up them. The children were facing away from her. She went to scoop them into her arms and press their cheeks into hers, but her arms passed through thin air. Confused, she tried again, but her hands swiped nothing.

As she watched, they vanished.

"They were not real, Taylan," said Arthur, looking up at her from below. "They were phantasms created by Morgan le Fay."

He took off his helmet wearily. "We failed. We will have to try again."

50

They laid Angharad to rest at the foot of Carn Menyn. After Wright and Bates had swum back to the boat, they'd stayed where they were, hoping to collect Taylan from the quayside after the Dwyr's assassination. Merlin had said he and Arthur would make their own way back.

Exactly at the moment the first charge exploded, Angharad's eyes had rolled up, and she'd fallen backward, hitting her head on the wooden boards. Wright had checked for a pulse and respiration, but she'd had neither. He guessed a stroke or heart attack had killed her. At least she'd had the satisfaction of hearing the sabotage had been a success.

Up and down the west coast of the BI, more of the Resistance's efforts had been successful, forestalling the invasion. As long as Dwyr Orr remained alive, Ireland would always be at risk, but they had bought the Irish and the refugees they were housing some time. The BA would be able to help them strengthen their defenses.

Wright looked up from Angharad's friends shoveling soil into her grave, and across to Taylan, who stood on the opposite side.

She was a wreck.

He knew she'd begun to bond with the fallen Resistance leader, unsurprisingly given their shared backgrounds. It was clear Taylan loved her homeland and missed it deeply. But there was more to her state of mind than shock and grief. He hadn't learned the entire story, but Arthur had mentioned something about illusions of her children appearing at the launch ceremony.

He didn't understand how that could be. How would the Dwyr know about Taylan's children, let alone what they looked like? And he thought she'd rejected the tech that would allow her to project a holo of them. It didn't make a lot of sense, but Taylan's face told him Arthur had it right. He couldn't imagine how she must feel, thinking they were nearly within her grasp, only to discover it was all a lie.

Should he suggest she returned with him to the *Fearless* to recuperate? There was no point. She would never do it. Colbourn wouldn't be pleased about losing her best Marine, but what could she do about it except berate him, and he was used to that.

The grave was filled. The men put down their shovels. One of them gave a short speech in Welsh. Taylan rubbed her eye with the heel of her hand.

When they returned to the hideout in the hill, Arthur and Merlin had returned from yet another mysterious excursion. To Wright's surprise, Taylan didn't even greet them. She took a detour around the pair to sit on the far side of the hollow. He went and sat beside her. Her head hung low, and she rested her elbows on her knees. The urge to pull the disconsolate woman into his arms was strong, but he resisted.

"What's up?" he asked quietly. "Isn't Arthur your friend anymore?"

He'd meant to be light-hearted, but the look she gave him struck the smile from his face.

"You didn't see the quayside, did you?"

"No, we had to get you away as fast as we could. Why?"

Her features twisted, as if she'd eaten something disgusting. "Something came over Arthur at the ceremony. He was a different person. You should have seen him. He was a killing machine. And the pulse fire from the guards didn't affect him. It washed over him, like he was made of asbestos."

He glanced at Arthur. Merlin was talking to him softly. The old king was built for fighting, there was no denying it. He didn't really understand what Taylan meant. "The pulse fire didn't affect him? How's that possible?"

"I don't know. Except it's something to do with Merlin. You remember how he wanted to call off the attack at the Dwyr's castle because he personally couldn't enter the grounds? Think about it. What difference would it have made if Merlin was there or not? He was never going to fight. I'm guessing he needs to be within a certain proximity of Arthur to do whatever the hell it is he does that changes him into an indestructible berserker."

If it hadn't been Taylan telling him this, Wright might have thought he was listening to an exaggeration. But she'd always been pretty straight. Too straight at times.

She pulled down her shirt collar. "He did this."

A long cut, filled with congealed blood, marked the lower half of her neck.

"Arthur did that?!"

"He was going to kill me too, along with the rest of them. He only recognized me at the last minute."

Wright didn't know what to make of it all.

What he did know was he was under orders to bring Arthur and Merlin back to the *Fearless*. The BA felt the two of them—and the alien in particular—were far too precious commodities to be allowed to roam the globe of their own free will. How he would accomplish returning with them if they didn't want to come, he hadn't quite figured out.

"There's something else I haven't told you yet," said Taylan. "Dwyr Orr knows who I am, and she's got it in for me. She said Arthur and I are her enemies. She seemed frightened of us."

"How could she possibly know about you and Arthur?" He wondered if someone in the BA had been feeding the Dwyr information.

She didn't answer. He had a feeling she was holding something back. What wasn't she telling him?

"If Dwyr Orr is after you," he said, "you'd be better off coming back to the *Fearless*. Nowhere on the surface will be safe for you anymore."

She bit her lip and shook her head. "I'm not leaving without my kids. I can't. She knows who they are too, or at least what they look like. They're at just as much risk as I am. I have to find them." She looked at him with such sorrow in her eyes, he couldn't help but reach out and touch her shoulder.

"There's something else," she said.

Here was the thing she'd been holding back.

"I think the Dwyr has a Merlin equivalent on her team."

"A...what?"

"She had a woman with her for the ceremony. The woman didn't say or do anything, that I noticed, but at the end, when everything was going down, Arthur was on his way to the Dwyr and the bombs went off, she kind of...evaporated. She became a mist, then she was gone."

Another alien like Merlin?

Wright was feeling overloaded with information. He needed time to process it all. But time was something he didn't have. A boat was leaving for Ireland in a few hours. The Resistance was taking advantage of the turmoil following the sabotaged launch of the EAC invasion to send more refugees across. The fighters themselves would remain in the BI, doing what they could to hold back the tidal wave that threatened to sweep across the Irish Sea.

He planned to be on the boat, with Bates, Arthur, and Merlin. Then he could contact the BA to be picked up from there.

"If you won't return to the *Fearless*," he said to Taylan, "at least come to Ireland with us. You said your children are there."

"No, I think I was wrong. I talked to Angharad about it. She said maybe they never left West BI, and that's why I couldn't find them. I was looking in the wrong place. I'm going to look for them here. She already sent out the word about them."

"But you'll be living in the shadow of the Dwyr!"

"I know, but, don't you see? It's the best place for me. She'll expect me to put as much distance between us as I can. She won't be expecting me to stick around. She won't look for me right under her nose. And I had another idea. While I'm looking for my kids, I can spy on her. Maybe I can get intelligence to the BA to help them in the war."

"It would make me feel better if you didn't sever ties with us completely," said Wright. "If I knew I might hear from you, or about you, from time to time."

They held eye contact, not speaking.

"If we're going to make that boat," said one of the Resistance fighters, "we need to leave now."

"We're ready," said Merlin, rising to his feet.

Arthur also stood up. He'd cleaned his sword, mail, and helmet, and was holding them.

Relieved the pair were coming with him without protest, Wright wondered how Arthur's new possessions would go down aboard a starship.

"I have to go," he said.

A man emerged from the short tunnel that led to the exit. He searched the room until his gaze alighted on Taylan. He said something to her in Welsh.

Her face transformed from dejection to joy. Clasping her hands to her chest, she replied in her mother tongue. Her eyes shining, she turned to Wright. "They think they might know where my kids are!"

"That's fantastic!"

"We have to leave, now," insisted the fighter who was taking them to the boat.

"Good luck, Taylan," said Wright.

"Thanks, and the same to you. Safe journey back."

He hesitated.

She waited, expectant.

Then the moment was gone.

He walked away from her, crossing the room.

"Goodbye, Taylan," Arthur called out before disappearing into the tunnel. Merlin followed him.

Wright stopped at the entrance, glanced back at the woman watching him, and then he left.

Taylan and Wright's story continues in

THE GALLANT

AUTHOR'S NOTES

So you made it to the end of the second book in the Star Legend space fantasy series. I hope you enjoyed the journey. Many thanks to Mike Phillips, military consultant, Liza Woods, editor, and to Mike Paddick, Welsh language consultant, for his help with the Star Legend audio books. If you're interested in some of the research and inspiration for *The Fearless*, read on.

The Corvettes

Naming starships is fun but challenging. It's hard to think up names that sound authentic but haven't been used before. In fact, Dr Who fans might have recognised the name of the ship in Star Legend, *Valiant*. That was a mistake, and not excusable as I'm a big Dr Who fan. Never mind.

The corvette names in Star Legend were inspired by the British Flower Class corvettes used during World War II by the Royal Navy and the Royal Canadian Navy. There were 294 of them, but only HMS Sackville survives, as a museum ship in Halifax, Nova Scotia.

Boulby Mine

The mine Kala Orr rescues Morgan le Fay from is based on

Boulby Mine, currently the deepest mine in the UK at between 1,100 and 1,400 meters deep. Originally a potash mine, its seams extend under the North Sea, where about one billion tonnes of polyhalite sit offshore. Due to the mine's depth, it takes seven minutes for the lifts to reach the bottom.

Morgan/Morgana/Morgaine

You may know the character Morgan as Morgana or, if you're an Arthurian legend scholar, Morgaine. I believe Morgana is a modern incarnation of the character's name invented by DC Comics (don't quote me). The Morgan of Star Legend is basically Morgan le Fay from Malory's Morte D'Arthur. In Malory's stories, she's one of Arthur's main antagonists. However, Malory doesn't make her Mordred's mother. That woman is Morgaine, one of Arthur's half-sisters from his mother, Igraine. Also, in Malory's version Mordred isn't Arthur's son. It's only in later interpretations that Morgan tricks Arthur into sleeping with her when he doesn't know she's his half-sister.

Iolani Hale

Iolani was inspired by Maria Sibylla Merian, a 17th century scientist, adventurer and artist. Maria was one of the first natural historians to show that insects didn't spontaneously generate from organic matter but reproduced and hatched from eggs. In 1699, Maria sailed from Holland to Suriname to study the fascinating local wildlife in the almost-impenetrable jungle. Iolani's dogs are named after Charles Darwin (of course) and Joseph Banks, another great naturalist.

Arthur's Armour and Sword

How cool it would have been to put Arthur in full plate armour, just like we see in Victorian renderings of him. Sadly, at the time he's supposed to have lived, plate armour hadn't been invented. The Celts are credited with inventing chainmail, and the remains of chainmail were found in the famous Anglo-Saxon burial, Sutton Hoo, so from the timing it's reasonable to assume Arthur could have worn it. His helmet is based on the one found at Sutton Hoo, and, naturally, his sword is Excalibur (which is not, by the way, the sword he pulled from the stone).

Was Arthur a Celt?

Destroying the assertion of the previous paragraph, it's questionable that Arthur was actually a Celt. According to genetic research, three-quarters of the ancestors of the British were hunter gatherers who arrived between 15,000 and 7,500 years ago, and a later invasion of masses of 'Celts' from the continent, supplanting the local population is doubtful. For more information, read Stephen Oppenheimer's *The Origins of the British*.

These are just a few comments on the many resources and inspiration gathered in the writing of *The Valiant* and *The Fearless*. If you'd like to ask any questions, talk about the books or just say hi, you can find me in the Starship JJ Green Shipmates Facebook group: https://www.facebook.com/groups/StarshipJJ-GreenShipmates. I'd love to see you there.

If you'd like to read Star Legend book three, *The Gallant* as an ebook a few weeks earlier than it will appear on Amazon, become a Patreon supporter: https://www.patreon.com/JJGreenAuthor

Sign up to my reader group for exclusive free books, discounts on new releases, review crew invitations and other interesting stuff:

https://jjgreenauthor.com/free-books/

DOWNLOAD YOUR FREE READERS' GUIDE TO THE SCIENCE FICTION NOVELS OF J.J. GREEN:
https://www.amazon.com/gp/product/B07HGV8WJV/